For my mother and for Sue

PREFACE AND CREDITS

The UK is about to break up, as Wales & Scotland try to claim independence and join the EU. Unexpectedly, the Coronavirus pandemic sweeps the planet, fake news abounds and voting goes on-line, in a referendum which is plagued with problems.

By Huw Johns © 2020
Cover illustration by Clem Wigley © 2020
Editor: Sal Anderton
Special thanks to Richard Anderton, Jayne Hodder, Gavin Pugh & Andrew Scarborough.

Chapter 1: Baked Potatoes

Peter was bemoaning his apparent lack of sex to his pretty younger wife, Justine. It was a conversation that cropped up from time to time and Justine imagined that it was more of an observation from Peter, rather than a complaint. The pretty forty-one-year-old brunette stretched her arms up towards the bedroom ceiling, yawned delicately and put her mug down, declaring she was exhausted and was going to sleep. Being a lawyer for a busy city centre firm was tiring. She and Peter had enjoyed a happy marriage for ten years and there was no need to have any sort of relationship conversation at this point, she told herself. Peter shifted around as if the matter had not been closed and that there was still some mileage in further discussion.

"Is there something you don't like, or something you would like, maybe?" he said, aiming at a suggestive tone but missing the mark and sounding like a French shop assistant trying to speak English. Justine was in a different mental zone altogether, as her reply suggested:

"I'd like a new duvet set – this one's looking a bit past it." she mumbled, half asleep, apparently unaware of the point of his narrative.

"Oh, come on, Justine – you know what I mean"

he said, demonstrably irritated. The increase in his pitch made her realise that the issue had to be dealt with now so that she could get her required seven and a half hours sleep needed to make her an effective well- respected, sought-after divorce lawyer. She sat up reluctantly and composed herself, as if she were in a client meeting.

"Everything's great Pete – I'm totally happy." she said and left a suitable pause of a few seconds, keen to get this over with, but not wishing to sound hurried and as if her only motive was sleep. "But if there were one thing, I think it would be that sometimes, well...., I think, it lasts a bit too long, that's all" she said softly.

"Too long?" he replied incredulously "Isn't that what most girls want? You'll be telling me next that there's too much foreplay!" he ranted, although deep down he wasn't that bothered with the genre of the complaint.

"It's just that I don't always need...." she searched for a metaphor "... a full three course meal" she continued hesitantly, leaving the words hanging in the air to be interpreted.

"So, are you saying you'd like the occasional McDonalds instead?" he demanded, seeking genuine clarification and becoming agitated at the same time. There was a pause.

"Well, maybe not McDonalds. I suppose I was

thinking of – well – I don't know – you know, somewhere like… ummmm, perhaps… Pizza Express?" she replied hesitantly.

Peter's agitation and irritation reached a peak and his reply was a higher pitched squawk.

"Pizza Express?"

Justine hadn't planned this and was now backed into a corner. She'd somehow gone down a bizarre food and sex metaphor alley that had ended up in her asking for more visits to Pizza Express. If only she could turn back the clock a minute or two.

There was silence. The two of them lay side by side in bed waiting for one to speak. Then, adding the banal to the bizarre, the exchange took a new turn.

"But we had lunch in Pizza Express on Saturday, when we were in the Bay." Peter suddenly said, as if trying to connect real life with this midnight metaphor medley. "And I walk past it on the way from the car park to the ad agency every day" he said, as if pondering the consequences.

"So?" snapped Justine, getting tired again.

"So, it's gonna make me feel different now, isn't it? Every time I walk past Pizza Express, I'm going to feel, well… you know!"

"For Christ's sake Peter! Are you accusing me of making you feel aroused by Pizza Express?" she demanded. "It's a good job I didn't pick McDonalds then – there are hundreds of them around! You'd never get to any client meetings, would you?" she spat. This argument was surreal. And then it got more surreal.

"Well you could have picked another restaurant!" retorted Pete angrily, now entirely immersed in this weird cameo and oblivious to its absurdity.

"Like what?" she shot back quickly, leaving him wrong-footed. There was silence for a few seconds as he thought.

"Spud-u-like!" he said triumphantly, smiling and then realising that his victory was a hollow one in the scheme of things. "There aren't many of them around anymore!" he continued unabashed as if he needed to back up his statement with some factual information.

"What the hell is Spud-u-Like?" hissed Justine, irritated.

"They're a chain of fast-food outlets that sell baked potatoes" said Peter – deadpan - as if this was all in context of a conversation about a love life and all quite normal.

Justine let out a long sigh, relaxed her shoulders and simply said "I can't believe you're comparing our love life to a baked potato restaurant, Peter." At which point she grabbed her pillow plunged her head into it and pivoted sideways turning her back to Peter, indicating that the subject was closed.

Peter remained sitting up, stunned and confused at how he lost an argument he hadn't started and been accused of comparing his love life to Spud-u-Like, when it had been her who had started the whole fast-food conversation.

"AGGGGGGGGGRRRRRR" he moaned, frustrated. Then he looked at the alarm clock with a further groan and resigned himself to preparing for sleep. What a bizarre ten minutes.

The alarm clicked, before preparing the CD for play. Peter's eyes flicked open and the neon green figures penetrated the bleariness: 06:30. Time to get up for work. He hated that despite buying a device which promised that he would awake to the CD of his choice ensuring a "soft landing" into the new day, what happened in reality was different. The click and the whir of the CD woke him and then a hiss or two made sure he was awake properly and then finally he got the music. Jesus – I'm ready to get up by the time the bloody music starts, he often thought.

 He jumped out of bed, keen to put last night behind him and to shake off his dreams of bikini-clad baked potatoes running away from him. He blamed the fact that he had relatively recently become a director of an advertising agency for this weird creative reverie and mused that when he'd worked as a civil servant at the Welsh Government, this sort of dream would never have occurred.

But Peter's life was changing in a big way. The Welsh Government had made a swathe of redundancies in the wake of cuts from central government funding and Peter's job had been on the line. He had begun to look around for other positions during the lengthy consultation process carried out by a smug Human Resources Consultancy. The HR Consultants had been hired by Peter's employers to ensure fair play during the hatchet job in which forty people would lose their positions. They had set up camp in the government building where Peter had worked and had squatted there for three months - rarely seen but menacingly ever-present. Pete had been keen to make his exit before what he and his colleagues had come to call "Judgement Day" when the redundancies would be announced.

Unfortunately, Peter had found that he was not qualified for life outside the public sector. A working life spent in local and regional government, he discovered, apparently only qualifies you for nothing other than more of the same. Businesses disappointingly took a rather a dim view of the abilities of an overpaid, clock-watching pen-pusher. But Peter had contacts. His position as Head of Economic Development regularly exposed him to the business community and indeed many such businesses had benefitted from providing services to Peter's department and its substantial coffers. Now it was payback time.

Peter had decided to embark upon a charm offensive with his contacts to further his quest for alternative employment. The result of a series of expensive lunches with business leaders was a handful of "good lucks", a smattering of "keep in touches" and one expression of interest, from Dougal Rogers - boss of controversial advertising agency, Creative Juices. Dougal had always recognised the extent and usefulness of Peter's contacts and had directly and indirectly benefitted from them via the many Welsh Government contracts that Creative Juices had won. Peter and Dougal had always got on superficially, with Dougal exploiting Peter's love of corporate hospitality and Peter seemingly reciprocating by identifying suitable business opportunities for Creative Juices within the Welsh Government.

Six months after the lunch Peter found himself staring at his new business card, which confirmed that he was indeed Business Development Director of Creative Juices. He was not really a director, of course. He had no share or decision-making power in the business, but his well-honed ego had meant that his title was as important to him as his salary. Dougal had recognised this in their early discussions about a position and quickly saved himself about ten thousand pounds by allowing Peter to call himself a director. Peter had insisted that it was purely for credibility reasons in that if he was going to be able to explore opportunities within the public sector on behalf of Creative Juices he needed to be taken seriously.

Peter had spent the first week of his new employment getting used to his new surroundings and trying to fit in with a working routine that was so far removed from his previous job that he may as well have been commuting to another planet to work. He had found it odd that the design studio frequently worked well into the night and occasionally - to meet a deadline- right through the night. He also found the constant presence of alcohol bizarre. The Welsh Government had not permitted alcohol to be consumed during working hours. By contrast, it seemed to be positively encouraged at Creative Juices. Account Managers were instructed to entertain clients at least twice a week and every Friday lunchtime the entire staff of Creative Juices were given unlimited access to the client bar in the boardroom on the third floor - for the whole afternoon.

But despite all the bonhomie and backslapping, Peter had spent the majority of his first week holed up in his modest office next to the toilet on the second floor. He did little other than wonder what he should be doing. The few phone calls that he did make had to be carefully orchestrated so that they did not coincide with a member of staff using the facilities in the room next to his office. Giving the impression that you are calling someone from a public toilet is not the best signal to send to potential clients - Peter had discovered to his cost.

Meanwhile Dougal was trying to strike a balance between letting Peter get settled in and getting him to start work and actually do something useful. His concern was shared by codirector Morris Well - a forty-four-year-old ex-door to door salesman turned Adman. Morris had suggested to Dougal that Peter was probably lazy and used to a cushy number - having been a civil servant. Dougal had made an expression that implied that this was probably true but that he needed help dealing with it not criticism and statement of the bloody obvious. It was quickly agreed that Peter needed to be thrown in at the deep end and dispatched to a series of organised business networking events. To make things more palatable for Peter, it was disguised and presented to him as a "director initiative" in which he, Dougal and Morris would all participate.

Morris had initially objected to Dougal when he had suggested the group networking tactic as a way of not being hard on Peter.

"I don't want to go back to those bloody lunches. They're full of time-wasting losers, like Life Coaches. I mean, if I want advice in where I'm going wrong in life, I can get it anytime from my wife!" he ranted.

" I know there are a bunch of tossers there, but we've always pulled work from these things, if just by playing *Spot the Odd One Out* and finding a successful business owner!" said Dougal. "But more importantly Morris, as we both know, Creative Juices is in financial difficulty and needs more work. Peter's public-sector work may take a while to materialise - as that lot seem to work at a snail's pace. So, we need to get a bunch of smaller jobs in to keep us ticking over- to keep the wolf from the door" said Dougal, with furrowed brow.

Creative Juices had recently lost its longest standing and largest retained client, Sansom Food & Drink Ltd. Creative Juices had originally been named after this account as it had sought - and failed- to specialise in the food and drink sector. Samson's boss, Dave Sansom had been a school friend of Dougal's father and the connection had been enough for Dougal to secure his first advertising account with the company twelve years ago.

But Dave had recently fallen into poor health

and his two sons had begun to take control of the business. One of them was married to a senior executive at The Marketing Works, a rival advertising agency, and before long the account began to slip away amidst accusations of incompetence and lack of creativity. Then Sansom announced that it would be reviewing all its suppliers including advertising services and within three months the prized account had been snatched by The Marketing Works, leaving Creative Juices weakened and vulnerable. It was at this point that Dougal had received Peter's invitation to lunch and been receptive to the idea of giving him a job as a way into his contacts and understanding of the public sector. Creative Juices needed ongoing work, the public sector was where they'd find it and Peter knew the public sector. Simple.

Peter arrived at the office around five to nine, after a thirty-minute journey from their three-bed apartment in Cardiff Bay. His journey to the office was easy (apart from having to pass Pizza Express) as all the traffic was heading the other way. The agency was based in a north Cardiff suburb in three converted Victorian houses which had been joined together, given a brass plaque and shared a car park with a firm of surveyors. Ironically, the perceived ideal location for an ad agency was Cardiff Bay, where Peter lived. A trendy area developed from the notorious docklands, it attracted the in-crowds, wannabes, ad agencies as well as a lot of television and media companies, feasting off the area's Dr Who fame.

Peter believed that Creative Juices needed to be in the Bay to be taken seriously, but Dougal owned their current premises and was enjoying a tax efficient personal profit from letting the buildings to the agency. Nevertheless, Peter felt it was time to raise it. The Welsh Government was mostly based in Cardiff Bay including its home, the Senedd. Peter's working life at Welsh Government had centred around the Bay, part of the reason that he, Justine and subsequently their son David lived there.

When he talked to his former government contacts, they expressed mild surprise that he was working for an ad agency that was not based in the Bay. Peter began to wonder if their perception might be blocking possible business opportunities.

"Nobody gets fired for hiring IBM." Peter explained to Dougal. "Public sector people are risk-averse. We - I mean they - don't get promoted for taking initiatives. They plod, keep their heads down, enjoy their flexi-time and look forward to their generous holiday allowance and final salary pension schemes. They don't take risks because they don't get rewarded for it and they don't want to lose the cushy number that most of them are on." said Peter, reflecting on how quickly he'd started to analyse and criticise his former colleagues. In truth it was mostly jealousy and regret.

"Think of the agencies that are in the Bay. " Peter carried on, oblivious to Dougal's bored look. "Sky-Pie 5!" he began.

"What the hell does that mean, anyway?" spat Dougal "At least Creative Juices has a bit of wit about it!"

Peter ignored him and began reeling off a list of rival ad agencies that were located in the Bay. "Urquhart Symonds Piers..." he paused.

"They just sound like some old fashioned 1960's style agency - lumping their fancy surnames together" Dougal retorted.

"Well it's a good job you didn't do that. We would have been Rogers Quickly and Well - a bit suggestive for me!" said Peter, pleased with himself for remembering the quip that he'd overheard one of the designers make. Dougal looked surprised that mild mannered, boring Peter had made such a perceptive and humorous comment. Then Peter played his trump card.

"Then there's The Marketing Works - based slap bang in Mount Stuart Square - right in the middle of the Bay!" Peter thrust his finger into the middle of the table as if Dougal might be in need of some geographical orientation to understand the concept of 'middle'. Dougal looked visibly upset at the mention of the arch rival agency that had stolen the Sansom account from them. Peter went in for the kill.

"How about we rent a small office in the Bay? Somewhere with a nice address, client room, projector, bar. A satellite office, if you like."

"The Bay is full of wankers" Dougal proclaimed suddenly, but his tone suggested that he had resigned himself to the fact that Peter's idea was probably what they would have to go with. He replied curtly:

"OK Peter - look into it. Not pricey. Get a deal. Call me when you've got a couple for us to see. Oh, and parking's a pain in the arse in the Bay - make sure we cover that off."

Peter smiled. Dougal grimaced. The meeting was over.

Chapter 2: Bananas

David Quickly's first day at Creative Juices was passing slowly. Aware that his father had got him the job and his girlfriend was counting on him to make a go of it, he was trying his best not to put a foot wrong.

David disliked new jobs mainly because they involved meeting new people. Part of the problem now he lived in Wales was his name. Back in Portsmouth he was known by his friends and mother - Peter's first wife - as simply David Quickly. Yes, he had encountered the odd jibe along the way when he had done something visibly slowly, like coming last in the 800 metres at a school sports event - but that was about it.

In Wales however, matters were different. David soon discovered to his chagrin that "David" is often replaced with the Welsh "Dai". Because it is pronounced "Die", David had been faced with the embarrassment of being known as "Die Quickly" within weeks of arriving at sixth form college in Cardiff.

He often used this name-calling as the excuse for flunking his A levels and ending up living with his father, Peter and stepmother, Justine until he was twenty. Living with them, his life had been punctuated by a series of dead-end jobs and short-term relationships, coupled with a general objective of living for the weekends which were funded by a growing overdraft.

But all that had changed a year ago when he met Alicia, an Office Manager in a stationery company in Cardiff. The pair had fallen in love and within six months - encouraged and largely financed by David's father and stepmother - they had moved into a small suburban flat.

That was seven months ago. Now, David was happy, but unemployed, having lost another job just before they moved in. And Alicia was patient but becoming more aware of David's negative side as the days went by.

He had been attentive when they had met and that she had loved. But domestically, she discovered, he didn't fit the bill at all. Since they moved in together, David spent his days watching Sky TV and his evenings playing around on Facebook and drinking beer, only summoning up the energy to apply for jobs when it became the cause of an argument. Within two months the relationship was looking fragile and David knew deep down that he was to blame.

So, when his father Peter managed to swing his

son a job as part of his own career move, David decided to turn over a new leaf and really prove everyone else wrong. This time he would get it all right. He would show Alicia that he could do it.

David's title at Creative Juices was "Account Manager / Business Development". He had originally been told that as an Account Manager he would be looking after a small number of "accounts" - existing clients - making sure that their work was carried out correctly and that communication was always maintained. However, during his 45-minute induction meeting this morning, Dougal had explained that there weren't really enough accounts to manage now that some had been "temporarily suspended", so David's primary focus was to be on "business development". David hadn't really understood the exact nature of the work but did his best to convey enthusiasm for it, not wanting to let anybody down.

Minutes later he found himself in a small room armed with a phone and a list of companies to ring to try to make appointments for Dougal. He wasn't an Account Manager at all - he had to find his own accounts to manage, if he ever got that far! It was like inviting someone for dinner and then asking them to bring their own food, he thought bitterly. But he was resolute and so he plodded on, thinking of Alicia and how impressed she would be at his adaptability and determination.

Finally, 1pm came and David could legitimately flee the office in search of food and relief from the tedium of telephone rejection. He accidentally catapulted himself into a crowd of shoppers on the high street as he rushed out of the office, tripping on a broken paving stone. Staggering on regardless, he looked to all intents and purposes like a man who had just escaped prison with guards in hot pursuit.

Spotting a pub, he made a beeline for it. A metre or so from the door he remembered his new resolutions, his new job and his new life. He hastily reconsidered and swivelled 90 degrees, nearly knocking over a small man, to head for a mini supermarket on a street corner.

Pleased with his restraint, David decided he could do even better. As well as the chicken salad sandwich and Diet Coke for his lunch, he bought some bananas, remembering that Alicia had said that they needed some. After collapsing exhausted on a park bench a few minutes' walk away and devouring his sandwich, David decided to text Alicia. He felt more relaxed now that the morning was behind him and with the benefit of some food inside him. He wanted to convey this positive vibe to Alicia and demonstrate that as well as completing a full morning of paid work he had also successfully executed a small domestic task by remembering to buy fruit.

"I've got bananas" he tapped into his mobile triumphantly.

Minutes later, a text from Alicia flashed onto his screen.

"UR useless. Just stick at it. Stick at something for a change. Even if it does drive u bananas."

Surprised, upset and confused David stared back at the mobile, hoping for some explanation. Actually, it was there - in grey and white. His new budget priced mobile obviously had some sort of odd predictive texting option which had changed "I've got bananas" to "I've gone bananas". This was too complicated to explain by text so David left a garbled voicemail which he hoped Alicia would a) believe or b) find funny or c) both a and b.

Unfortunately, the outcome was neither a, b nor c.

***

David dawdled back to work, head down as he shuffled into the back door of the agency he bumped into Dougal, who was heading out for a business lunch. Noticing David's low mood, in an impromptu gush of pre-lunch altruism, Dougal asked how David was getting along. Sensing from his reply that more than a quick few words in a doorway was needed, he suggested that David spend a little time with each part of the agency over the following week. This would, Dougal hoped, relieve the tedium of telesales and give David some industry perspective that might help him sound more knowledgeable on the phone. David's mood brightened and Dougal promised to make the necessary arrangements later that day. As he pulled away from the agency in his black Range Rover, he pressed the hands-free button and clicked the icon that read "Claire" to connect him to his PA. Claire would be making the necessary arrangements for David's grand tour. Keen to take credit for this inspired, human resources initiative, Dougal made a mental note to email David as soon as he had parked to tell him to report to Claire for instructions.

Later that day, David arrived at Dougal's office to find 28-year-old Claire printing out his itinerary for the next week. Claire seemed older than her years. She exuded an air of confidence and competence that made David feel uncomfortable.

Her wiry frame gave the impression of someone who was always moving or doing something - probably exercise or work. Claire was a long-distance runner and clocked up as many as five marathons every year, many of which she ran to raise money for her favourite charity, the RSPB. Claire lived on her own with a small assortment of pets and the occasional female visitor.

David wondered why the agency printed everything. After all, people like he and Claire were in their 20's. No one prints stuff anymore, surely? Why didn't she just email me? he thought. But Creative Juices was old fashioned and stuck by the old school rules of paper notes and typists. Every contact report, agenda and status report had to be written by hand and given to a designated typist, who created the document on Microsoft Word and printed it out. There were only a few computers to share amongst the account handlers and management staff, though fortunately all the designers were equipped with the latest Macs. Indeed, David's first department to visit was to be the design studio, where he would envy the plethora of technology that had been bestowed on them.

David read Claire's itinerary: He was to spend tomorrow morning cold calling again. His visit to meet the studio people - many of whom he already knew superficially - was marked for

12.30pm in the Urchin and Seahorse. This was a pub just a few doors down, owned by the rapidly expanding craft brewers BayBrew who were based near Cardiff Bay, a few miles away. Odd - he thought and looked up at Claire for clarification.

"They like a little drink" she offered by way of an explanation. David subsequently found this to be somewhat of an understatement.

He decided that it might be a good idea to call into the studio during one of his many morning breaks in order to check they were expecting him in the pub. As he descended in to the bowels of the building about 10.30am, he found himself sharing the stairs with Wendy Williams, the Creative Director, in effect the boss of the whole department, though Derek Hoskin as Art Director effectively managed a small team of designers. Wendy managed Derek, Octavia - the Production Manager who scheduled all the jobs and Tim Hughes, the copywriter.

Wendy was a warm, perceptive intelligent fifty-something with a look that suggested a cross between hippy and chic. Designer jeans, tight leather jacket, multi-coloured hair, piercings, unlit cigarette behind the ear. A plastic bag jangled its contents as she took the stairs to the basement.

"If I'd known you were coming to visit us before

this afternoon, I'd have asked what you wanted to drink." she said to David, beginning to unload the contents of the bag into a nearby bench in the studio. There were three bottles of wine, about a dozen miniatures - all gin and tonics - and two cans of bitter for Tim. David tried not to show his surprise. After all, they were probably for some after work party, he reasoned. His speculation was quickly confounded when drinks and change were dispensed by Wendy who then poured herself a large gin and tonic before calling the team to order to brief them on the day's work.

The team was depleted in number from its usual quota - Wendy explained - because there had been an "all-nighter", hence the late briefing. An "all-nighter", David discovered was what the studio did a few times a month to catch up and make deadlines. He suspected that it wasn't fuelled by homemade cakes and lemonade but thought the better of saying so.

Wendy peeled back another metal cap from a fresh mini-gin, adding a dribble of tonic before swigging it and allowing the alcohol to hit the spot as she introduced David to the team. She flicked her yellow, purple and red hair not noticing the unlit cigarette fall to the studio floor and stick to the carpet of Spray Mount glue that was used to attach visuals to boards. Good job the cigarette wasn't lit, thought David. The stink of strong glue and stickiness underfoot suggested a possible fire risk of an enormous kind.

"This is David Quickly." Wendy announced. "He joined us a few weeks ago as an Account Manager and we'll be seeing him for our lunchtime briefing where I hope you'll all make him feel welcome." she said, sounding more like a stage-weary rock chick than an advertising professional. Lunchtime briefing, thought David. It might be serious - I'll have to take a pen and paper. He needn't have.

The studio team had obviously taken Wendy's instruction to integrate David seriously. Fast forward to 3pm and they were ordering their fourth round of beers, suggesting playing drinking games before nipping back to work for an hour or two and then going for a curry. David felt well-integrated, indeed.

"It's ok" said one of the designers - a young, chubby redhead with a swarthy look. "We were in work until 1am last night and we'll probably be there again tonight. Sometimes it's like this - not all of the time, though." he said wearily.

David became concerned as to how he should play the afternoon. After all, he was on an organised departmental tour. And in the company of the departmental head - even if she was standing on a chair playing a pool queue as an electric guitar whilst singing along to "Highway to Hell". Then there was Alicia. Turning up the worse for wear might not be a good idea, he thought. So, he opted for a pre-emptive text to her to explain his predicament and assure her that he was "integrating well". An hour later he nearly was "integrating well" with Caroline, one of the design-girls who had taken a shine to him over lunch - if you can call four pints of lager and a Jaeger bomb, lunch. But he dodged her hand-hold, said he'd see her again and needed to get back for an urgent call, or twenty.

David was buoyed by the lunchtime drinking session, the attention from Caroline and an encouraging text from Alicia which said "Not2 worry/Njoy/integr8 xxx". On his first telephone call he spoke with a medium sized business that were considering a re-brand. He convinced them to have a meeting with Creative Juices describing its studio capabilities as "legendary". Perhaps he was thinking of their legendary drinking capabilities. Hopefully the potential client wouldn't make a speculative visit to the studio that afternoon, he thought. He emailed Dougal, Morris, Wendy and most of his lunch companions to disseminate the good news and create some positive PR for himself. The feedback to the email was encouraging, with Dougal expressing his "delight" that the agency integration programme had borne fruit so early. Even in his inebriated state, David recognised that Dougal was taking part of the credit for his success and that he had also elevated the status of spending a few days in other departments to "an agency integration programme."

There was a collective email reply from the studio people suggesting that David's success should be celebrated that very evening, with a drink or two after work. According to David's watch this was a very short time away. He declined with a perfect and true excuse: Alicia was picking him up. Alicia's offer of a lift was not entirely altruistic. She had thought it wise to extract David before things got out of hand and had also planned to go to do the week's shop at a supermarket not too far from Creative Juices.

So David celebrated his first business win not by drinking beer and eating curry but by pushing a trolley up and down the aisles of the supermarket while a sober Alicia sped ahead plucking food items from shelves and dropping them into the trolley when David eventually caught up. This sometimes took a while as the combination of a malfunctioning trolley wheel and a slightly inebriated David at the helm meant that travelling in straight lines wasn't easy. The situation was exacerbated by Alicia's speed and the crowds of shoppers in each aisle. David tried to concentrate on Alicia's bottom as a navigation tool. She was wearing tight red jeans making her shapely scarlet buttocks seem like beacons that David could aim for whilst navigating his trolley in the crowds. He eventually caught up with the navigation beacons at the checkout, wishing that he could be following them a little longer. Perhaps later, he thought, somewhat ambitiously.

Later that evening, David received a phone call from his father, Peter, to congratulate him on the business meeting he had set up yesterday.

"I think we are making an impact now, after learning the ropes." he said warmly. "In fact, I might have a little win of my own if things go well at the Senedd next month." he added, referring to the Welsh Government's parliament building. When Peter hung up a minute or two later, he reflected on the conversation. Perhaps he shouldn't have told his son about the meeting, as it was still early days. But he had received a call from Piers Jackman an old friend in the inner sanctum of the Welsh Government. Piers was an advisor to the Minister for Business and as such was frequently party to news before it went public. What Piers had told Peter could potentially lead to something which would make Creative Juices a substantial amount of money.

Peter needed to organise the office in the Bay fast. If there was a sniff of business from the Senedd, it was likely that agencies in the nearby Bay would stand a better chance, all other things being equal. He needed to view a couple of offices, pick somewhere a little quirky and get hold of a sign company and interior design company that could both turn things around in a few weeks. Even though it would probably be not much more than a meeting room and a reception. So even this small job could be a tall order. Then Peter remembered a young woman he had chatted with briefly at the networking event. Hadn't she been an interiors person? After scouring his briefcase and suit pockets Peter eventually found the card in his wallet. He made a note in his diary to call her in the morning and added another one to call the agency's preferred sign makers.

Chapter 3: Poached Eggs & Pistachios

Morris surveyed the room of business networkers cynically. There were about fifty of them gathered for an early morning business breakfast in a function room of a hotel just north of Cardiff. They were a mixed bunch, Morris thought. There were the usual suspects donning suits and skirts - probably solicitors, accountants and financial advisors. Then there were three people in their early twenties, all dressed informally. Web designers or social media people, Morris guessed. The third genre of business was much easier to spot: A stereotypical carpenter with a tool belt, a builder sporting a hi-vis jacket and a plasterer wearing a plaster-splattered baseball cap and heavy-rock sweatshirt. They were going straight to site by the looks of it. Morris amused himself with the thought that with the addition of a cowboy and a sailor, a cross selection of the attendees could have passed for the Village People.

Morris's sales background rendered him fairly immune to worrying about talking to people. He'd never had to attend these events to get his door to door career off the ground and he viewed the whole thing as a bit of a soft option compared to knocking doors with boxes of burgers in Pontypridd and being told to piss off. He mused that a bit of door to door sales might toughen some of this crowd up, but knew he needed to stay polite and positive. Telling a fellow business networker to sod off just for asking what he did for a living just wouldn't be the done thing.

He was here to babysit Peter on his first networking outing. The thinly disguised attempt at jump-starting Peter's work ethic had to be seen to be a business development drive by all three directors of Creative Juices. But Peter was late. Actually, Peter was parked at the furthest end of the hotel car park, pretending to be on his mobile phone and pretending to wait for the rain to stop, delaying his attendance at the networking meeting. Finally, he knew he couldn't put it off any longer and after switching his mobile to silent, he headed from the comfort of his car into the morning drizzle and made for the hotel. Oh, how the mighty have fallen, he thought, thinking back on his revered position at the Welsh Government. As he approached the tatty-looking building, a broken illuminated sign displaying the word "reception" winked intermittently at him as if to mock his downward spiral.

Meanwhile, Morris had struck up a conversation with someone. A combination of ego and disdain, rather than fear meant that he hadn't wanted to lower himself to talk to others. So, he had simply stood in the middle of the room sipping a luke-warm coffee and waiting for others to approach him. It hadn't taken long and within a few minutes he had been verbally accosted by a photocopier salesman and a woman selling a natural health product. Neither had asked about Peter, they had simply grabbed his hand in sequence and introduced themselves. Name and job title were followed without a pause for breath by a statement of what they offered, why they were competitive and what benefits he might expect if he exchanged his money for their services. The natural health lady was rather determined and seemed to be claiming that her product could cure pretty much anything. Noting Morris's raised eyebrow, she back-pedalled and admitted that it wasn't much good for life threatening illnesses. Probably. What do you suffer from? she asked. Whatever it was - her product could cure it. The only catch was that it didn't work immediately. No, that's the drawback with some of these miracle cures, you have to take them for 6 to 12 months before they have a possible effect, you see. Six months was £500 but twelve months, by which time he was bound to have been cured of all ills, was a bargain at just £800. And he'd thought the breakfast was expensive at £18!

By the time Peter joined Morris, the "open net-working" session was over and the group had been called to breakfast. Peter mumbled his excuses and apology for his tardiness and the pair tried to locate their designated places for the next part of the meeting. The organisers had devised a complicated system of matching coloured dots to corresponding tables which in turn had a seating plan. This system, they explained, would work for everybody except those who had booked online. Ironically, those networkers who thought that booking online would have been the speediest option were wrong as they all had to be allocated seats last on the tables where there were spaces left. Morris and Peter had been booked online and spent the following minutes milling around looking for free spaces in the melee of morning confusion.

The host cleared his throat as if an influential keynote speech was imminent. The potential gravitas of the moment collapsed quickly though, as he explained that it was most important that no-one took more than two poached eggs from the breakfast buffet. Then he remembered to welcome everyone.

Peter turned to Morris as they were ushered to seats - rather unfortunately - next to each other at the breakfast table.

"High level networking this, isn't it, Morris? Poached egg quota imposed - get it wrong and it could upset the equilibrium of the whole Welsh economy." Peter said sarcastically.

"We shouldn't be sitting together - we're here to meet people." Morris hissed back grabbing at a passing waitress - nearly inappropriately - to request a table transfer.

Peter's cynicism was still switched on as the waitress looked around in vain for a spare place on another table.
"You might have missed the transfer window, Morris!" he shouted as Morris was whisked off.
"I told you - this networking is serious stuff. Poached egg quotas, transfer windows..."

The speaker cleared his throat over the P.A. and a hush fell over the room. Morris was hungry and hadn't anticipated that the speaker's slot would be before breakfast. The only sounds were the distant clanging of bain-marie lids in the kitchen and Morris's rumbling stomach. He fished in his pocket for a small bag of pistachios that he kept for precisely these sorts of emergencies, rubbing his midriff to gesticulate to the others on his table that it was necessary that he consumed the nuts at this point. He gave an exaggerated look of self-pity that suggested the nuts may be needed for medical reasons.

The speaker – Professor Ken Moorland – was from Cardiff Business School. He spoke about the growth of India and China being partly fuelled by the world at large outsourcing the manufacturing of seemingly just about everything to them. He quipped:

"In the business world, it seems it's Shanghai, Mumbai or `bye `bye!" There was a ripple of amusement that didn't quite make it to laughter.

Moorland went on to talk about a Welsh entrepreneur who the business school worked with. He designed and prototyped products in the UK, sourced some components from Germany, but ultimately manufacturing took place in China. Moorland demonstrated the mathematics of the logic behind this by creating a comparative example of producing in the UK versus China. Even with the huge cost of shipping removed, China won hands down over the UK. Because of 3D printing, even prototyping was beginning to shift Eastwards – Moorland explained, going on to explain that technology like 3D printing was fuelling even quicker growth in the East.

Over breakfast, Morris met the two people

seated on either side of him on the big round table. Peter latched on to an accountant who sat to his left. His wife worked for the Welsh Government so there was common ground. Peter felt safe and the accountant seemed relieved that he wouldn't have to talk about business.

Morris exchanged pleasantries with the estate agent to his left and then became engaged in a conversation with a Scottish hypnotherapist called Bryan who was sat to his right. The hypnotherapist explained in a partly decipherable Glaswegian drawl, that under no circumstances must he be mistaken for a hypnotist. Oh no. "Those phoney sideshow performers who make you believe that you were a monkey chasing a snake just give us all a bad name." he declared.

"Fun though?" said Morris, provocatively.

"It's not about fun. If you want to think you're a monkey and behave like one - that's fine by me, if you know what I mean."

Morris didn't, but it was useless to object as Bryan already had him down as a wannabe primate who didn't have the intellectual capacity to differentiate between a stage hypnotist and a clinical hypnotherapist.

To diffuse the tension, Morris used the open-ended questioning technique he had perfected as a door to door salesman to ask Bryan more about what he actually did - and what sort of customers he was looking for. It appeared that Bryan treated a range of phobias and addictions as well as stress, but his specialism, he announced dramatically, was "past-life regression". Morris had nodded all the way through the bits about phobias and stress but his facial expression must have involuntarily changed when past-life regression was mentioned. Noting the scepticism, Bryan moved in to counter it, whispering conspiratorially under his breath "Most have us have had other lives before, my friend!"

Morris twitched uncomfortably, wondering how he'd ended up in the middle of a Harry Potter book when all he'd wanted was to flog some design and print services to local businesses. He was also struggling to understand all of what Bryan said because of his thick Scottish accent. He couldn't help but wonder if Bryan could only hypnotise Scottish people. Surely, if you can't understand all the words the hypnotherapist is saying, it won't work properly? he thought. Then Bryan delivered the big line. This was the big line that was intended to convince Morris of the absolute credibility of past lives and their ability to be accessed. The big line was coming. Then the big line was delivered with sincerity, belief and also, unfortunately, with great volume, causing the other eight people on the table to look up from their breakfasts with shock.

"I've killed people." said Bryan, seemingly unaware of the attention he was attracting from the others around the table and addressing only Morris. He repeated his big line. "I've killed people. Not many, maybe ten." (There was no collective sigh of relief from the others thinking oh, only ten then, well that's ok) He continued "I was a soldier, 2000 years ago. I was just following orders." His soliloquy came to a dramatic close.

Morris wasn't sure how to follow this as the others looked on for some enlightenment or context as to why the adman was sitting next to a mass murderer who seemed quite happy to confess his sins at a business breakfast. The event organiser saved Morris any further dilemma as he took to the mic once again to announce that the poached egg allocation and collection had been perfect and that the event was shaping up to be one of their best ever. What an odd way to measure success, Morris thought, before grabbing his jacket, nodding to the others around the table, shaking hands with the mass-murderer and explaining that he had to shoot off early to pick up his dry cleaning on the way to work.

***

"What happened to Peter, after?" asked Dougal as Morris was overstaying his welcome in Dougal's office and helping himself to the pistachio nuts in a big green bowl on the thick mahogany desk. Morris was oblivious to the fact that Dougal was very busy and gave him a full eight-minute account of the whole networking event, punctuated only by pauses for pistachios. Dougal carried on sifting through his client file, nodding when appropriate and shooting Morris the occasional sympathetic look as if to say "I'm sorry you've had to spend the morning with some tossers." By the end of the discourse, Morris had consumed eleven pistachios. He was only stopped from eating more because his hands were so full of shells that he was incapable of picking up anything else. He bent forward and lobbed them into Dougal's empty waste bin, creating the noise of automatic gunfire.

"So, what about this hypnotist? Does he need anything? Website? Video? Brochure? Logo?" said Douglas, anxious to get something tangible from Morris's pistachio-fuelled self-pity.

"That's just it. They all NEED stuff, but none of them can afford it, Dougal. If we want to deal with these small guys, we've got to package stuff up so it looks like a bargain. We can still charge the public sector and the bigger firms decent money but these little guys won't swallow it." he said, swallowing his thirteenth pistachio, as if to lend visual aid to his words.

"Cheap is OK if you're overheads are low, Morris, but ours aren't. We employ twenty-eight staff, run ten cars, own and maintain a building and thanks to the government we now have to start paying bloody pension for every bugger too! It's gonna take a lot of two-sided leaflets to pay for that, but I welcome your thoughts on the opportunity. Why don't you discuss it with Peter and the others and we can meet later in the week and talk about it in more detail?" said Dougal, getting up to put his jacket on, stepping on a stray pistachio shell and walking out of the room with a "subject closed" expression on his face, accidentally turning the light off and leaving Morris in darkness.

"I thought that went quite well." said Morris pompously and quietly to himself, helping himself to another pistachio. His self-indulgent reverie was soon broken by the entrance of Rebecca Jones, one of the agency's Account Directors. She screamed, having flicked the light on in Dougal's office only to find an ex door to door salesman covered in pistachio shells slouching in one of the client chairs in the dark. But Morris was one of the agency bosses, so hers was not to question why.

"Oh, I'm sorry, Morris, I didn't see you there... I mean I wasn't expecting you in the dark..." she stuttered. Morris quickly asserted his authority by brushing away some of the shells and explaining that he thought better in the dark and that it was a technique he had learned while travelling in the Far East as a young man. She seemed impressed, or at least blagged it well. He studied her. Rebecca was about thirty-three with a pleasant figure that was adorned with a snug-fitting grey and black dress which finished an inch or so above her knees. Aware of his stare lingering too long she flicked her dark hair sideways and shot him a warning look with her green eyes.

But Morris was one step ahead.

"Rebecca. I have been tasked with heading a team to evaluate suitable approaches to the micro-business market for Creative Juices, and I'd like to you to be part of it. It's a small team - there will only be four or us: You, me, David - Peter's son - and Iestyn - our new Financial Controller. Rebecca looked slightly embarrassed and then pleased and then flattered. She cocked her head flirtily, smiled slowly and simply said "I'd be delighted. Just tell me where you want me." Damn - she'd been going for mildly flirty and accidentally gone overboard with a faux pas that could have been taken the wrong way. "I have to go." she said quickly, blushing as she left the room at lightning speed propelled by the desire to give her cheeks the chill of the cool air in the company car park.

Morris congratulated himself again and celebrated with a final pistachio before heading to the kitchen to make himself a coffee. He found Peter there, putting his tin-foiled sandwiches into the fridge. The two exchanged stories from the morning's networking meeting, with Morris quick to point out that he had spotted some potential and that Dougal had entrusted him with the development of "Project Micro", the initiative to attract smaller sized businesses. Morris was aware that he was exaggerating Dougal's instructions, but subconsciously he wanted to get one over on Peter. It didn't work. Peter simply smiled and wished him good luck, adding that he - Peter - might have some profitable news soon. Mindful of the need to convert his ego-driven, partly-fictional Project Micro into reality before Dougal intervened, Morris walked to his office and emailed Rebecca, Iestyn and David to arrange a meeting to kick off the initiative.

The following Thursday at midday, the meeting was convened. Morris had decided that the project was worthy of a sandwich lunch and had duly ordered a generous buffet which he hoped would fuel the imagination of the newly-compiled team. It had the opposite effect as Rebecca was on a low-carb diet, so nothing in the range of mayo-laden sandwiches, crusty quiches and sausage rolls, really accommodated her needs. Iestyn, it turned out, was a vegan but had been too shy to say. David had enjoyed a mid-morning Starbucks snack and wasn't hungry. So, it was with some humiliation that Morris dispatched the trays to be offered around the rest of the agency, after he had filled his plate.

Morris called the meeting to order and outlined the objective: "As an advertising agency we have been very successful supporting larger businesses and the public sector. The economy and the political landscape are changing and this is having an effect on our business. We are surrounded by small businesses. In fact, I spent a morning with fifty or more of them last week at a local business networking event. However, these companies are small - sometimes just one or two people - and they cannot afford a great deal. Our challenge is to find a way to engage with them profitably at a price that is worthwhile for us, but still attractive to them."

There was silence for a while, as the team watched Morris pick up a sandwich which promptly de-constructed itself in Morris's hand, leaving curried mayonnaise dripping down his wrist. He tried to use a serviette to rectify the situation but in the process of grabbing it encouraged a large lump of coronation chicken breast to leap from the sandwich onto his lap. The audience of three clearly found all this much more absorbing than trying to find an answer to the small business problem. Eventually, someone spoke.

"Maybe we need to cut our costs for the small guys." David piped up, pleased that as a relative newbie he was first in. "From my limited experience, it seems that having every client serviced by a Designer, Account Manager and Account Director is a little bit of overkill?" he ventured. But Rebecca was quick to defend the account handlers, being a senior one herself.

"I disagree, David. You can't have clients talking to designers, or even worse seeing them. God knows what would happen. They might end up telling the client the truth, talking them out of bigger brochures into a little leaflet, for example. Especially if it's after midday, if you know what I mean!" she added with a barb, referring to the studio's frequent liquid lunches.

Morris was keen to diffuse the age-old rivalry of studio and account handlers so turned to Iestyn, who was the new Financial Controller and so belonged to neither department.

"What do you think Iestyn? How can it work with margins? What could we offer?"

Iestyn replied that he needed some time to study margins on various services and get a handle on how long fixed-fee jobs took, and the potential consequences if they overran. The group discussed the various ad agency services and what might appeal to very small businesses. It was beginning to look like a dead-end meeting, then Rebecca cut in:

"What about video? We could film here against a green screen, drop some background graphics in, get the businesses to do a pitch themselves or charge more and give them an actor."

There was a little buzz around the meeting room. Video was not new, but it had come down considerably in cost and some of the studio guys had begun to dabble with the free editing software that was available online.

"OK, not exactly a high-end production company, but no extra overheads and we could film a few in a day." Rebecca suggested as the three men stared at her. She smiled modestly and flicked her hair self-consciously. Morris was to have the final word.

"I think this has legs" he said, smiling. He pressed on. "The devil is in the detail. I suggest we all give this some thought and let's meet again to talk more."

Chapter 4: Sausage Rolls

Peter had quickly realised that there were a number of vacant offices in the Bay. Mark Flawless, the owner of Flawless Sales and Lettings had assured him that there was a huge demand for offices and that they were in short supply. None of this tallied with the glut of viewings that Peter had been offered. But that's estate agents for you, Peter thought, eyeing Mark's trendy suit suspiciously.

"Look Mark, I'm not trying to achieve some sort of world record in seeing how many vacant premises I can visit in a morning, so let's just cut to the chase and show me the best three, please. And that's not the three that you want me to have, it's the three that most closely fit the criteria I gave you." Flawless gave a practised oily smile. He used it whenever he was being insulted by a customer, which was fairly frequently. The smile created a forcefield of resilience for him and gave an air of "I know much more about this subject, but this is a common reaction from someone as ignorant as you."

Half an hour later, Peter was on the fifth floor of an old merchant bank in a square that was crammed with buildings that would have been the epicentre of trade during the industrial revolution. There were merchant banks, a coal exchange and a shipping company's emblem still engraved into the stone of an elegant building. You could almost feel the buzz of the square in all its former glory. Peter's reverie was cut short by Paula, to whom Mark Flawless had assigned the task of the show-arounds. Peter sensed that Mark had become impatient with him and that Paula's appointment was intended to show some sort of downgrading. In fact, Peter couldn't have been more delighted. Paula was a bubbly thirty-something with a dark bob and a pretty face. He began to wish he was seeing all the premises he had been offered.

Peter peered out of the window and noticed a rival ad agency in the building opposite, two floors lower. He grinned at Paula.

"I quite like the idea of being up here and looking down on the competition." beckoning her to come over to the window. She scuttled up and stood unnecessarily close to him as he pointed down and explained how much rivalry there was in the advertising business. Paula smiled and bent forward, leaning over a desk near the window to get a better view of the building opposite. Peter was aware how flirtatious Paula was being but didn't flatter himself by suspecting it was anything more than her wanting the sale and the commission that inevitably went with it.

After a couple more viewings of offices and even more of Paula's rear, Peter felt that there was a clear first choice office to show Dougal. The second and third hadn't any parking and were smaller than the first so the decision was not a difficult one. Not only did the first look down on the competition, it boasted a large meeting room, two offices and an impressive reception area. As a satellite office it needed to be small but not just a token meeting room that looked as if it might have been hired by the hour. So, this was perfect, Peter thought. He confirmed the terms of the lease with Paula and checked that Creative Juices would be able to customise the office, with signage and interior work. Paula beamed and agreed to everything. Peter wondered if he could have asked for more, she seemed so accommodating. His mood turned as he began to wonder if she might be very desperate for the money -the commission she would earn from the let of the office. He looked at her, but the quality and style of her clothes didn't suggest that his assumption was right. Designer skirt and jacket, black, fitted, but with an unusual slightly exotic but understated trim. The shoes and top also looked good quality, though Peter was no expert. As they parted, he promised to email her with some possible dates for Dougal to carry out what he hoped would be a rubber stamp second viewing. Paula stressed that the office would be in great demand so the viewing should be as soon as possible. Which Peter translated as Paula wanted it in this month's sales figures. His suspicion was confirmed with her parting flirt.

"Peter - we've got on well and I like you, so I will try to hold these offices for you but Mark won't let me do it for long. I'll help you if you can help me and come back to me quickly." She shook his hand professionally to end the meeting but added in a little giggle and wink to hopefully seal the deal.

Nothing happened for a few days because it snowed. Snow in the UK brings everything to a halt. If aliens studied the behaviour of adults when it snows, they would think the whole nation was mad. Snow divides people into two groups. Those who have urgent commitments and to whom it will be a great cause of hassle. It might involve having to find childcare because of closed schools, checking on elderly relatives, or for some working in the emergency services, dealing with the serious consequences that extreme weather can bring.

Then there is the other group. Their kids are old enough to go out and enjoy the time off school. Their employers have sent everyone home.

They have a sudden memory lapse of their recent comments about never having enough time to get jobs done around the house, finish the book they've been reading or watch a film. So, when the snow gives them the gift of freedom, what do half the British population do? They go to the pub. Not only do they go to the pub, they go early and they drink for the entire afternoon, bonding with fellow snow-day neighbours, discussing the same topics: "How long will it go on for? How deep will it get? Will we get cut off? Where were the gritters? Will it freeze? Will there be floods when the ice melts? How much food is in the supermarkets? Are people panic-buying or is it necessary?"

Then the biggest question of all is asked. The one that will bond everyone sipping their beers, wines and spirits on that freezing, blizzardy afternoon.
"What if the pub runs out of drink? The delivery might not get through!"

Silence, shock, concern. The landlord is promptly heckled and requested to reassure his punters that he has enough stock to take their money for many more days if necessary. He tells them to carry on enjoying themselves and that there is plenty to go around. It mightn't be true, but who can prove it? The pub breathes a collective, boozy sigh of relief and carries on the merriment discussing snow, TV and shops that are hiking the price of bread by 300% or 400%. "Disgusting!" people say "Taking advantage of people like that. They should boycott them!"

Dougal and his wife Nadine found themselves in that very snow-day situation, pub-bound and snowed into their pretty little village in the middle of the Vale of Glamorgan, half an hour from Cardiff and deeply covered by a thick white blanket. Dougal and Nadine weren't really motivated by the drinking on that particular afternoon, although the village camaraderie was enjoyable so they indulged. They were actually there because they were running low on food after three solid days of snow so reasoned that a pub meal or two might be a wise precaution. The agency was shut so Dougal had decided to enjoy spending time with Nadine who he saw relatively infrequently due to her role as an international sales manager for a cosmetics company. When the nation had gone into red alert mode and Dougal had needed to decide whether to shut the agency for a couple of days, Nadine had also been incredibly busy trying to close a big deal in London before dashing back just in time for snow curfew. As a result of their busy lives, neither had thought to stock up on food. Nadine had quickly stopped at a mini M&S at a service station on the M4 and grabbed a chicken, some broccoli and a bag of potatoes.

Dougal had dashed into a Tesco Express and pro-
cured twelve bottles of white wine, four tubes
of Pringles and four ready meals - two lasagne
and two cannelloni. Then he dashed back from
his car before leaving to supplement his rations
with four bottles of red wine, which he felt
would be a better match for his microwavable
Italian food.

Meanwhile, in Cardiff David and Alicia were also
snowbound, but in a more "pretend it's more
serious than it is" way. Alicia decided to do
some cleaning and suggested that David might
do some ironing. David was not in the best of
humour as the band that he played guitar in had
two gigs that weekend and both had been cancelled because of the snow. David strongly suspected that in both cases it was a case of a
landlord not wanting to spend money attracting
people to a pub that was already full.

The band was called Pub Dog and played cover
versions of all types of songs from the 60's to the
present day. Playing guitar had provided David
with pocket money during his unemployment.
He had previously played for a ZZ Top tribute
band but got fed up of wearing a long wig and
huge beard under blazing hot stage lights on the
cabaret circuit. The band - ZZ TopNot - were
popular as they lampooned the 80's band as well
as covering their songs. But David had never

felt particularly cool in costume and was frequently laughed at. Which of course was the point, but when you're insecure and looking for female company it wasn't a good place to be. So, he quit what was quite a lucrative earner by music standards and joined Pub Dog, who gigged a couple of times a month, when it suited everyone. He earned much less but he didn't feel like a prat.

Keen to avoid or at least postpone the ironing, David told Alicia that he was going to treat her to lunch. Before she had chance to look forward to sitting in a warm, chic restaurant nibbling on steak and enjoying a glass of Malbec, David clarified that the source of the meal would be Lunchbake - the chain of bakers. Lunchbake is the high point of the day for office workers up and down the country, many of whom seek to relieve the tedium of their employment by indulging in a tasty, desk-bound takeaway. Sheer physical laziness often means that rather than making the walk to Lunchbake part of the lunchtime routine, enjoying fresh air and exercise, most workers delegate the "fetch-lunch" task to one colleague. As a result, it can be quite deceptive to see a queue of four people each of whom are ordering on behalf of ten fellow workers. The staff don't mind and seem to enjoy witnessing the impulse purchase decisions.

Fundamentally the shop sells three things - sandwiches, hot pastries like pasties and bakes and also cakes and sweet stuff. Here's the rule of thumb: Most people go in determined to have just a sandwich or roll and even take advantage of the healthy options. But somewhere along the way they become overwhelmed by the aroma of freshly cooked pasties and sausage rolls and in a quandary of either hot food or sandwich, some-how become overcome with confusion and order both. Then - in resignation - they add some kind of little cake for an afternoon treat.

When David arrived at the store, he was fancying a warm Cornish Pasty.

"We don't serve them" he was told. He argued the point and explained that he had definitely had one at a* that very shop in the past. The server looked disbelievingly at him as if he might only be convinced of the validity of his claim on pro-duction of photographic evidence, which David didn't have.

The teenager went on to tell to him in hushed tones that he could have what they used to be able to call a Cornish Pasty, as long as neither of them referred to it as a Cornish Pasty and as long as he promised to forget all about the incident afterwards. David agreed. The assistant went on to whisper to him that pasties could no longer be called Cornish unless they are made in Cornwall. I asked him where his were made.

"Barry" he replied.

"So, can we just call it a Barry pasty and get on with it?" David said impatiently, though he couldn't help thinking that a Barry Pasty just didn't sound as good.

David checked out his story on his mobile as soon as he got back to the car it turns out it was absolutely right. The Cornish Pasty was indeed given Protected Geographical Indication (PGI) status - in 2011. The PGI status is the same one that protects champagne, Parma ham, Stilton cheese, Arbroath smokies and Cornish clotted cream. You can make Cornish Pasties wherever you like but you can't call them Cornish unless they are made in Cornwall.

 All of this made him think about how important words are in making food sound more appealing. Studying a menu in a restaurant a few days later he noticed "trio of sausages" on offer. Surely, a trio sing or play music? David would have been extremely surprised if the bangers could have done either particularly well. He thought about the likely reaction had he asked for a "trio of beers" for his mates in his local. He told his story to an amused Alicia over lunch on his return:

"And now everything is "pan fried" rather than just 'fried' which just doesn't sound good anymore. I mean, what else are you going to fry it in? The same of course is true of "oven baked." In "Oven Baked Fillet of Sea Bass" the word "oven" is unnecessary but somehow adds a little romance to the dish and probably justifies an extra few quid for it. And then there are the sauces. Gravy has been driven into virtual extinction only to be replaced by the far more palatable "jus". "Jus" is rarely just left to be sloshed all over the plate as its predecessor might have been. Instead, jus is usually "drizzled delicately" or perhaps even "doused with glee", again putting another £3.50 on the desirability factor of the dish.

Finally, there is the description of how the dish is presented. Never can the chefs of today be content with leaving to our imagination the relationship between the chicken breast and the rice and how they got together. No, the chicken must "nestle" on the bed of rice, or even worse be served "alongside a timbale of delicately steamed rice" Whatever next? Will the chicken "sit confidently astride the rice", "nuzzle up next to the mash" or perhaps even be parachuted into a giant Yorkshire Pudding by a team of dancing butterflies?"

Alicia giggled. David concluded with his punch-line: "So I've made a resolution to seek out a plain English establishment that describes its fayre honestly. This is the sort of thing I want to see

"Small, salty cottage pie made in a commercial kitchen in Birmingham a few weeks ago, blast frozen, quickly microwaved and presented with a salad garnish to make you think it's home-made. £14.50." Alicia laughed again and began to enjoy a newfound respect for David who seemed to be growing in confidence by the day since starting at Creative Juices.

"Shall we forget about the rest of the housework and have fun today?" she suggested.

They headed out for the afternoon festooned with brightly coloured wool garments, their bodies bloated by layers and their agility reduced to zero. Even turning a head to talk required a body turn of 90 degrees to overcome the mobility-reducing effects of wearing eight layers of clothing.

The afternoon was spent slipping and snowballing, laughing and looking for places to shelter from the bitter wind. Many retailers had shut up shop but some were open - either the national chains that probably had "snow policies" or the self-employed cafe-owners who worried that the loss of a few days takings could take their businesses under, so narrow were their margins. Alicia jumped 90 degrees to face David, looking like someone doing the Timewarp in the Rocky Horror Picture Show. A conversation was necessary so David jumped to the right to face her.

"Look at that sign up ahead - I think it's open. Is it a coffee place?" said Alicia, jerking her head sideways in the direction of what was previously ahead before she had jumped 90 degrees. David jumped to look. A small "A" board about 40 metres up the high street of the north Cardiff suburb read:

Happy Snow Day! Free coffee with every cake. It's warm in here!

It's great to see a hard-working entrepreneur giving it his all to make the best of what could be a bad situation. The cafe - called "Not Another Coffee Shop" was packed and the owners - a couple in their thirties - were taking full advantage handing out takeaway menus and promoting special events to their captive audience. Alicia and David tried to squeeze into a tiny corner booth. In their haste to nab the table they had forgotten that their multiple jumpers, t-shirts and bubble jackets had swelled them to twice their normal volume. They quickly shed a few layers and tucked into the booth to examine the small, laminated menu whilst glancing at the television on the wall relaying pictures of stranded motorists and crammed airport lounges.

"Why is this place called Not Another Coffee Shop?" said Alicia.

"It made me laugh." said David "I think it's two things: One - it's suggesting that this is much better than your average coffee house. And two, it's having a pop at how many coffee shops are opening every month." he declared.

It was probably true. The British were having a love affair with coffee for no particular reason. It probably started in the USA as it seems do most things. If they are good things, we ignore the fact that they originated in the US, but if we want to deride something - like the proliferation of coffee houses - we blame the Americans. When David's father had been David's age, he would have been content to go to a "greasy spoon cafe" and order a " strong milky coffee" from the "girl behind the counter". Now you had to go to a "coffee house", order a "skinny decaf latte with a double shot" from someone who's job title is "Barista". The result is much the same but the latter comes with a fancy glass a £5 price tag and numerous attempts to up-sell you to a bigger drink or a cake, to keep the drink company.

But this place was different and seem to delight at taking the mickey out of the large national chains with slogans on the back of the menu that included: "The place where it doesn't COSTA fortune to drink coffee". And "Starbucks is mega-bucks - we're cheaper and more fun". David disliked the ubiquitous national coffee chains, always supported the underdog and so this place immediately gelled with him. Emma, the co-owner came over to introduce herself and take their order. It felt good to be valued. After all the national chains are owned by masses of share-holders and accountants who try their best to avoid paying tax, David thought. What could be more genuine than being served by the owner of this lovely little place and given a run-down on its history? It turned out that Emma and husband Mark had both trained as accountants and after a spell in one of the big accountancy firms had decided that there was more to life. With the benefit of training in acute fiscal planning, they set about researching and planning their catering venture which launched seven months later. David tried to be casual about asking if they used a marketing company, but it came over as a loaded question. Emma was diplomatic enough to take his business card and Alicia regarded the whole situation with equal measures of embarrassment and pride.

David glanced at the TV. The weather news had eventually petered out and was being replaced with a speech by the First Minister for Scotland, Cameron Dunbar. David suddenly realised that this was not a minor news item but breaking news. He tapped Alicia's arms and pointed to the subtitles and summary on the screen.

European Union backs Scotland's bid for 2nd independence referendum.

Dunbar's predecessor, Fiona Campbell, had presided over the original independence referendum that had seen a narrow majority in favour of remaining in the UK. Since then, a wave of separatist support had been sweeping across Scotland, initiated and fuelled by the Scottish Nationalists. The party were gathering political allies both in Scotland and in the EU, an entity that resented the UK's exit from its membership and welcomed Scotland's pro-European stance.

David and Alicia shrugged in unison. After all, what did it mean for them?

"Another coffee?" David suggested.

Chapter 5: Laverbread

Despite the announcement of the EU backing a second Scottish referendum, nothing significant happened for a week. As expected, Cameron Dunbar made a brief speech at Holyrood shortly after, but zilch since. In his speech he welcomed the EU's stance on the matter and acknowledged the importance of free trade, free movement of citizens and international security. By highlighting some of the key principles of the EU he wasn't directly saying he supported being a member state, but it sounded a lot like it. The speech had been well-written. Had it been delivered by Winston Churchill it might have even been classed as rousing, but Dunbar's monotonous vocal took away any possible gravitas.

Cameron Dunbar was not blessed with an interesting voice. Despite vocal coaching in his early political life he now resigned himself to what he occasionally perceived to be a handicap. That said, his Robbie Williams-sized ego usually overcame any bouts of self-doubt and found him preening his immaculate jet-black hair and reflecting on his brilliance within minutes. The voice was the combination of being tone deaf and brought up in Perth by a mother from Orkney and a father from Glasgow. The vocal result was an odd monotone that could probably put a foreigner to sleep but to a Scot was just an indication of a dour, hardworking man with strong beliefs and a resolute attitude. To the English, Welsh and Irish, Dunbar sounded pessimistic but to the Scots has was dependable and gritty.

Although to the public it appeared that not much was happening by way of a response to the EU's comments, behind the scenes in Edinburgh intense discussions were taking place between Dunbar, his political advisors and publicists. Questions abounded. Do we have mandate? Can we call a referendum? What will London's response be? London was how the ruling Scottish nationalists referred to central government at Westminster. And "Bastard Torres" was the expression frequently used when referring to the ruling Conservative party. The publicists usually raised eyebrows at this, worried that ministers might become so used to using the term in private that it may suddenly slip out in public.

To make a referendum legal, permission had to be granted from London in what is known as a section 30 order. The UK government had granted that permission for the initial independence referendum, but after the people of

Scotland voted to remain in the UK, the temporary devolved power to hold such a referendum had been withdrawn by London. Dunbar had hit a brick wall. There seemed to be no legal basis for a second referendum.

He ushered Dunkan Bride, his chief legal advisor and Alistair Mc Fadden, his communications manager into the oak-panelled office. The atmosphere was tense - time was running out to capitalise on the EU's comments. Bride spoke first.

"Having explored all the constitutional avenues we believe that the only legal basis on which we can request a section 30 order to allow a second referendum on Scottish independence is on the grounds that the UK has left the EU but the people of Scotland wish to remain. Only by becoming an independent state can Scotland begin to negotiate membership of the EU."

"And if we are refused?" said Dunbar flatly. It was McFadden rather than Bride who answered.

"We may need to court our friends in Brussels to add weight to our argument. If we can make our intentions clear and leak the story in stages to the appropriate media, London may be forced into a position of issuing the section 30 order, if public opinion is behind it."

The three men discussed the various options, searched in vain for constitutional precedents that could be used and eventually agreed that Bride's suggestion was the best, if not the only option. Certainly, London would not be surprised, but it was better to go with a robust, obvious strategy rather than a flimsy, surprise tactic which could quickly collapse.

A few journalists were leaked snippets in the weeks that followed. Dunbar's meeting with the EU in Brussels was the first. The media were fed the reason for the meeting being "to discuss Scotland's ongoing relationship with its EU partners". The broadsheets gave their interpretation of the phrase and explored the potential consequences. The tabloids didn't bother with the subtlety and ran the headlines "DOOMBAR!" and "ScOUTland?"

The campaign was underway as snow and night fell in Edinburgh

***

Back in Wales, the snow had melted, the cogs of the economy had reluctantly begun to turn again and Creative Juices had resumed yellow alert, having happily put their heads in the sand during the snow crisis.

Mark Flawless rejected Dougal's offer for the premises in the Bay. Paula showed Peter some smaller offices a block away from the main square, bordering the former red light and docks area. Eventually a deal was done and the office was ready to be tarted-up. Peter wasn't best-pleased with the final choice of office, having imagined something more grandiose than two cubicle-type rooms, a shared reception and a bathroom - which was bigger than one of the cubicle rooms. Perhaps the bathroom could double as the meeting room - he thought sarcastically. He was used to big Welsh Government budgets, not the shrinking coffers of a troubled small business.

He was having a celebratory coffee with Paula after the lease had been signed, in a café not far from the new office. The eatery was a mix of African artefacts, live music posters, strong-smelling coffee, fresh flowers and quiches - including an improbable pine nut, green olive, beetroot, feta and laverbread one.

"It makes you wonder whether the café was designed by committee, or if it's a representation of the owner's eclectic life?" said Peter. The place was staffed by student-types, so the lack of an owner to interrogate brought his investigative mood to a close. Paula gave the appropriate "thank you for the business and good luck" and Peter began to feel slightly downhearted, guessing that Paula's interest in him had, after all, been purely professional.

"You don't seem very happy, Peter, considering you have just signed a lease for your new Bay office!" said Paula.

Peter hesitated, realising that his low spirits weren't entirely based around the Paula situation. He confessed that the office didn't quite live up to what he had in mind in terms of a trendy ad agency pad. Paula raised her eyebrows in a look that said "you get what you pay for" and Peter shrugged in a way that said it was out of his control.

"You'll get the rent money from the studio flat above as well - and that could help add a little fun to the place." said Paula, before Peter poured cold water on the suggestion by pointing out that the flat was not even let and contained only a bed and a wardrobe and had peeling wallpaper and a defective shower.

"I had lined up an Interior Designer to handle the transformation." explained Peter. "But Rogers has scuppered the plan and has suggested we could do it for a fraction of the price at IKEA!" he continued in an exasperated tone.

"IKEA have some good things, Peter." Paula chipped in. "If you need a hand, I'm not bad with interiors and I'll come with you and point you in the right direction. After all, I know the property, as well. It won't take much. I know a cheap decorator too."

Peter's mood quickly elevated and he smiled, grateful for some positive conversation and the surprise chance to spend more time with Paula. She checked her watch, announced she was running late for a viewing and within seconds was gone, leaving Peter staring at her empty cappuccino, flecked with coffee residue and topped with lipstick. Feeling tired and hungry but buoyed by his conversation with Paula, he ordered the odd-sounding pine nut, green olive, feta, beetroot and laverbread quiche - in the scheme of an early lunch.

"I'll settle up now for everything before I eat, please." Peter said to the server, who took his note and handed back a few coins in change.

"What is laverbread anyway?" asked Peter, pocketing the money without thought for the tip jar in front of him.

" Seaweed. It's Welsh. Apparently, it's an acquired taste." retorted the affronted Scottish drama graduate triumphantly, before moving quickly on to the next customer and preventing Peter from changing his mind about the seaweed quiche.

***

Back at Creatives Juices, Morris had convened another meeting on the video ad project, this time dispensing with the buffet. Iestyn had been tasked with running the numbers and assessing the viability of the project, which was creatively led by Rebecca, assisted by David. David was pleased to be involved - as a newbie. He threw maximum enthusiasm into it, not least because he hoped it was his escape route from telesales-tedium, if he could make himself indispensable.

Morris gave a quick recap of the purpose of the meeting before inviting Rebecca to outline her proposal. She rose, dressed smartly in a black skirt and snugly fitting grey jacket and nodded to David who by contrast was sporting rather informal attire, old Levi's and a blue Fat Face fleece. His job for today was to man the data projector and distribute the hand-outs. Rebecca nodded to him and he awoke the sleeping projector which beamed the Creative Juices opening slide onto the screen, casting an orange hue across the faces in the dimly-lit room.

"Thank you, Morris for outlining why we are here and what the objectives of the project are. I'm going to go over the operational and creative side of what we propose. In short, we want to make TV style online video ads affordable for micro businesses. But what does affordable mean? To get a benchmark I've talked to all our account handlers and also everybody who has attended networking events recently. The consensus is that the ad needs to cost under £1000. Iestyn will go over our costs per sale, margins and necessary sales volumes later, but I'll give you an insight of how we propose to keep costs to a minimum."

Rebecca went to on to explain that the cost of actors was potentially prohibitive, so the proposal was to use aspiring talent, many of whom - she suspected - would perform for under £100, just to have something to include in their showreel. The filming would need a large room, to cover all possible scenarios, though most of it would be filmed against a portable green screen, which allowed other backgrounds to appear realistically behind the actors, giving the impression that they were on location somewhere. It would be necessary to hire a venue, like a hotel conference room for the day, during which it was estimated they could film four ads, Rebecca said.

Morris looked doubtful at this point.

"What about the actors? Will they be the same throughout the day?"

"No - there will be different ones for each ad." replied Rebecca. "David will act as producer and co-ordinate actor arrival times, scripting -Tim Hughes, our copywriter - I hope, can write these - and props. David beamed at the prospect of getting out of telesales.

"Props?" quizzed Morris.

"Yes. To give you an example, we have created an outline ad for an IT support company which David will take you through" explained Rebecca.

David overcame his slight nerves and loaded the next slide. He coughed, then began.

"My father - who you know - is a big fan of Fawlty Towers and we regularly watched re-runs of it as kids. Many of you will have seen it on TV, I know. So, if you have, do you remember the episode where Basil gets infuriated with a broken-down car and beats it with a large branch?" Everyone nodded, some more emphatically than others.

"The idea is the we have an office worker, becoming gradually more annoyed with a slow computer which eventually freezes altogether. Their mounting anger is demonstrated as they disappear off-camera and return with increasingly bigger implements with which to beat the computer. Finally, the PC is destroyed with a huge over-sized mallet... or something similar." explained David to an audience, who were beginning to look sceptical.

"That sounds expensive." said Iestyn, employing one of his favourite phrases. "We'd have to cost out the computer, the mallet, everything. I know you're probably thinking of an old or defunct PC but still, what if we don't get it right first time?"

"First take." mumbled Rebecca, not intending to correct Iestyn but wanting to demonstrate her glossary of important terms for the business, all of which had been recently gleaned from Wikipedia. Rebecca was thrown a little by Iestyn's negative comment as they had done the general costings together for the project, which Iestyn was about to present. Unfortunately, the Fawlty Towers-inspired example ad had been a very late addition to the presentation and Rebecca had omitted to discuss it with Iestyn. She flashed him a smile. It didn't work, as he was looking down at his figures and frowning. He went on to dig into the detail and before long the whole concept was being picked apart.

Morris sensed an opportunity passing and suggested a comfort break. Comfort breaks – or bio breaks - are part of today's business "must-know" phrases. They really mean "I'm busting for a pee and I'm sure many of you are too. Or maybe you want a fag or just a break from this tedious meeting." But of course, it's not the done-thing to say that. David had learned much of this a few jobs ago at an American call-centre operation. He had only been a sort of glorified filing clerk and tea-boy, but overheard some choice conversations, many of which bemused him at first.

There was the phrase used when someone has left their workstation for a toilet or fag-break, or because they were pissed off. The phone rings and in their absence, it is picked up by a colleague, who announces to the caller that the individual is "not at their desk at the moment." Ah, gone for a piss then, thinks the caller, never daring to say it. And then there was the classic line that was used every time someone was fired, or walked out - both of which were common: "I'm sorry, John's no longer with the company." I mean, you can't tell the truth, can you?

"I'm sorry John turned up to work stoned last Monday. Sadly, no-one noticed until late morning when he began taking his clothes off announcing that the only way to liven up such a monotonous job was to do it naked. He was escorted off the premises shortly afterwards, singing and wearing just his underwear. He is currently trying to sue the company for unfair dismissal based on his work-related stress. He'll probably succeed."

Other essential work-speak includes Q and FY, David remembered. When you propose a plan, it is essential to let people know when it could be realised. Only rookies say October-December next year. Proper etiquette is Q4 (quarter four), FY and then the financial year it applies to.

Another popular one, David had found at the American company, was to talk about their a "flat org. chart." David had supposed this to be a negative thing until he had discovered that a "flat organisational chart" just meant a lack of managerial and supervisory layers. Furthermore, it was important to "reach out" to someone rather than ask them something and to "ping" emails rather than simply send them. Wankers - David had thought. His negativity was probably the reason that this segment of his employment history had not turned out to be a large one.

David realised he had wasted his comfort break pontificating about business-lingo as the others returned to the room, looking refreshed, for various reasons. Iestyn gave his presentations on financials and even included a more positive financial appraisal of the Fawlty Towers ad, thanks to a charm-offensive by Rebecca in the break. The truth was that this project needed to proceed. Morris knew the business was in trouble. Rebecca wanted recognition. Iestyn fancied Rebecca. And David just wanted to get out of telesales.

For all those reasons, it was decided that a pilot project would be launched in Q2 - 4 weeks away - subject to approval by the board, which Morris would handle.

David decided - as a newly appointed Film Producer - he could afford a short celebration with the studio in the pub at lunchtime. He hadn't been back since his inauguration, so he thought had better check he could join them. A quick detour on the way back to his desk found him in the studio. He was walking quickly - keen for his detour not to be too obvious. As he entered the studio, his pace slowed, due to the layers of sticky Spray Mount glue residue that layered the floor. Spray Mount was used to attach visuals to board to present to clients. Although many clients were quite happy to have the visuals for their ads, mailshots and websites by email, doing it "old-style" with printed visuals stuck to good quality board, often made a difference to the clients' reaction and also gave them something to keep.

The studio was empty. Or at least it seemed to be until a voice emanated from behind a partition. It was Derek - the Art Director.

" Hello David. Are you looking for Wendy? They're all in the Urchin and Seahorse - it's just me and Octavia holding the fort. Yes - we'll sort the production schedule out while they get creative in the pub!" he said, though in good nature. Octavia appeared behind him and made a face which suggested that her view of things was not as positive or generous in spirit.

"Thanks Derek. Is that the pub I would have gone to before with them?" asked David.

Derek kindly offered to call Wendy on the mobile to double-check they were in the Urchin and Seahorse sensing David's caution and shyness. Within a short space of time David was pub-bound. On the way his eye was caught by headline news courtesy of a huge TV in the window an up-market home entertainment shop.

"Scotland: Independence Referendum to go ahead - says Dunbar." David began to wonder what the fuss was all about, with so much news coverage in past weeks being devoted to Scotland and Cameron Dunbar. It didn't affect him, after all. Why couldn't the media be more relevant?

The Urchin and Seahorse felt more like an Irish bar on a Friday night than a suburban Cardiff public house on a Tuesday lunchtime. The atmosphere was buzzing, the juke box loud and retro, the conversation animated. In fact, it took David a while to find the studio, who were playing pool in the back room, to the well-amped soundtrack of Deep Purple's "Smoke on the Water".

David was greeted like a long-lost hero with whoops and cheers and offers of drinks. Caroline simply smiled at him. Wendy thrust a gin and tonic in front of him and David accepted it, despite the fact he wasn't really a gin fan. He sat in the only empty seat, next to Caroline.

"What about this Scottish thing?" he said, trying to make conversation, but realised he sounded rather dull and boring, so hastily added "It's on TV all the time. Bit boring. How long have you lot been here?"

"I don't really follow politics" Caroline said apologetically. "I like art and theatre."

Roadblock. David was stumped for an answer, knowing virtually nothing about either subject. Unwisely, he ploughed on, nonetheless.

"I went to see the panto at the New Theatre last year. Jack and the Beanstalk. Really funny. Very good!"

It was Caroline's turn to be lacking inspiration for a reply. An awkward silence would have happened were it not for the juke box blasting out the opening chords to Lynyrd Skynyrd's 'Freebird', drowning out the difficulty. Tim thrust a pool cue at David announcing that it was his turn to play the winner. The afternoon rocked and rolled on.

**

Peter and Paula were in IKEA. It had been slightly difficult to arrange as it really had to be a weekday rather than a weekend to make it legitimately work for Peter. Paula, on the other hand, had needed to find an excuse to take a couple of hours off on a Wednesday morning. Even though Creative Juices were tenants of the property the agency was managing, she wasn't sure that their obligation extended to taking the tenant furniture shopping. Paula felt slightly guilty and began to wonder why she'd offered to help Peter, suppressing the notion that it was anything other than business.

They met at the newly-let office, Peter thinking that it was better than he remembered. Clutching a red file, he explained how he envisaged the space - not that there was much of it - working. Paula looked up at him smiling and feigning interest. The she took a tape measure out and began to put it to work, scribbling numbers on a well-thumbed pad between the swooshes of the tape retracting into its case.

IKEA was busy.

"IKEA is always busy." said Peter, always feeling he was ten steps behind Paula as she darted into various alcoves to check prices, measure objects and assess colours. She had suggested to Peter that instead of buying artwork, the rooms should be adorned with Creative Juices branding and portfolio work and that the meeting room should sport a full coffee and juice bar. With much of that already in hand and the painting done, today's job was about the tables and chairs, some storage and a few accessories.

Peter wasn't a regular at IKEA and when he did come it was usually a forced visit with Justine, the reward for which was Swedish meatballs in the IKEA cafe. It didn't feel right doing the same thing with Paula. And as she had been so generous with her time, he supposed he should at least take her for lunch somewhere. He probably hadn't envisaged the amount of self-assembly work that would be needed, forgetting that IKEA was flat-pack crazy. By 10.30am they were all done and the oversized cardboard cartons had been loaded into a van that Peter had borrowed from a printer for the day.

Peter thanked Paula and insisted that lunch was on him as a token of appreciation. Paula pretended to think about it and check her diary before agreeing to meet Peter at 1.30pm, in a pub he'd never heard of but which she explained was near a property she had to show a client at 1pm.

They parted and Peter focused his mind on flat-pack. By 11am, his temper was frayed and he was surrounded by torn cardboard, tiny screws and bits of plastic that didn't fit together.

The instructions on the side of the box had said: "Assembly in 15 minutes by one competent person". So how long will that take me then? wondered Peter. As if to underline the whole competency issue, next to the text there was a graphic of one stick man holding a screwdriver next to an oval with a big "15 mins" in it. Peter's mind was thinking back to school and to maths problems: If John has five apples and Sarah has four, how many pears does Mike have?"- type of thing. So, if it takes 15 minutes for one competent person to put this together, how long would it take an incompetent, pissed off person? Do you double the time of everything then add on an hour... I mean, is there a formula?

"I wonder what my graphic would look like? Peter thought angrily. "A crying stick man with a broken bench and an oval saying 'All Day'?"

He should have known it was going to be a difficult day when he found himself in the DIY store at 7.30 that morning, searching for an apparently rare type of nut/bolt to fix a loose cupboard door in the office. Appropriately, U2's "Still Haven't Found What I'm Looking For" had come over the P.A ."Ah - a company with a sense of humour." thought Peter, who didn't find what he was looking for.

People have taken to turning to You Tube when life throws them a challenge that they are ill-equipped to deal with. Peter's challenges were frequently, though not exclusively DIY-related. It seemed that was no end of bedroom-dwelling, web-cammed American teenagers offering solutions from everything from great guitar riffs to getting by in German. There's probably one for brain surgery if you look hard enough. They all start with the teenager—usually called Josh, or Brad—saying "Hi—how y'all doing? Today we're gonna learn how to [insert task: e.g. do brain surgery]… it's real easy—we'll have it done in just a few minutes!"

Peter took out his mobile and pressed speed dial number 5. Within seconds, Bob, his regular handyman, answered. Peter explained the problem and Bob made sympathetic noises as if to suggest that no-one apart from experienced tradespeople were capable of assembling IKEA furniture. Surprisingly and on the inducement of a sum of extra cash, Bob offered to defer his afternoon job and come to the office to assemble the furniture. Peter was delighted but couldn't help wondering if he'd gazumped a little old lady whose central heating had packed up - or some-one else equally needy.

Feeling satisfied at his self-perceived mastery of the self-assembly situation, Peter jumped in the car and sped off to meet Paula in the Red Lion. As he pulled up at the pretty white building, adorned with hanging baskets, he noticed a text from Bob. It explained that he'd arrived at the property and would have it all done in a couple of hours. Peter's expression was a mixture of jealousy, irritation and relief.

Lunch was unusually good - both Peter and Paula had prawn salads - complete with homemade Marie Rose sauce and homemade bread. It was on the recommendation of the specials board that had announced that the pub was "famous for its salads". Peter's newly-found understanding of ad-land made him sceptical.

"I wonder if they change that according to what they want to get rid of?" he said sarcastically.

Paula laughed, sipping her wine and soda while Peter confessed to his DIY disasters. She made her excuses as the clock turned 3pm, saying she needed to catch up on some office paperwork back home. Peter's mobile chirped a text alert. It was Bob - who was half an hour off finishing. Bob always sent these texts, it was his way of sending a bill for cash on delivery of the job.

"Do you want to drop by and see how it looks, Paula?" It won't you take long and it seems a shame as you've sorted everything not to unveil it!" he grinned. While Paula thought, Peter answered a call from Dougal, enquiring about progress, having noted Peter's recent length of time away from the main office. Peter gave an unnecessarily comprehensive account of his time, referring to Paula as "the letting agent".

When Peter and Paula returned to the new office in the Bay, unprompted, Bob conducted a demonstration of his work, describing in detail the specific challenges he had encountered, as if to justify his price. He topped it off skilfully by adding that the job he'd cancelled had to be done on Saturday morning, when he normally took his boys to football. Peter wondered if trades-people learned these bill-loading techniques as apprentices or at college. Being fairly incompe-tent at DIY, he'd met a number of tradespeople in his time, several of whom made a far more im-pressive job of justifying the bill than they did carrying out the work.

Peter handed Bob a small wedge of notes and Bob disappeared like some sort of genie. Peter and Paula inspected Bob's handiwork and un-packed the accessories that Bob hadn't spotted or had deliberately ignored. Under Paula's direc-tion, Peter hung a picture or two and suitably placed some ornaments. There was one left - a rather ugly looking picture that Peter had found - on offer. It was a print of an oil painting of the Hayes - a well-known city centre street in Car-diff. Paula turned her nose up as if to suggest she wasn't responsible for it and that it wouldn't "go" anywhere.

Keen to get the upper hand, Peter suggested that it might be a good addition to the completely bare flat that was attached to the property - an-other project awaiting attention. Paula cocked her head as if to question his suggestion. Peter shrugged and returned to his car to fetch a new packet of picture hooks.

"What do you think?" said Peter, nodding his head to the stairs that led to the flat, wondering suddenly what might happen next.

"I think we should try it" said Paula, leaving Peter confused as to whether they were still talking about the picture of The Hayes or the opportunity afforded to them to take their friendship a step further. Annoyingly, Paula's mobile went off and a ten-minute conversation with a potential client ensued. Peter began to wonder if the moment had been missed or if it had even existed at all. Paula's mood changed to one of commission-driven estate agent and the call seemed to go on and on and on. Peter poured himself a chipped coffee mug of water and pondered what may or may not happen next.

Paula ended the call, seemingly satisfied with outcome and walked over to Peter confidently, as if reading his thoughts. As she came close, he could smell the mixture of her breath and perfume for the first time.

"I'll leave you to wash up." she said, nodding at

the chipped coffee mug. "I'll wait for you up-stairs."

***

Chapter 6: Stinking Bishop

Peter noticed two missed calls. He had switched his mobile to silent in the flat an hour ago when he had been with Paula. It wasn't until he got into his car that he noticed the notifications. One was Justine, the other, Piers Jackman - his old friend and advisor to the Business Minister in the Welsh Government. Knowing he should have prioritised Justine but figuring that if it had been urgent, she would have left a message, Peter tapped the screen on his phone to return Piers' call, his hopes mounting that this would be the conversation he had been waiting for about a potential opportunity for Creative Juices within Welsh Government. Piers had eluded to something a while back and hinted that it could be big, before he realised he'd gone a step too far and then downplayed it. As it turned out, it was bigger than Peter could have imagined.

"Peter - thanks for coming back. I'll get to the point. Is anyone there with you or are you alone?" said Jackman conspiratorially. Peter confirmed his solitude and Jackman pressed on, choosing his words with great precision.

"We think Scotland will get the second referendum. And all the polls suggest they'll get independence. They'll go with the EU." said Jackman in hushed tones, as if he feared that Peter, though in his car, might have put him on speakerphone, gone to a drive through McDonalds and opened all the windows.

"That will be the beginning of the break-up of the UK." continued Jackman before pausing dramatically. "And Wales will follow suit." he concluded.

"How so?" asked Peter.

"Plans are at an advanced stage to hold a referendum on Welsh independence. If Scotland get it, there will be a clear precedent, which will make our job much easier. Hence the waiting game." said Jackman.

"Off the record, we've been putting out a lot of noise on social media and through some of our other usual media outlets about nationalism, Welsh Heritage, rugby wins, Calon Lan - that sort of thing, just to stir up a bit of pride. The social stats suggest its going down well so we'll ramp it up in the coming months. Of course, it wouldn't do for us to be one-sided about the outcome. There will be a NO campaign as well as a YES campaign. But my minister - and others - will be backing the YES to Welsh independence." explained Jackman.

"I see. So how can I help?" said Peter, slightly shocked at the news and confused as to how he was to play a part.

"It's quite simple, Peter. We need a multi-channel ad campaign that will deliver the result my minister wants. And that's where Creative Juices comes in. I want you to deliver it - subject to agreement of fees, signing of NDAs – you understand." said Jackman formally.

"Sounds interesting." said Peter, trying to play it cool. Jackman ignored the tone.

"You can't be contracted or employed by Welsh Government as that would be seen as bias and we can't use public money to back one side. So, your contract will be with the official YES campaign group. Subject to formalities, you will meet the chairman of that group Gethin Jones-Evans, next week. "

"And the NO campaign?" asked Peter.

"There will be one, but as yet with the whole thing under wraps, it's in relative infancy. So, I want us to get the big guns ready and line everything up so we can steal a march on the NO campaign when this all goes public." Peter suspected that Jackman knew more than he was letting on, his tone was so assumptive.

"We know the farming community will support independence if it means we can get back into Europe and get our grants again. As will a lot of other factions of society - particularly in poorer areas. We think about half the business community or more could support it as well. We can discuss that at a later date. The Tories will try to play it out that we are breaking up the UK. That could be a tough message to counter, but if Scotland go first, they'll cop most of it for us, weakening that argument. The Tories got us out of Europe so the last thing they want to see in Westminster is Scotland and Wales going back in."

Peter agreed. He asked Piers about next steps and whether they would be pitching against other agencies. Piers replied negatively explaining that confidentiality was top priority and creating a pitch scenario would likely compromise this. He was to discuss it with Dougal and no-one else. They would both be invited to Piers' home in the country where they would be presented with two envelopes containing the Non-Disclosure Agreements they were to sign, before anything else could be discussed.

Conversation over, Peter checked his watch to see if it was worth heading across town to the office. His mind was racing with optimism, fear and pride. Unable to wait to deliver his news in person and unwilling to navigate rush hour traffic on the chance that Dougal was still in the office, Peter called Dougal's mobile.

He repeated the question Piers had asked him minutes earlier. Was Dougal alone? No - he was in a supermarket - replied Dougal, slightly irritated and blissfully unaware of what was about to unfold in the coming months. At Peter's request and due to the supermarket's proximity to the Bay, the pair rendezvoused at the new bay office, with an impatient Dougal wondering what was going on and muttering that it had better not be just to show off some new tables and chairs.

The news that Peter imparted to Dougal late that afternoon was to change both men's lives considerably.

***

Peter's mobile rang. It was Justine, who was fuming that she hadn't been called back. Peter explained that he had been in an important meeting which had resulted in a huge chunk of work for the ad agency. Justine mellowed.

"Anyway, I was calling to see if you wanted to

go out to dinner tonight. On me." she said, more calmly, making Peter feel somewhat guilty.

"I've just had a successful settlement for a client and I thought it might be nice to spend more time together." she continued.

"Great. I accept - thank you. Where shall we go?" said Peter confidently, feeling that life just couldn't get any better today. He was wrong.

"Don't mind." replied Justine, before giggling and provocatively adding "Maybe Pizza Express?"

***

Friday, 10am. Peter pulled up at Dougal's in his leased Mercedes. Dougal lived near the village of Bonvilston in the Vale of Glamorgan. The decision had been taken to arrive at Jackman's house in one vehicle. So, having scrunched to a halt on the spacious gravel driveway nearly crashing into Dougal's cherry tree, Peter jumped out of his car. Dougal clearly wasn't going to invite Peter into his house - he was already waiting for him in the Range Rover, with the engine running.

Piers lived just outside Cowbridge, so the pair took the A48, the main artery though the Vale of Glamorgan from Bonvilston towards the busy, up-market town of Cowbridge. Despite the SAT

NAV, the house wasn't easy to find. "Just outside" Cowbridge had been somewhat of an exaggeration, the property having turned out to be a good fifteen minutes from the town. Cowbridge had been busy with traffic backing up behind two tractors, moving at a snail's pace. up the high street. Peter anxiously checked his watch as they crawled past the Horse & Groom, The Duke of Wellington and The Bear Hotel.

"Are there any shops here, Dougal - or just places to eat and drink?" asked Peter sarcastically.

Dougal - seemingly less worried about being on time and perhaps still a little cynical about the size of the contract replied that actually Cowbridge was indeed full of independent shops.

"It's a Mecca for women in particular. There are lots of little clothes shops tucked away here and there. Every year they hold a fashion week with red carpet on the doors of every shop. You can flit from shop to shop and generally just enjoy it. Nadine likes the clothes - I just enjoy live music and the free fizz that most places dole out. It's not free, I should emphasise! Nadine spends £500 on a pair of Jimmy Choos and I get half a glass of warm Prosecco worth about £1.50!" he laughed, obviously oblivious to the importance of the meeting ahead.

The Range Rover navigated the narrow country lanes before arriving at a tiny village with just a small shop and a post-box.

"It's the other side of this village." said Peter, reading directions from a small, crumpled piece of paper.

 Jackman's house was an impressive, new timber-clad building which looked newly constructed and unique, as if perhaps Jackman had bought the plot and built the house on it.

"He said to go around the back." said Peter, getting out of the car. Dougal grunted, becoming weary of the secrecy and increasingly doubtful of what would come of it all. Almost reluctantly, he followed Peter's footsteps at the side of the house, past what looked like a large Biomass boiler and around to the back. The expansive patio was flanked by what must have been twenty-five metres of bi-fold doors. A small part of the run of doors were ajar and Peter proceeded as per his instructions. Dougal wasn't far behind him. Their eyes struggled to accustomise to the change in light as they stepped from the patio into the tiled lounge area, which looked as if it would have been more in place in Spain or Portugal than in Wales.

As their vision crystallised, it became evident that three men were sitting around a wooden table at the rear of the room, clearly in mid flow of a meeting. The men broke off their conversation and shuffled their papers away. Peter knew Jackman but the other two faces were not familiar

"Good morning gentlemen." Jackman rose but the other two remained seated, only giving cursory nods.

"I will make introductions in due course, but before we do anything we must attend to some formalities, please." He nodded to a pair of white C4 envelopes on a huge coffee table, seemingly made of railway sleepers.

The non-disclosure agreements, or NDAs, as they were better known were accompanied by two cheap ballpoint pens. Peter and Dougal slid the four-page documents from their respective unsealed envelopes.

"Take your time if you need to." said Jackman from what appeared to be an adjoining kitchen. There was suddenly a smell of coffee.

Dougal had signed many NDAs in his career, but in truth without the presence of a solicitor he was usually a bit in the dark. The principle was always confidentiality, but the detail he often found a little boring or incomprehensible. Peter had been instructed to go through the NDA thoroughly, being more of a detail-person than Dougal. In less than two minutes he had seemingly digested it contents and nodded to Dougal, who began to wonder if Peter had seen the NDA before, his reaction had been so quick.

The pens were quickly brought to work and the contracts signed. Jackman appeared, checked the signatures and beckoned the two men forward.

"Let me introduce you. This is Gethin Jones-Evans, chairman of the YES campaign. And this is Eric Urquhart-Williams, Chief Executive Officer of the private bank Urquhart-Williams Honiton, that you will both – have heard of. We are grateful to Eric for the support he has pledged." Jackman said obsequiously.

Handshakes followed, but strict formality was observed with neither the banker nor the YES-man making any effort at small talk nor exuding any warmth towards the ad-men. Jackman felt that it was his duty as host, matchmaker, introducer and facilitator, to break the extremely cold ice that was evident.

"Let's have coffee in the kitchen." Jackman smiled and four men followed him to the source for the coffee aroma, the ad-men wondering what small-talk might be appropriate, if they even got the chance.

***

An hour later Dougal and Peter were on their return journey, talking excitedly but in low voices, as if there might have been a hidden microphone in the car. They had agreed to do two things. As well as putting together costings for the management and execution of the campaign, they were to provide a confidentiality statement, explaining what steps would be taken in order to guarantee that the campaign would remain under wraps until it went live. It would include background checks on staff, further NDAs and an extensive briefing which would be recorded and reviewed by the Yes-men before instructions to proceed were given.

The security element was potentially more challenging than the campaign itself. Advertising work, after all, was the company's raison d'être. Security on the other hand, was not. And then there was the multi-channel campaign. In Jackman's house, they had briefly talked about billboards, bus shelters, social media, media releases and video. But the scale had been left open-ended, with the YES-men declining to commit to a budget. "Just quote for what is necessary to get the job done properly." had been the mantra, which in ad-land equated to an open cheque book.

A meeting of all three Creative Juices directors was convened for the following morning at nine. Morris had scheduled a video meeting and was peeved to have been over-ruled and told that the directors' meeting was of colossally greater importance. He felt a little deflated, having perceived he was running an extremely significant initiative.

Dougal brought him up to speed with recent events and Morris looked impressed, particularly when Dougal placed him in charge of security and staff liaison. His ego swelled again and he rummaged in his pocket for a half-finished packet of pistachio nuts which he duly and inappropriately offered to the other two men. They shook their heads in decline, both wondering what sort of man did this in an important meeting. The truth was that Morris had used the sharing of food technique in many an awkward meeting, to break the ice, or diffuse a difficult situation with a customer. It didn't always work. It wouldn't have worked with the three YES-men at Jackman's house, but get it right and it was a winner, thought Morris, who used a packet of mints when nuts weren't available.

They went on to discuss the campaign. Rather than starting with working out which routes to market to prioritise, Dougal started with how much money they could make from it. Ad agencies typically make money in addition to their fees by buying third party services - like print or advertising - at a discount and selling onto the client at a higher price - sometimes higher than the client would have paid had they bought the service direct. Some unscrupulous agencies justified it as paying for their time, but then went on to charge for that time anyway.

The margins on third parties were taken as read - the question was how much would they amount to. The campaign was to have maximum impact and as it seemed that the banker - and probably others - were bankrolling it. Logically then it was volume turned up on all channels? Peter suggested caution and suggested that the campaign comprised a gold, silver and bronze option. That put the choice in the hands of the YES-men, which was better, he explained.

"Of course, we need to charge a substantial set up fee, extra charges for the security and risk - plus a monthly retainer." said Dougal greedily, having already assumed that this opportunity was his passport out of financial difficulty.

Again, Peter cautioned restraint, suggesting, with his considerable purchasing experience (which he made clear) that charging for general non-disclosure and confidentiality as a separate entity may raise eyebrows and that they were better to increase the retainer so that difficult questions were not asked.

Having drummed up the sort of money that they would need to make from preparing and managing this campaign over a period of several months, they moved onto the detail.

"Messaging." said Dougal. "What do the public need to hear to persuade them to vote YES?"

"We will need some pretty good research to ascertain that." Peter chipped in.

"I think we all know that Wales benefited more than most from the EU grants, so why not pitch it that way? You know, Back to the Future of Wales, type thing?" suggested Morris - impressed at his off the cuff creativity. The others made "Perhaps, but let's think about it" humming noises.

"There is a danger of basing our approach to this on anecdotal evidence." said Peter, keen to keep a logical and scientific flame burning in this dark den of greed and haste.

"Yes, but why spend tens of thousands on market research just to be told what you probably already know?" Morris raised his voice. Peter answered.

"What neither of you realise is that people like this - people like me if you like - are risk-averse. So, we cover our arses by spending money to that we can always justify what we've done in case shit happens down the line. We are accountable, so we have to. Don't worry about spending money on research. I can assure you, they'll be fine with it."

"OK, so research, messaging, implementation. Let's line up meetings internally with Rupert and Sandra."

Rupert was head of digital and social and Sandra the sole media buyer. There wasn't always media to buy so Sandra doubled as an account manager for some of the older clients.

"We need to push the security measures through for them, first." said Dougal.

"That will delay things. They don't have to know who the client is, surely? At this stage it's just a costing exercise. Tim Hughes and Wendy can deal with messaging later on after the research is done. For now, we just need rough costs and a timeline so we can get this work in the bag." said Dougal sounding a little impatient.

"And the security plan." added Morris.

"Yes, but we can't charge for that!" snapped Dougal.

"I'm not sure you are right, Dougal." interjected Peter. "We will have to implement a watertight cyber-security policy. Our IT guys are going to charge us for that. And there'll be other costs - and time spent as well."

"We already have a cyber security policy." said Dougal.

"Yes - but it isn't going to be good enough or well-documented enough to satisfy the people you are now dealing with." Peter explained, sounding frustrated, as if he was fed up of stating the obvious to these money-hungry, short-cut crazy cretins.

Dougal shrugged as if to admit that this was Peter's league and probably not his. Then he remembered that Peter had said they could charge for it and he began to smile.

"How much do we charge for it?"

"I will cost it out." said Peter. "I'm not plucking a figure out of the air!" he said, the realisation dawning on him that costing exercises in
ad-land were very different to the public sector
that he had been used to. Technically the YES
group were a campaign group not a public sector
organisation, of course, but many were senior
civil servants, or worked in the public sector or
government at some level.

It seemed to Peter that Dougal based his quotes
on what he wanted to make.

"I mean what does he do? Cost out his foreign
holidays for the next year, come up with the increased income he'll need, double it, add fifty
grand, put a nought on the end and then present
it to the client?" thought Peter slightly bitterly,
feeling that his ethics had been compromised.
A text from Paula suddenly popped up on this
mobile which was resting on the desk. Maybe
he wasn't one to question morals after all, he
thought, grabbing the phone quickly not knowing if the message had been seen by the others.

"The letting agent." he said, guilt forcing him to
offer an explanation when one really wasn't necessary.

"Seems to be a lot of admin and follow up with that lot. What do they want? Surely not more things to sign or pay?" asked Dougal.

"I don't think so." mumbled Peter, thinking of a way to change the subject. Morris took his nuts out and put them on the table, which was enough of a distraction to move the conversation on. The project was given a code-name of Knapp & Co. after minimal discussion. To-do lists were carefully written under the instruction of Morris, who insisted that they were sufficiently open-ended so as not to breach the confidentiality rules, which he had scribbled down in the last few minutes. The meeting ended as three chairs were pushed noisily back under the table and the men left the room, charged with enthusiasm.

***

Rupert looked sceptical. He'd been head of digital and social for four years and had never had such a loose briefing.

"Well who are Knapp and Co?" he asked Dougal, who was beginning to wish he'd waited for security phase to pass and then simply told the team the truth.

"Because they don't come up on any Google searches" said Rupert, in the way that people in their late teens or early twenties worshipped Google as a beacon of wisdom.

"Of course they fucking don't, Rupert. Because they're not fucking real." spluttered an exasperated and worn-out Dougal. "This is just a code-name for a confidential client."

Rupert looked hurt at Dougal's outburst and Dougal began to think he may have overstepped the mark in terms of employee relations.

"Look, Rupert, you're a digital whizz-kid. We'll be counting on you for this campaign. Everything will become clear in the next few weeks. Just hang in there. And thanks for your support, mate." That should do it, thought Dougal, feeling proud that he had rectified the situation.

"Neanderthal prick." hissed Rupert, after Dougal left. "His generation don't have a fucking clue about digital marketing."

Rupert had never imagined he'd end up in marketing. An out and out science and maths geek, he had excelled at school but had never felt the inclination to go to University. He'd begun to dabble with selling things on eBay and then quickly to the sexy-creative marketing industry was evidently changing and things moved online. Now people like Rupert were in demand as marketing became what he thought was more of a science than an art.

Creative Juices had been a summer job for Rupert whilst at school, his July and August spent carrying out menial administration tasks. But a chance conversation with Dougal one day in the car park had led to a rapid escalation in Rupert's career prospects. Within twelve months, Rupert had become cocky and arrogant. Keeping a close eye on industry salaries, he had begun to feel left behind and started to keep an eye on the job sites. Before long, he had been offered more money elsewhere, forcing Dougal's hand to match his salary. Since then, their relationship had been slightly strained. Rupert was a key part of Creative Juice's armoury, but he knew it and he made sure everyone else knew it too. Somewhere on Douglas' to-do list was finding a replacement for him.

***

Three weeks later the security arrangements had been rushed through. Everyone in the company had signed a non-disclosure agreement and a full cyber security audit and risk-assessment had been carried out. There were numerous recommendations in it, all of which had to be implemented quickly and with an eye-watering degree of cost because of the request for it to be done at speed. During this period there was an odd atmosphere in Creative Juices. No-one, apart from the directors knew the reason for confidentiality measures being put in place. There was a quiet buzz of anticipation throughout the building.

David and Alicia had been at Peter and Justine's for Sunday lunch when David had raised the subject. Throughout the meal, Peter had avoided all work-talk to circumvent the possibility of the topic coming up.

"Come on then Dad. What's going on in work?" David asked, as Justine slid the cheeseboard onto the highly polished table.

"Nice try, son." said Peter, using one of a selection of bizarrely-shaped cheese knives to help himself to a chunk of Stinking Bishop. Peter had only really bought it because of the name, but actually, it tasted pretty good, with the Ships biscuits and green grapes that Alicia had carried in for Justine.

"You'll find out in good time. It's all positive." he changed the subject. "Stinking Bishop anyone?"

David realised that he was getting nowhere so decided to liven things up in his own humorous and observational way.

"What do you think, then? Is the rumour true? Does cheese affect your sleep patterns? Alicia and I found out about it, by accident in the small hours of Monday morning." he started. Alicia grinned, enjoying David's confidence.

"Oh - what happened?" replied Peter, grateful that the work-talk had been put to bed. David continued.

"We awake suddenly - it's like, I dunno, the sound of a dog barking, a police helicopter overhead or a burglar breaking a window—I can't remember which. At the time, I think I thought it was all three! So...we are disorientated, fretting and struggling to manage the transition from our dark reverie to consciousness. Both of us—it turns out—are trying to shrug off rather unpleasant dreams. I am is being chased by Pac Man through the streets of Cardiff and all Alicia's family have turned into giant orange Space Hoppers and moved to Norfolk! So, she goes to the kitchen to make a drink, I pick up the iPad thinking last night's cheese and biscuits we ate are to blame and looking to see if I'm right. She looks at me as if I'm completely mad, buries her head in the pillow and goes back to sleep. Guess what I find? It turns out there's a British Cheese Board" Funny, eh? Board, cheeseboard - get it?"

Everyone laughed.

"So this British Cheese Board have written about it. Couldn't believe it but it turns out that not only does cheese affect your dreams but different cheeses give you different types of dreams. Who'd have thought, eh?"

Everyone wondered why the British Cheese Board would endorse the rumour that their product induced nocturnal-nasties. David explained that it was their way of dealing with the problem head on. So, they had commissioned some research with few hundred volunteers who were asked to eat bits of cheese, half an hour before going to bed and to make a note of their dreams!" said Peter, as if still surprised.

"So, what happened?" asked Justine, leaning forward, genuinely interested and amused. Alicia nodded as if to infer that the next bit of the story was even better. David continued.

"It turns out that Cheshire cheese gives only mild dreams, but Stilton induces bizarre dreams. Eat Red Leicester and you dream about the past, but Lancashire eaters all dreamt about the future. And if you want to dream about celebrities—it's cheddar you need, apparently." he concluded.

Everyone looked amused and surprised. Peter topped it off.

"What about Stinking Bishop?" Everyone laughed.

"Don't mind if I do!" said David, seizing another odd-shaped cheese knife and impaling the wedge of cheese. More laughs.

"Where did you get these knives anyway, mum?" asked Peter, picking up one of the curved knives, staring at the intricately carved handle adorned with what looked like brass pieces."

"They were a wedding present from your Uncle Mark - he used to travel a lot overseas with work." answered Justine. "Your dad and I only found them the other day. We were clearing out the loft. I think they are African. Sort of tribal, you know." she mused.

"Well I bloody don't." said Peter. "I think they're from Splott market! And what African tribes live off cheese anyway? Let alone carry around a stack of different knives to cut it with!" exclaimed Peter, rolling his eyes, though in a good-humoured way. Justine smiled as if to say "well, you never know."

Alicia and David offered to wash up. Or rather Alicia volunteered them both. She had enjoyed herself, but was the designated driver and Peter and David were enjoying their wine and the conversation was becoming more raucous. Justine diplomatically and helpfully suggested that she would help Alicia and they would leave father and son to their bottle of red. Alicia agreed, turning to David and agreeing a timescale for departure. David looked at his watch as if to negotiate, but Alicia was already helping Justine load the gravy-stained plates into the dishwasher.

"So when WILL we know then, Dad? You know, about the secret?" said David, fancying his chances of prising the information from his father, a few glasses of wine after his first attempt. But Peter just smiled.

"No dice, David. I might have had a wine or two but this is very confidential stuff. You'll find out in good time. Probably this week." Peter had let a provisional timescale slip out, but in the grand scheme of things, it didn't matter.

Alicia handed David his jacket, remaining standing and conveying gratitude to Justine and Peter for their hospitality. The atmosphere was happy-sleepy and the aroma a mix of cheese, gravy, steamed vegetables and wine.

"I think I'll open a window." said Justine to Peter, after they heard David and Alicia's car start-up in the driveway.

Chapter 7: Prosecco

Alistair McFadden was not a patient man.

It seemed that Scotland would comfortably back a leave vote, but London were delaying and dithering about the Section 30 order. There was avid media discussion about constitutional implications and the potential consequences of the break-up of the UK. Journalists south of the border were thriving on the drama, keen to explore every angle and in some cases, exaggerate every possible outcome.

The work McFadden impatiently looked forward to was the running of the media campaign to persuade the people of Scotland to break with England and become a separate state. Although the campaign was already in advanced stages, none of it could be made public until London granted permission for the referendum to happen. So, much of Alistair's time was spent commissioning market research and selectively promoting the results that showed a sizeable appetite for independence. The monotony had been broken the previous week when he had been warmly received in Brussels by a senior administrative team, including Jean de Malo, a senior civil servant.

***

McFadden felt overwhelmed by the scale of the EU. Whilst always at ease in Edinburgh, he felt somewhat of a fish out of water looking up at the enormous slab of the EU HQ. His visit had been at the invitation of the office of Jean de Malo with the brief of "exploring mutual opportunities and cultural synergies." The three-day itinerary was set for him and his accommodation paid for in a five-star boutique hotel. In fact, no expense was being spared. McFadden spent his first day in meetings, discussing everything from Scottish fishing rights to North Sea Oil, single malt whiskies and mutual tourism opportunities. He was beginning to feel that the whole trip was nothing more than a "hands across the sea" public relations exercise, but decided to enjoy the hospitality and make any useful connections he could.

The meeting with Jean de Malo was scheduled for the end of the programme. McFadden thought it strange that he hadn't even been allocated a cursory five minutes with de Malo on his first day, having dealt only with his minions. On arrival at his hotel room, McFadden found a gold-wrapped box of artisan Belgian chocolates with a hand-written note from de Malo, welcoming him to the country and assigning him a personal assistant for the duration of his stay. Her blue and yellow EU business card was included with the note: Helene Marenelly - it said - but gave no job title. McFadden's phone pinged and almost magically it turned out to be a text from her, welcoming him to the city and explaining that she would be picking him up in an hour for a brief tour and dinner. She arrived perfectly on time in a chauffeur-driven Mercedes and nodded to the Concierge, who summoned Alistair from the lobby.

The tour and dinner were business-like affairs. Helene, he guessed, was about forty. She exuded the casual evocative charm that is the preserve of many French women. Dressed professionally but with a twist of chic, her black and red dress was complemented by a small hat. It takes an attractive woman to be able to pull off a hat, McFadden mused. A single man since his divorce a year ago, he was more than happy to have Helene's company for a few hours. Any aspirations he may have had were quickly extinguished by Helene's formulaic conversation and lack of warmth. He began to wonder if she had been a chatbot in a former life or whether the whole process was completely automated and controlled by some sort of central computer deep within the EU building.

Over dinner, Alistair sampled two Belgian beers recommended by the waiter. His aperitif had been a Bière aux Framboises - a weakish beer made with raspberries. With the meal he sipped a stronger, straw-coloured wheat beer. She consumed only sparkling water. He wondered how many times a week or month she went through these processes with various visiting politicians and civil servants from across Europe. The conversation had begun to bore McFadden, who was glad eventually to see his hotel room where he flopped on the bed, exhausted. He woke four hours later, still fully clothed, at 2am. In the scheme of trying to initiate some normality, he decided to read his emails, most of which were from members of his staff. Glancing at the subject lines his eyes were immediately been drawn to one that stood out. It said "Welsh Government - P. Jackman." The text in the email was brief. It relayed a request from a Piers Jackman on behalf of the Welsh Government to have a confidential telephone call with him.

In Brussels, McFadden finally met with Jean de Malo after two days of semi-automated charm-offensive by his minions. Jean de Malo turned out to be far more open and friendly than his team, who were obviously used to protecting information. Despite a few attempts, McFadden had managed to glean nothing from them about de Malo or what his department was really responsible for. He had requested some background on de Malo from one of his Comms executives back in Scotland. There had been plenty of general background available - school, university, date of birth and so on. But nothing on his role in the EU. Like everyone else he met, de Malo spoke perfect English with only a hint of a French accent.

After formalities were exchanged, de Malo beckoned McFadden away from his vast wooden desk across to a coffee table with two chairs either side of it and a commanding view from the fifteenth floor. McFadden didn't care for heights and immediately took the chair with its back to the window, slightly impolitely, leaving de Malo to take the other one.

"I'm not sure that you will be aware of my principal role?" said de Malo sipping his coffee. McFadden lifted his espresso cup and correctly assumed it to be a rhetorical question.

"My department looks at opportunities and threats to the EU, evaluates them and recommends courses of action to our ministers. These are discussed at committee level and recommendations are made or escalated for further debate and legislation if that is required. It depends on the nature of the opportunity or threat." McFadden looked bemused and was surprised that a department existed on such a scale. De Malo continued:

"Scotland. We like it." he said obliquely with a flat tone that in which he could have been referring to a pizza topping, rather than a country.

"We see Scotland joining the EU as a big opportunity. For you. And for us, too." de Malo continued, with more warmth.

McFadden nodded his head. "We have much to offer, as well as the traditional industries you will be aware of our service sector and shale gas operations are some of the most significant in the UK." De Malo smiled as if McFadden were in a job interview and had given a good answer.

"And of course, with the rest of the UK out of the trading picture, you'll have a bigger slice of the European opportunity pie." smiled de Malo. McFadden wondered where a non-native English speaker had got the expression " European opportunity pie" from.

Mutual back-slapping over, the meeting continued and de Malo made it clear that Scotland would be welcomed by the EU. Obviously, it wasn't something he could guarantee, of course as it was a decision for the member states. But

- off the record - he explained - many of them were not very happy about the way the UK had left. And so, whilst a decision would be made on merit, he didn't doubt that the members of the European Parliament had long memories, if McFadden knew what he meant.

McFadden smiled. Ah - the EU's chance to stick two fingers up to London. And a virtually guaranteed rite of passage for Scotland into the EU, barring any major diplomatic or geopolitical catastrophes. De Malo leaned forward conspiratorially.

 "You know Alistair, London, the UK - they vote leave then they stay in. They - how do you say - bugger around? For years this goes on with the EU and then try to leave without paying their bill! It is no wonder the members were not 'appy!" said de Malo demonstratively, waving his hands and finishing with a "Bofffff!" - a very French ending to virtually any sentence. McFadden nodded, sharing the disapproval and disbelief that the UK government could behave in such a childish manner. He smiled inwardly.

***

Back in Edinburgh, McFadden was catching up on the few days he'd been away. His staff had been putting many of the finishing touches to the campaign. Unlike in Wales, the Scottish independence campaign was a more partisan issue with the political parties issuing the rallying cries, rather than taking their side but making all the noise through the back door via yes or no campaign groups.

The ruling Scottish Nationalists and their coalition partners, the Labour Party, both supported a vote for Scotland's independence, whilst the Conservatives wanted Scotland to remain part of the UK. McFadden disliked the ego of ministers, but they were his masters. Despite being a Labour man through and through, he had needed to take a broader view of the coalition with the SNP in the interests of his job and - he told himself - his country.

The campaign was to be unleashed through every conceivable channel from Twitter, Facebook, Instagram and You Tube to billboards, newspapers, radio and TV. FISH - the ad agency - had come up with the slogan: "Be proud again. Be Scottish again." after lengthy and costly market research. "Our wealth. Our choices. Our country." had come a close second. The weekly meeting with FISH had been postponed last week due to McFadden's Brussels trip. They had wanted to hold it with other members of his team, but being somewhat of a control freak, McFadden had opted for a written report by email and to postpone the meeting until he could attend in person.

The meeting usually alternated between McFadden's offices and the ad agency's premises. He arranged it that way for the sake of balance, though secretly he much preferred escaping to the quirky ad agency, especially if it was a high-pressure week in his office. The agency was based in an old warehouse, out of town. Play was actively encouraged as a creative stimulant, so the place was full of fruit machines, pool tables, treadmills, VR gaming stations and even canoes. McFadden often wondered if there were prostitutes on call or perhaps hidden away somewhere. He thought to himself that it was a fucking wonder that anyone got any work done as he passed the Creative Director whooping at his high score on a particular game, oblivious to the fact that he was in the presence of a higher civil servant and a major client.

A millennial creative-type bounded up to McFadden.

"Table tennis or Space Invaders?" he asked, as if this was the agency's equivalent question to "Coffee or tea?" McFadden wanted to tell him to fuck off, but remembered his position and politely declined, leaving the creative-type deflated and surprised.

The agency meeting room was designed as a virtual aquarium, with 3D images of moving tropical fish projected onto all four walls. The agency had called itself "Fish" as a reference to what it did for clients - fish for new business, votes or some other sort of engagement. One of the walls morphed the fish images into a Power-Point presentation titled "FISH: The Weekly Think-Tank with [insert client name]: Scottish Government." It probably sounded good when they were dealing with companies. Maybe "FISH: The Weekly Think-Tank with GWB Office Supplies." But somehow the gravitas of the Scottish Government juxtaposed with the childish arsing around of an ad agency just didn't work. But McFadden smiled. He enjoyed the break from the world of political madness to this world of fishy, tosser-ridden madness, often leaving feeling as if he was plied with drugs and had been hallucinating for the entire duration of his visit.

The meeting was fairly normal, considering the surroundings. With most of the creative content signed off, it was a question of channel planning. The three principle channels were radio, social media and what was called "outdoor" - billboards, bus shelters, buses, taxis, railways stations and the like. Whilst the creative side of advertising amused and entertained many clients, the research and planning often didn't.

McFadden was interested, but didn't really feel the need to know the ins and outs of everything and often wished he'd sent one of his team to these types of meetings. Radio was often bought on what is known as OTH, which stands for "opportunities to hear" - a calculation of how many times a listener is likely to hear an ad. Similarly, outdoor is bought on the basis of OTS, which stands for "opportunities to see". McFadden found the stats a little boring and often amused himself that in some of the rougher parts of the city, the posters were so frequently defaced that they probably attracted more attention than the original billboard ad. He could almost predict the graffiti amends to the new slogan, as "Be proud again. Be Scottish again." would be morphed into "Be pissed again. Be Scottish Again." Fuck, it was almost bound to happen.

The billboard sites had to be audited. This was a sensible, grown up term for the agency taking the client out for the day to tour all the billboard sites and sign off each one of them, based on location, appearance and condition. Long lunches and short tours were the order of most of these types of audits, McFadden had found over the years, but accepted it had to be done. Again - one to delegate to a team member.

Radio was always interesting. Their way of selling more ad airtime was to give clients the showbiz feel. Yes, you may just be buying cheesy-sounding ads, but really you are in showbiz now. You can schmooze with the DJs, hang out in the funky boardroom clad with signed music memorabilia from famous artists. Who knows, you can probably even shag the receptionist if you spend enough money. It was the way the radio seduced clients. It was well-practised and clearly so effective to all but the most seasoned marketers.

Then there was Billy, the "Comprod" - an abbreviation for Commercial Production, the writing of radio ads and the commissioning of voice-overs, choosing of backing tracks and so on. Billy had been cornered in a rough old pub a few years ago by a drunken Glaswegian thug who had somehow gotten wind of what Billy did for a living over a winner stays on pool marathon.

"So, you're the fucker who writes all the cheesy fucking shite words and fucking irritating jingles that make me what to fucking spew!" he had shouted, hanging onto his pool cue for balance. Fortunately for Billy, he had indeed needed to spew, which had provided a getaway opportunity. Billy hadn't until that point considered that Commercial Production Manager for radio station would have been classed as a dangerous occupation.

The problem with comprod people is that they are tuned into cheesy mode for so long they just can't help themselves. Every solution to an ad becomes a horribly cheesy jingle that you can't forget, or a cliché rhyme that rings in your head all day. What do these people behave like at home? Surely, they can't just leave the job at work?

"Honey, you look great today, but let's not buy our car insurance any old way... "

McFadden frequently found that he had to reject a few rounds of creative comprod proposals before they would get out of autopilot mode and actually begin to think about the real problem rather than just chunk out the cheese. He was due to hear the latest campaign suggestions today. Normally the radio stations provided demo recordings of potential ads, but due to some sort of technical error, this hadn't been possible. So instead, the agency (who were managing the radio campaign and making a healthy profit on it as well), had only scripts to provide to McFadden. Half an hour before he had arrived, they had realised that this wouldn't really be good enough so decided to try to act them out. This turned out to be a fairly big mistake. McFadden watched open-mouthed at a dire interpretation of the Comprod Manager's script played out by three people who were utterly inept actors. It reminded him of being at his son's school plays and Christmas concerts, except that this time he didn't need to pretend it was good.

"Fuck, that was dreadful." he smiled, glad to be back on his own patch and in charge again after his Brussels trip. "Let's just wait for you to sort out the tech problems and get the proper demos. There's no rush. But thanks for making my day anyway, I wished I'd videoed it." he beamed.

The account manager and two young account execs who had enacted the scene looked both relieved and offended. You can only imagine the conversation they might have had over dinner with their partner - perhaps a nurse or doctor - later that day.

"How was your day, darling?"

"Tricky. We lost two patients, we are still struggling with bed capacity and staff shortages. You?"

"Well, this afternoon the radio station couldn't produce a demo of an ad, so I had to act it out with a few colleagues. I was a lion and I had to roar at various points in the ad. I think I made a bit of a dick of myself and the client wasn't impressed either."

That's the thing with ad agency-land. It's only when you put it in context of the real world that it seems ridiculous.

"Today we made a major breakthrough in medical science." Compared to:
"Today, I hired a low-loader truck so I could balance a van on it. The sole point of this costly and time-consuming exercise was to make the company logo on its side more visible for a twenty-second social media video."

***

Peter and Paula were meeting once or twice a week. Originally, they chose The Red Lion, but it was deemed too popular and they risked being seen. So, after trying a less popular pub where they had sat in virtual isolation eating plastic food, Paula had suggested she prepare lunch at her place next time. It turned out for the best and the pair enjoyed time together before lunch in Paula's smartly-decorated bedroom. She lived with her only child, Tom - a seven-year-old - who was in school. Separated from her husband, Alan, a year ago, her divorce proceedings were underway. This was a rented house - an interim measure - until the financial settlement was through. Money was a little tight at the moment as Alan wasn't paying maintenance until the lawyers reached an agreement and spent most of their money in the process. Peter quickly picked up on this and insisted he fetch lunch from Marks & Spencer on his way there.

Peter parked fifty metres short of the house and walked up the terraced street. He looked for the sign that it was safe to proceed. Yes - the brightly painted vase from Murano in Italy was still in the window. Were it to disappear, it would be the signal that Paula's son was unexpectedly home or that something else was afoot and he was not to proceed or to text her. The lunches were always late, so they didn't coincide with the school lunch break, thereby avoiding a potentially embarrassing clash. When their affair had begun, Peter had bought a pay as you go mobile so that he didn't have to receive texts from Paula on his usual mobile. She rarely remembered to text it, much to Peter's annoyance.

He knocked the door with the hand that wasn't clutching the M&S bag and Paula ushered him in.

"It might have to be a quick lunch - I need to be back for a meeting." said Peter.

Paula was taking the Wensleydale cheese and apricot chutney sandwiches from the bag as he did. She handed his sandwich to him.

"If it's going to be a quickie then let's not waste time with lunch. You can eat yours in the car later." she said, beckoning him to follow her.

Peter's life was becoming a matrix of secrets as he alternated from making sure that Justine didn't find out about Paula and the agency staff didn't let anything slip about the campaign. It was inevitable that the two secrets would meet at some point and they did, one afternoon in Paula's house. Paula and Peter had shared a bottle of Prosecco over a late lunch. With Paula on a half day, she could afford to indulge a little. Flitting around the lounge in a short blue dressing gown, she had teased and flirted with Peter as she tidied up some of Tom's stray toys, bending sideways and revealing her laced blue underwear as she did. They had chatted as Paula went about her chores, with Peter looking on in anticipation. Paula had asked Peter about the agency and why his workload had increased so much in the last couple of weeks. Having confided so much in Paula in the last few weeks and enjoying her so much that afternoon, Peter had confided in her. After all, they had a shared bond of secrecy anyway, he had assured himself. Peter had told Paula about the yes campaign, the referendum, Scotland - in fact, everything. He had felt relieved afterwards, having unburdened himself of the weight of such a monumental secret.

"I'm so impressed." Paula had said, in awe. The stories that came from the ad agency were often entertaining but this one dwarfed the others. Her husband, Alan, was managing director of an engineering company that sold cigarette packaging machines. It was highly profitable, but it didn't produce many interesting stories - or maybe he had just never told them to her. Not that Paula had minded. She had been happy with the comfortable lifestyle, only working two days a week for Flawless and balancing that with looking after Tom, keeping fit and shopping. Then she had discovered Alan's affair with a girl half his age - one of the machine operators in the factory. After that, things had quickly begun to deteriorate. He had involved a lawyer within a week, despite insisting that he and Paula could work things out between them. She had been forced to find a lawyer as well after it was clear that fairness was not top priority for Alan. So, the lawyers had fought it out, sending expensive letters to each other's clients whilst Peter and Paula watched their bank balances nose-dive. Unable to live under the same roof, they had separated and the lawyers had vultured-in to arrange divorces and financial settlements.

This was still going on, which is why it was so important that Alan didn't find out about the affair. If that happened, it would add ammunition to his case, even though Paula hadn't even met Peter when she and Alan had separated. In Paula's, one afternoon, Peter noticed a neat pile of letters on the kitchen table, addressed to Mrs Paula Haines, with the letterhead bearing the logo of a well-known and expensive law firm. He wondered what he had got himself into and whether he wanted to get into any further. But by that time, it was already too late.

***

McFadden was in a meeting with his PA, Alison, who was trying to tick off as many tasks as she could in the hour they had scheduled together.

"Jackman - Welsh government. Have you contacted him yet?" asked Alison, knowing he hadn't, as the office had received a second communication from Welsh Government chasing a reply to the first. Alison had emailed back to explain that Alistair was away on urgent European business. He was contactable in emergencies otherwise he'd be in touch in due course. McFadden had forgotten about it, having been immersed with all the preparations for the campaign ramping up in the last week or so.

"I have arranged the call for tomorrow morning." said Alison, giving away the fact that she already knew that contact had not been established yet. Alistair smiled. Having a brilliant P.A. helped mask his inadequacies in terms of administration, and sometimes, attention to detail.

It was unusual for higher civil servants to talk directly with each other. Normally messages are passed via minions. So, McFadden had been surprised at the request from his opposite number in the Welsh Government to have a personal telephone call with him. As soon as he put the phone down from the call with Jackman, he realised why a personal call had been necessary. The possibility of Welsh Independence. Wow. He hadn't seen that coming so fast. Dunbar needed to know about this - and fast.

"What about strength in numbers?" said the First Minister. "If London is under pressure from two devolved powers that must make success more likely for us?" he ventured.

"The Welsh don't see it that way." replied McFadden. "I get the impression that they want us to take the flack for breaking up the UK, pull off the referendum and then ride on the coat tails of our success."

"I see." said Dunbar quietly. "Can we gently start some media activity around how the other devolved administrations might react to a Scottish win on independence?"

"Already underway, First Minister. I've got a team working on it as we speak. To be honest I'm not sure how effective it will be, but if it gets traction in the nationals and on social, it'll make London sit up and take notice. We just need to make sure the Welsh don't find out it was us who started the whole campaign." said McFadden.

"What difference does it make?" retorted Dunbar, shrugging.

"I think we would be better off keeping Wales on our side, First Minister. It may be useful in the long run." Mc Fadden replied

**

Wales: Jackman received Peter more warmly in his office than he had in his house with the two other YES men present. He made a small reference to that day and appeared to apologise for the formality. Peter shrugged as if was of little consequence. He was here to update Jackman on progress at Creative Juices and as happy to report that everything was ahead of schedule. The campaign concepts would be ready in the next two weeks, but they didn't want to set a date to present them yet until they were completely confident of an exact date. Jackman raised his eyebrows in mock surprise and irritation, before reaching into the top drawer of the desk that separated the two men and producing a thin, bound document which he slid across to Peter.

"Read it at your leisure. But time is about to become more relevant. The NO campaign has begun to emerge. Mainly Tories. Headed up by a guy called Alan Haines - a Tory businessman who owns a couple of manufacturing companies." said Jackman dryly.

Peter was shocked. Surely it couldn't be the same Alan Haines that was Paula's husband? It was incredulous. Paula had mentioned a business, but it had been a factory. Then it struck him like a thunderbolt that Paula was privy to inside information about the YES campaign. What had he done?

Jackman commented on Peter's silence, so Peter changed the subject trying to put the Haines situation out of his mind until he had the chance to think properly.

"Looks like we are going public soon then?"

"Yes. We have no way of knowing how advanced the NO campaign is, but time is of the essence. They can't really go public until the

YES campaign do or we table it for debate it in the Senedd. We would rather debate it in response to a groundswell of public demand, if you see what I mean, so getting the campaign up and running early would be helpful. But it does change the message. We can't be asking for a vote yes yet, because there isn't a referendum! This needs to be in two phases. Firstly, it's about Welsh independence and Wales re-joining the EU. Then it's about vote YES when we get the referendum."

Peter imagined that had Dougal been there he would have pointed out that changing the brief at this stage would incur extra costs. Doubling the cost, probably, knowing Dougal. But Peter didn't feel at all comfortable mentioning this, instead he'd leave it to Dougal to load the monthly invoice as he saw fit and get on with comprehending the fact that they had to pull the cat out of the bag in terms of a campaign in a much shorter timeframe than they'd expected.

The he remembered Alan Haines.

"I'd better go Piers. I'll be in touch later today." Peter said, shaking hands with Jackman and leaving briskly. Relieved to have some personal space to digest the information he had just learned, Peter sat back in his car seat and exhaled loudly. Then he found the small pay as you go mobile reserved exclusively for Paula and sent her a text. "Call me. Need to ask you something. Urgent xx"

Paula called back within a few seconds. She was confused at Peters sudden interest in her husband's occupation and didn't have the answers Peter wanted.

"Well, I don't know - yes one company, I think." she spluttered, thrown by the line of questioning. "There was also something in Vietnam he was involved with though. I thought it was the same company but it could have been another one. We didn't discuss it apart from when he went there, which was only about once a year. Some sort of factory - engineering supplies? I think." she said, piecing the bits of memory together.

"What about politics?" Peter persisted.

""Well yes, he is a true-blue Tory, that's for sure. He was a member of the party but he'd only joined for the odd jolly with some mates at fundraisers. Nothing more than that." she said. "Or that's how it seemed..." she said quietly, her voice full of self-doubt.

Chapter 8: Greek Salad

Creatives Juices went into virtual lockdown overnight. Long hours and over-nighters were in order to fast track the development of the YES campaign. David was still working on the video project with Rebecca and there were half a dozen existing clients to service as well. New enquiries were sporadic, but there had been an invitation to tender from a housing association for a re-branding exercise. It was decided that regular clients wouldn't get in the way of the YES campaign work. In most cases the production schedules could be amended to delay delivery of certain jobs without them even being aware. Then a few white lies about the availability of certain poster sites and a day or two's fictitious delay at the printers and Creative Juices had bought enough time to focus the lion's share of its efforts on the independence campaign.

The video project had been a success, but it was time-consuming. The price point was too low for the effort that had to be put in, as Iestyn had alluded to originally. There were actors to audition, scripts to write and re-write, props to source, clients to deal with and shoot days, when filming as many ads as possible was shoehorned into one day. If the margins were low, the volume and demand was high. The real problem was that the person behind the camera all day was Derek, the Art Director. He was a keen amateur photographer and had recently got into video as a hobby, so possessed the necessary kit. Morris had spotted the potential saving and wooed him into the project over a few beers. The upshot of that was a shortfall in the design studio, with Derek on three shoot days when he was really needed in the studio. Cancelling the shoot days wasn't a viable option as that meant reorganising actors who would probably claim they had turned own other work to be there on that specific day. Then there were the clients who might just change their minds and pull out.

The video ads were on special offer at £500, reduced from £900. Orders were flying in. The video-ads did their own publicity because of the contractual "Juice-TV" branding and web address on the end screen of each ad. Clients could opt-out of that but Morris had decided that doing so would add a prohibitive amount to the price of the ad, therefore discouraging such actions. As a result, nobody opted out. But Juice-TV really wasn't very profitable when you considered how many agency staff were involved as well as the cost of the actors. So, the price of the video-ads was gradually increased until demand began to level off. It was cheaper than market research. Just increase the price - or lower the discount - every two weeks - and stop when the drop off occurs. The ads got to £749 before demand began to plateau and the discounted price became anchored there allowing the project to roll on.

David and Rebecca had been recognised for the success of the Juice-TV project and for David in particular, this was a big step up. He was feeling mature, confident, well-humoured and in love. Now the time was right to propose to Alicia. It had to be right, though. A special restaurant. He had thought of booking a restaurant in the Bay, overlooking the harbour, but most of the restaurants in the Bay were chains - none of the independents could afford the rents and rates. The best independent restaurants were found in the Roath and Heath areas on City Road and Crwys Road, where rates and rents were much cheaper. You didn't get a view of the Bay but you got decent and often highly original food, even if your vista might be a launderette or a chippy.

David booked a new Greek restaurant, called 'The Santorini Surprise' – a moniker that turned out to carry some irony. He and Alicia had been to the island of Santorini the previous May on a last-minute cheap deal. The holiday had been wonderful - a mix of scooter-riding, shopping and wonderful Greek food against the spectrum of blue, terracotta and white that was the ever-present colour palette of the beautiful island. Neither of them had been to Greece before and Alicia had really taken to the Greek salads - a mixture of black olives, Mediterranean tomatoes, Feta cheese, cucumber and oregano with other additions, depending on the taverna. Sometimes she had ordered it as a main meal, other times as a side dish with Souvlaki - a pork kebab dish - as a main. Once she'd discovered what she liked, she stuck to it, ordering the same combinations most days. David had been more adventurous, sampling Stifado, a sort of casserole, Dolmades - stuffed vine leaves and Kleftiki - a slow-cooked stew of lamb. So, when a Greek restaurant called Santorini opened its doors a few months ago in Cardiff, David earmarked it as a treat for Alicia. He upgraded it to a proposal venue having checked that the necessary Greek salad was on the menu and would be available on the night.

The ring had been tricky. David knew nothing about rings, prices or sizes. Did they come in small, medium and large? Or did you have to have an actual circumference in millimetres? And if the latter, how did you go about measuring the finger girth inconspicuously? David had a modest amount of savings that had been left to him by his late grandmother. But whilst he wanted to make things special, he didn't want to blow the lot on one ring. And what about the stone? There were, it seemed, endless complications and choices to make. He didn't really want to ask his father in case the whole idea of marriage might be poo-pooed, based on their age, compatibility or some other random reason. So, Google needed to provide the answers. Sure enough, it was all there in the "People also ask" panel.

"How much are wedding rings?"
" What sizes do wedding rings come in?"
"What colours are precious stones for rings?"

...and so on.

Armed with advice and knowledge from people he didn't know, David headed for a jeweller's in the city centre. After browsing, he pointed out three rings that he was initially interested in. Immediately, he was whisked into an upmarket waiting area and offered a glass of champagne, which he accepted. He began to wonder if he had misread the price, given the red-carpet treatment. Or was there a tiering system? Squash for cheap rings, wine, then prosecco then Champagne as you moved up the price ladder? After two glasses of champagne that he guessed were costing him about £200 each, he purchased a ring made of Welsh gold with a small sapphire, which he would tell Alicia reminded them of the ocean in Santorini.

Proposal night arrived. David and Alicia taxied to Santorini where they were greeted warmly by the owner. There had been a few problems in the kitchen, he explained, with the grill and oven. They were now working, but as a result, there were delays, but free Retsina wine or Ouzo would be provided by way of compensation. He gesticulated around to the rest of the restaurant where people sat foodless, but tipsy. David wondered how long the problem had been going on for. It was 8.30pm, so the other people might have booked for 7.30pm, perhaps?

A waiter showed them to the quiet table in the corner that David had requested. A Retsina and an Ouzo appeared quickly and they decided to order quickly as they were already at the back of the queue, so to speak. There was talk of just ordering two Greek salads, which unless the chef broke normal protocol or was drunk, would not need to be baked or grilled, but David insisted that as a "special night", they would have a two or three course meal, or even a Meze - a traditional Greek mix of dishes. The waiter again explained the delay factor and the couple nodded as if to say this was understood. David had planned to make his move after the meal but suddenly realised that this might be some time and Ouzos away. So, he seized the moment.

"Alicia. I want to ask you something important." he said gingerly. He had planned a short preamble but forgot it and plunged in with a "Will you marry me?". He slid the box containing the ring across the table. She looked taken aback. Then flattered. Then beautiful. Then happy. Then about to speak. Then the fire alarm went off. Instinctively they both looked around, only to see smoke belching from the kitchen door. The owner was shouting.

"Go, go! Wait outside! Not drill. Real fire! Grill on fire!" There were sounds of a fire extinguisher being implemented and more smoke as David and Alicia fled the building along with the other Ouzoed and Retsinaerd would-be diners. It was pouring with rain. They heard sounds of fire engines as they walked quickly away from the building that was now billowing smoke from the door. The couple tried to disentangle themselves from the crowd of escapees but the narrowness of the pavement seemed to keep them all moving as one body. David felt Alicia tug his arm sharply and suddenly they were both disengaged from the crowd and squashed in the small doorway of a closed shop. Looking at each other expressions changed from relief to surprise, to uncertainty - as to what should happen next. Alicia grabbed David, swung him around pinning him to the graffitied roller-shut-

149

ter door. The words "Marty is a wanker" were spelled out in red spray paint just above David's head. Oblivious, Alicia whispered "yes". Then again slightly louder, then louder again, then very loudly beaming. "Yes, yes, yes!" Passers-by in the dark and rainy night might indeed have mistaken what the couple were doing in the doorway, given what emanated from it. But she finished with a quiet "Yes, I will marry you!" and smile and then a long kiss pressing David hard against the roller shutter door. So hard, in fact, that the burglar alarm went off - its shrill tones fusing with fire engines in the confusion of the night.

In the morning Alicia woke and leaned over to David who was already awake and reading something on his mobile.

"That was quite a proposal. Given a beautiful ring. Evacuated from a restaurant which was on fire. Accepted proposal in a shop doorway and finished the night nearly being arrested for breaking and entering. That certainly was a Santorini Surprise!" she grinned. "We'll never forget that night for as long as we live. And live together." she beamed staring at her ring which she had worn to bed, clearly delighted to be engaged.

"Well I did plan something memorable." said

David. "But that surpassed even my expectations!"

Alicia used the remote to switch on the TV as David went to the kitchen to make tea and coffee. BBC News sprung to life mid-story, with something about a serous virus that was killing people in China. Alicia was a very empathetic person, gave regularly to charities and took an interest in the environment and other people's plight, whether in the UK or overseas. David, on the other hand, was more offish and selfish, but Alicia didn't interpret it as a negative, just a personal difference. She listened to the reporter, explaining that the outbreak of Coronavirus had now resulted in several hundred deaths in a matter of days. David returned, carrying his regular Red Bush tea and her lemon infusion with honey. He never understood her love of a drink that he only consumed when he had a heavy cold. And even then, with a slug of whisky in it. She told him about the Chinese virus but he simply shrugged and said he hoped they would manage to sort it out, before opening Facebook on his mobile and navigating to his feed.

***

Creative Juices were pulling all the stops out to deliver the YES campaign. They needed to produce two campaigns, one which would promote

Welsh Independence, the other that would encourage a yes vote. A workshop had been set up to begin to distil the result of the market research and derive a matrix of prioritised messages that would be part of the campaigns and reflect the research that their research agency had undertaken. Some of the message could be expressed succinctly, in one phrase. Copywriter Tim Hughes was a critical part of turning the stodgy research report into attractive soundbites. "Back in Europe. Back in Business. Back Independence for Wales." was a forerunner for the main campaign theme, but there needed to be alternative headlines that could play out to other segments of the market, addressing their concerns. So, the campaign matrix was complicated. Then there was the messaging work to be done underneath the main headlines - web copy, flyers, e-shots and a social media calendar. All this was extremely time consuming to do, even though only in draft format.

With a day to go before the presentation to the YES group, momentum was given a huge boost as Scotland announced that a second referendum was imminent, now that London had bowed to public and political pressure both in the UK and overseas. Scotland's First Minister, Cameron Dunbar tried his best to make his voice sound enthusiastic and Alistair McFadden ensured his drab delivery was compensated for by a brilliant TV ad campaign using upbeat actors to promote the positivity of independence.

They had won. Or at least they had won the first stage - getting the referendum. But they still needed the country to vote in favour of independence. The first vote - had been a close call with the NO vote only just tipping the balance. Sure, the polls indicated a win for YES this time around, but polls can be wrong and every effort had to be made to get the YES vote over the line.

McFadden spoke with Jackman over the phone. When were the Welsh going to get the whole independence project moving? For McFadden it could only help encourage more yes supporters in Scotland now that things had moved more quickly than he thought. And Jackman stood to gain from the fresh news of potential Scottish independence. They discussed how they could use the synergy to best effect. But the critical factor was timing. Wales had to go public on the independence campaign to light the stick of dynamite that could eventually obliterate the UK.

Jackman conveyed this to Peter who in turn conveyed to Dougal who in turn, conveyed to the entire team at Creative Juices, all of whom were exhausted and trying to make the deadline for the presentation the following day. It had been intended to be motivational but hadn't been taken that way by the battle-weary staff who had worked long hours anyway. There was nothing more they could do.

The presentation took place at Urquhart-Williams Honiton. There were seven people in attendance in the boardroom of the bank, apart from the team of three from Creative Juices. Gethin Jones-Evans, chairman of the YES campaign, Eric Urquhart-Williams - whose boardroom it was, Piers Jackman plus four other unidentified individuals. Dougal, Peter and Tim Hughes were the presentation team for Creative Juices. Throughout the presentation of ideas, schedules, creative and budgets, Eric Urquhart-Williams remained focused on detail, with the others asking more general questions. Some had clearly sat through ad agency presentations before and others, from their more surprised looks, had not. The meeting lasted nearly three hours and at the end of it all eyes were on the banker. It became clear that he was playing a significant role in the funding of the campaign so naturally had a bigger say in how it was run. He looked around at his colleagues and only glanced briefly at the agency.

"This seems in order to me. I'd like the answers to the questions on the radio timeslots and demographics and also the extra mock ups on the campaign to farmers, but in principle, let's get on with it." For someone bankrolling a YES campaign he was surprisingly reluctant to use the word himself to signal his approval.

The Creative Juices team had barely had chance to catch up on sleep before the next phase of work was beckoning. With the campaigns virtually signed off the enormity of the implementation was upon them. Within a fortnight the so-called "nationalism campaign" was live on billboards - or 48 sheet posters as the agency called them - across Wales. The Western Mail, Wales Online, the South Wales Echo, the Daily Post and a host of regionals were also carrying ads as were the radio stations. There had been talk of a phased approach to give the impression of gradual momentum rather than a sudden deluge, but the Scottish situation had prompted the decision to fire all the guns at once.

Back in Europe. Back in Business. Back Independence for Wales - was everywhere. As Dougal had said, anyone who missed it was either asleep, on holiday, or dead.

***

Jackman read the headlines again on his iPad, sitting in the lounge next to the half-open bi-fold doors, sipping a specially-blended coffee. A shaft of winter sunlight warmed his face on this otherwise cool day. The news was as bleak as the day. The Chinese virus was in Europe. He'd followed the Coronavirus story over the last few days never thinking that it might spread outside China. But there were now reported cases in Italy. He was stunned. Not only did it make him think about the plight of those who had died, but also the fact that he was part of a movement that was encouraging a yes vote and a return to being part of Europe at the same time as Europe might have some incidences of a mystery killer disease. Probably, it would all blow over, he thought, hopefully. He switched off his iPad, placed it on the coffee table where the NDAs had been a few weeks previous and elbowed the bi-folds open, still carrying his coffee. Wandering across the patio, he couldn't help but feel troubled. A lot was happening all at once. First, Scotland getting the referendum. Then the rush to push for Welsh nationalism and getting the movement moving. And now a deadly disease on mainland Europe. His analytical mind tried to work out possible outcomes and scenarios, but his subconscious mind needed time to digest the odd melange of events before his conscious mind could process solutions properly. He decided to go to the gym.

The media were quick to pick up on the Welsh Independence story. In fact, they had been all over it even before the ad campaign had gone live. Social media posts had preceded the main campaign and key journalists had been briefed in order to create the impression of an unintentional leak of a great story. All this had been well planned for by the YES team, many of whom had recently attended a media training day, where they had learned how to deal with the media to the best effect and how to craft messages that were consistent. The course tutor had given them stock phrases to use to emphasise points, like "Let me be clear."

"Let me be clear, our intention was never to break up the UK. We want unity. But we want unity with our European friends, a unity that will bring economic prosperity back to Wales."

Wales' First Minister, Alun Roberts, had deliberately distanced himself from the YES movement with Jackman being used as the fall guy. The intention was that Roberts would throw his weight behind the campaign as soon as it gained public support. Inevitably that would have to be quick, as he would be asked to comment on the matter both in the Senedd and by the media. As soon as the story broke, he announced his political support for the YES movement. Within a day, the NO campaign was unleashed on social media with Alan Haines giving interviews on both Radio and TV. Their message was to keep Wales in Britain and not break up the UK. The

UK was a powerful global nation, but Wales on its own would be a small fish in a very big pond and would wither economically.

With the Scottish referendum just two weeks away, the drama spread across the UK. It made better television than dramas or soaps as coverage switched from Scotland to London and back again, like political ping pong. The Wales story was usually brought in every time the phrase "breaking up the UK" came into play. TV channels dispatched reports to all parts of Wales to record "vox pops" - impromptu short interviews with members of the public. It always seemed necessary to find people with extreme opinions, very strong accents or in an unusual location. But it made good TV. Not everyone complied, of course. There was the thirty-something coming out of public toilet in Neath who was asked how he felt about Welsh Independence. He had looked furious and spluttered

"I've just been for a fucking piss, that's all I wanted! Not to be fucking ambushed by you TV twats as soon as I've done my fucking flies up!"

"Can't use that one, then." the reporter had mumbled under his breath.

Then there were the Welsh speakers, who refused to answer in English. In Carmarthenshire it happened a few times. When it didn't, the accents were occasionally so strong that the interviewee may have been speaking Welsh anyway. BBC Wales and S4C fared better than their London-based counterparts with all of their reporters being bilingual.

Opinions were divided, which is exactly what the producers wanted, so they could make a long game of the campaigns in terms of coverage. If there were a clear winner from the outset, the coverage wouldn't be as long, but a good two-sided battle, well, that was different. What divided the responses in the vox pops was not only support for a referendum or the lack of it, but a critical understanding of the whole matter. Some people were honest and simply shrugged, saying that they would leave it to the politicians and that was why they elected them. But those were a tiny minority. Most people expressed an opinion, no matter how informed or ill-informed they were.

"I think it'd be great to have a Welsh passport. A red one, I'd like, I would. With a dragon on it. Lush it'd be." one woman had said, elongating the pronunciation of the word 'dragon' as if it had fifteen 'a's in it and using the great Welsh superlative, "lush".

"We d'like going on our holidays in Europe. Turkey, we do. So yes, I'd vote yes, I would." a man outside a travel agent had said with great gusto, before losing confidence and following up with " Turkey is in Europe is it? Or have I made a knob of myself? Cut that bit out, isn't it?"

"Isn't it" is a Welsh way of ending pretty much any question or sentence, even though it is completely unnecessary to have the sentence make sense. Another Welsh linguistic idiosyncrasy is the desire to augment a verb by preceding it with a "do" - usually shortened to "d'" and then the verb is repeated at the end again. So, instead of "We like chips." it would be "We d'like chips, we do". Again, the additions are utterly superfluous, but seem to make more of the sentence and add some Welsh character.

Of course, not everyone spoke like this. There are a wide variety of accents and idioms across Wales, but capturing a cross section was important for credibility. Some vox-poppers in the South East of Wales had sounded almost English, indeed some were, which made for interesting responses. Interviews were conducted across a range of employment types. Farmers, tradespeople, business owners, students, the unemployed were amongst the segments being covered. Because of the ever-increasing focus on equality and diversity, these audiences needed to also include various ages, disabilities, gender reassignments, races, religions, genders and sexual orientations. All in all, it was a complex matrix. Especially when it came to the farmers, who were nearly all married white, male Christians. But as long as the sample of the audience was representative, it didn't matter.

The next stage of messaging that Creative Juices was about to unleash was the "education phase." These messages would give the public tangible reasons to support the YES campaign now that the "nationalism phase" had run its course. It would be back again in phase three of the campaign, but it was important to keep the debate lively to keep the public engaged. The education phase from YES set out the main reasons to vote for Welsh Independence and included the economic and political benefits . All were centred around being back in Europe, with the promise of more money, more jobs and better security.

***

Despite the nation's preoccupation with the question of independence, David and Alicia had a wedding to plan. Alicia began to come home from work with wedding magazines and invitations to wedding exhibitions and David began to wonder who was going to foot the bill for everything. He hadn't thought this bit through, imagining that he and Alicia would simply get married somewhere simple and then go on honeymoon.

His ideal solution was a long engagement, which gave time to save and think. But Alicia was in a wedding whirlwind and David was beginning to wonder what to do. She started with the desire for a big white wedding.

"What, pay all that money and get into debt just to dole out rubber chicken to a bunch of people, most of whom you hardly know?" David had said, deflating her dream. So, over the two weeks that followed the engagement, her mood turned from elation to frustration as various options were discussed. Her parents took some thinking and calculating time before offering her a generous sum towards the wedding. Peter and Justine also committed their sum, which was equally generous and had also followed many discussions between them.

Fortunately, Alicia was practical enough to realise that she had a budget to work towards. The budget would cover a superb wedding for a few dozen people or a modest wedding for more. But it didn't quite give her the extras that the wedding magazines told her she must have. So, the choice was hers. Take a loan for the difference or make a choice between smaller or bigger wedding. David was stuck in the middle of this, wondering what to do. He'd figured that he had done the hard part, what with the ring and the proposal. He hadn't envisaged this. Then a sympathetic friend suggested a wedding abroad, which David hadn't considered. In his lunch break the following day, he headed for the travel agents, only a minute's walk away from the office and quickly armed himself with a dozen brochures, much to the delight of the travel agent, who took his number and told him not to book on the internet. Armed with a weighty pile of potential destinations, he arrived home later that day and proudly fanned them out on the kitchen table. The Seychelles, the Caribbean, Mauritius, Sri Lanka, Italy and Mexico were amongst the top destinations, the agent had told David.

Alicia initially thought they were honeymoon brochures, which softened the blow a little. It took her a while to come around to the possibility of getting married abroad, with questions about guests, parents and other relatives attending.

"That's the beauty of it." said David. "It's up to them whether they come or not. Your parents and mine would come as their donations would cover their travel as well as the wedding. It takes the hassle out of who to invite to a big rubber chicken event in Wales and we get two weeks in the sun."

Alicia went quiet and then decided to have an early night. Things didn't bode well, David thought. But, in the morning she was brighter and announced over breakfast that she had warmed to the idea and that they could have a really up-market wedding which matched their budget, without having to borrow any money. Over the days that followed, a happy equilibrium was restored and the couple spent the next few evenings perusing the tropics and its wedding resorts. She was a little bit concerned that the beach wedding system could be a bit of a production line, so they looked for the most upmarket options available. There was also the need to check availability of rooms for their parents - all of whom wanted to come - and any friends, though as they would bear the cost, that was looking unlikely.

Alicia had become very amorous since the engagement and particularly since the wedding plans were reaching some sort of harmony, so evenings of wedding planning were followed by early nights. David was always in the office at 7am, dealing with Juice-TV matters and sometimes working from the Bay office, just to get some peace. It was rarely used for anything more than the occasional meeting. Juice-TV had shoot days fully booked for the next month. They couldn't add more in, because Derek was needed on the YES project and it became clear that a back-up videographer and editor may be necessary if they were to scale Juice-TV. Freelancers were ruled out as once they got too close to the project, they could easily steal the concept and do it for themselves albeit that Juice-TV had been the first to the market. So, reluctantly, the board authorised the appointment of a videographer for Juice TV, which although busy and profitable wasn't a runaway money-maker. After analysing what seemed like hundreds of showreels, Derek and David interviewed two hopefuls and put the favourite in front of Dougal for the "culture-fit" interview. The first assignment was to be for the YES campaign which seemed to place even more importance on getting the right person for the job. John Jarvis - a Media Studies graduate with a year's experience with a production company - was eventually appointed. The choice was made partly because of his showreel and partly because of a government grant that paid half his salary for the first six months.

Chapter 9: Pig On A Stick

Referendum day. Scotland. Both sides of the campaign were still out on the media and on the streets, trying to convince floating voters which box to cross.

McFadden's team were in overdrive. First Minister Dunbar made his scheduled media appearance at his local polling station at 7am to cast the first vote. Stakes were high - a "no" vote at the polls could spell trouble for his career. A "yes" could put him in the history books. He spent the day in his office, glancing up constantly at the huge OLED TV that relayed the latest coverage. Occasionally he flicked from BBC to Sky and then back again. There were calls every twenty minutes or so from various members of the team - other ministers and civil servants. When he wasn't consuming election coverage or taking calls, Dunbar worked on two speeches - one for victory, the other for defeat. He had always liked to write his own speeches, sometimes fact-checking them with his team, other times - where it was more personal - just practising the delivery of the speech, using his voice to the best of his ability. He also knew that he needed to conserve energy as there may be a long night ahead, during which he wouldn't get much sleep, as the counting process took place.

All eyes were on Scotland, particularly in Wales. McFadden received a text from Piers Jackman wishing him luck. Dougal was glued to the new TV in his office for most of the day. Morris consumed seemingly half his body weight in pistachios. Alicia wondered what it would be like to get married in Edinburgh. And Peter and Paula spent late afternoon in bed, with a bottle of Chablis and an assortment of Paula's new underwear, with Peter occasionally glancing up at the subtitled TV for updates on Scotland.

The count was on. Exit polls pointed to a win for "yes", but not by a huge majority. McFadden arrived at Dunbar's office with two of his team, ready to work through the speeches for impact and also to practise them on camera. One of the men was an editor, who would proof check the speeches and suggest amendments, the other a videographer who was setting up to film Dunbar practising his speeches. McFadden supervised the event, chipping in occasionally to demonstrate his experience and usefulness - in his own eyes. The assembled group said very little over the next ten minutes. The only sounds were tapping of keys and the clicking together of video equipment. The editor typed out amends to the Word documents speechwin. doc and speechlose.doc. The videographer assembled the tripod and rigged up the radio mic. McFadden pecked at his mobile - emailing and texting. Dunbar paced, his eyes looking up as if in hope of divine intervention.

Europe looked on with anticipation. A selection of de Malo's team spent the day plugged into numerous media channels, distilling the latest news and summarising for de Malo to digest. It was sent to him via WhatsApp every ten minutes or so.

The night's TV coverage was electric, with results coming in every half hour or so and both sides running neck and neck until the small hours. YES began to nudge ahead as the clock sailed past 3am. Alicia and David fell asleep. Paula and Peter woke up, having accidentally fallen asleep at midnight. Jackman paced the lounge, pausing for a power nap at 1am. Wales waited with baited breath as Scottish history was poised for the most seismic change for over 300 years. Maybe.

Fireworks went off across Scotland, even though it was morning. Dunbar was at party HQ, watching the events unfold with two hundred or more supporters.

It was over. The waiting was over. It was the end.

They had won. Streamers exploded from nowhere, Dunbar was rushed to the stage to receive his mandate to take Scotland out of the United Kingdom. With 66% of voters behind him there was a comfortable majority, though others would doubtlessly argue to the contrary.

"The Scottish people have spoken. And they have said in a clear voice that they want freedom. Freedom to make their own decisions, freedom to enjoy their own wealth, freedom from Westminster interventions and freedom to apply to join the European Union, if they so wish." said Dunbar, wanting to make all the key points before his coalition partners stole any limelight.

TV cameras beamed the speech around the UK, mainland Europe and even the USA, though many didn't really understand where Scotland was. The American education system seems to focus heavily on nationalism and an America-centric attitude to the world. Ask your average American about Wales and they'll probably say they've never heard of it. Scotland fares a little better, but only if you explain as regards anywhere in the UK that it is "near London". This seems to comfort Americans, most of whom seem to have been there. So, putting it in the context of what they know seems to help and compared to distances in the USA, Scotland is near London. So, maybe they are right, after all. You can imagine Mr and Mrs America watching TV...

"Hey Bill, watch this, there's a party in Scotland, England. They're independent now."

"Independent from where?" replies Bill.

"Well, I don't know, honey! Where is Scotland anyway?"

"London."

"Do they speak English there? I would love to hear somebody speak English."

"Honey, we all speak English."

"Oh really? I feel like such a dork."

"Uh, huh."

In Wales all eyes were on the Welsh Government. First Minister Alun Roberts made a short speech congratulating Scotland's YES campaign for their hard work and reiterating that the people of Scotland had indeed voted to be independent. This prompted immediate media questions about Wales' own intentions. Deliberate silence had been agreed - at least for a few days. Let Scotland take the limelight and then when the story dies off announce the intention to ask London for a referendum. No point splitting the media coverage at this point and the celebrations in Scotland would hopefully fuel the fires of the YES campaign in Wales.

Behind the scenes conversations had been going on between Cardiff and London for the last two months about a Welsh independence referendum. Central government knew the issue was brewing and having early conversations may prove prudent. Ministers from both sides had held two meetings behind closed doors in Westminster, debating the constitutional ability for Wales to break away. Wales had "reserved powers" - devolved law-making powers, granted by Westminster going back to 2006, but they only applied to certain areas of legislation and not the ability to hold a referendum. Technically this meant that Westminster had to grant permission, similar to granting Scotland a section 30 order. Indeed, the situation was much the same and the stakes were even higher with the complete dissolution of the UK on the political horizon.

Piers Jackman had arranged for a media briefing for First Minster Alun Roberts on the Tuesday following the Scottish Victory. The intention was for Roberts to announce his intention to hold a Welsh Independence referendum, following the Scottish win. There was to be no mention of needing Westminster's permission. Of course, political commentators, journalists and others in the know would raise it, but not before it had hopefully spread through the nation's communities and picked up a wave of optimism and nationalism. Wales had declined economically since the UK left the EU, because of its reliance on EU grants to subsidise its economy, which was too public sector biased. Research suggested that there was now a feeling of resentment towards London for driving the exit from the EU.

Alun Roberts was a well-educated, optimistic man. A Welsh speaker, born in Llanelli, he had studied Politics Philosophy and Economics at Oxford. From a long line of labour supporters, the combination of his intelligence, education, connections, labour background and positivity had led him to the Assembly, where he became First Minister after five years serving as Minister for Communities and Minister for Education. Monday's speech was ready, it didn't need to be long. He and Jackman made final changes to it late Friday before breaking for a restful weekend, leaving the media to concentrate on the aftermath of the Scottish vote.

The weekend was anything but restful. On Saturday morning, a story broke on social media about Alun Roberts smoking cannabis whilst at University. The source was cited as an anonymous "college friend". It wasn't true and it was quickly denied and silenced on Twitter, but the damage had been done. People might forget it, but not in a matter of a few days. If he were to be unlucky, the mainstream media might pick it up as well. Even if the fake news was reported in a third-party fashion, it would only add to the damage.

Blow number two happened a few hours later when the NO campaign came out of nowhere and exploded with activity across social media channels and Wales Online. The message was clear: "Taking Wales out of the UK will affect our ability to defend ourselves as a country. It will break up centuries of being part of a world superpower, only to render Wales an economic backwater."

The second blow was, in a way, more devastating than the first. The first could be quashed as fake news, leaving some doubt in people's minds, but the second alluded to a subversive deception of the Welsh people. That could be much more serous if it spread. It did, multiplying exponentially on Twitter, Facebook, Instagram and within hours it was picked up by the broadcast media, who were soon looking for a statement.

They already had plenty of footage of Alan Haines as leader of the NO campaign, whose face was all over everything for the entire weekend. Jackman was on the phone to the First Minister within minutes of the NO story breaking. Alun Roberts hadn't even seen it at that point and was still recovering from the cannabis fake news.

"Haines must have had inside information." barked Jackman at his minister. "And I bet he's behind the dope story!"

"But we cannot prove that." replied Roberts gently. "We need to mitigate the problem."

An emergency cabinet meeting was convened for 9am Monday. The cabinet largely supported independence, with only one objector and one abstainer, both of whom declined to attend that morning for "family reasons." Clearly the First Minister couldn't make the speech he had intended to the following day so the content and the media statement that was released on Monday simply confirmed that Wales was in discussion with Westminster about the possibility of a referendum following growing public pressure. It was made clear that these were early stage conversations largely theoretical and constitutional and as yet there was nothing to report. So, the impact was weakened, but the collateral damage was minimised.

Then, more fake news on social media: "Welsh Government plans to phase out funding for Welsh language. They will no longer sanction funding of bi-lingual publications or road-signs. "What next?" said the post. "Will they ban the Welsh language?" The posts went viral in Wales on social media. It probably would have been dismissed as cranky a few days ago but with a tide of negativity swelling against the First Minister, the media seagulls were circling, looking for easy pickings. The next three days were spent defending the First Minister and the Welsh Government against the blows. But for Roberts there was only one way out, as senior civil servants, including Jackman, had confirmed. He had to resign. Resigning would mean that he would be the fall guy, take the fake news with him and leave the Welsh Government intact to move on with the Deputy First Minister, Tomos Davies, in charge.

Within a day, Roberts had reluctantly announced his resignation as First Minister, citing personal reasons. His short speech said that Wales was on course for great things, but he had to concentrate on his family. Speculation was rife in the tabloids as to why Roberts had resigned and while the journalists were competing for better stories, the YES campaign arrived overnight with a bang. Gethin Jones-Evans, chairman of the YES campaign made an announcement at midnight on social media, live from his offices in Cardiff Bay, filmed by Juice-TV. The timing was critical. Wales needed to wake up to the news and the clips of Jones-Evans speaking from his office with the dark skies visible in the background giving a feeling of authenticity.

His speech was well-honed and themed around honesty. An ex-head teacher by profession, he spoke well. Creative Juices had advised not filming live so any mistakes could be rectified in "post" - post production - but there was no time. In his speech, Jones-Evans talked about his passion for Wales, the great partnership between Wales and Europe, a rosy economic future and also fake news.

"Let me be clear. There is no movement to quell the Welsh language." A phrase which he translated into Welsh, adding in the same tongue that he was fluent Welsh speaker and an avid supporter of bilingualism. Switching back to English, he spoke of the need to consult with both Westminster and Brussels and reach a "broad and sensible consensus of the way forward based on democracy and pragmatism." The tone had deliberately been shifted from punching out the benefits for Welsh Independence to a call to imbue trust and faith in the YES leader. Indeed, the speech was so empathetic and well-delivered many may have wondered whether they were looking at a future First Minister.

If Jones-Evans hadn't trumpeted the benefits of independence too loudly during the next days, the paid-for media would have. These few days had always been the go-live of the biggest phase of advertising and as newsreaders played the Jones-Evans speech from dawn, so billboards across the region were being transformed from their previous incarnation to a YES advert. The campaign played out on local radio stations and local press as well plus online via a series of pre-recorded mini videos, courtesy of Juice-TV, that were released daily. In addition to John Jarvis, David and Derek had recently taken on a full-time editor and another cameraman to cope with the work, which was now blossoming beyond the mini-ads. The social media ads for YES lasted no more than a minute and always started with an arresting visual image or statement. With social, there is such a short time to capture attention, the first two seconds are critical.

The NO campaign seemed to have been caught off-guard by the scale of it all. They had won the first round and ousted the First Minister but the public had been quickly wooed by Jones-Evans and bombarded by the multi-channel ad campaign for YES. The opposition could catch up in terms of advertising but it would take many days to arrange poster sites and book radio airtime to supplement their social media and press campaigns. For a while YES had the edge. And that was thanks to Creative Juices.

***

"How did he know Paula?" Peter raised his voice, as soon as the front door was closed and the coffees were poured. "How did your ex-husband know about the timings?" he said, trying not to sound threatening or accusatory.

"Are you accusing me?" she replied, in either fake or genuine astonishment. Peter tried to calculate which.

"We only speak via lawyers - you know that!" she said, clearly irritated.

"I know. I wasn't accusing you, Paula. I was just asking for your help - after all you know him." said Peter

There was a pause. Then she spoke.

"A friend of his - Evan Tomkin - is a cyber security and expert. He's allegedly - though he doesn't admit it - an ex-hacker. He helps organisations protect themselves from cyber-attacks."

"So, you think we might have a security breach?" asked Peter.

"Look, I don't want to point fingers, but have your stuff checked over at the campaign. Alan's friend, I know, is part of the NO campaign, so it might be me being paranoid, but your emails could have been hacked."

Peter looked concerned and thoughtful. Then he thanked Paula and they walked out into the garden, coffees in hand. They talked about the campaign, the roller-coaster events on the media of the last few days, though Peter was guarded in giving away any additional information to Paula. After lunch, he made excuses and headed back to Creative Juices for a board meeting. The agency's billings were now back on target and if the battle continued they could well be 50% up. The YES campaign looked as if they were about to commit to more activity based on staying ahead of the NO campaign, Juice -TV was now filming all over Wales and the West and enquiries were coming in daily. The board decided it was time to reward the staff. There was discussion about the best way to do it. Bonuses can set expectations for the future, it was argued, but then company days out can seem like thinly disguised work. In the end a combination of both was agreed - a bonus plus a company away-day, mid-week, representing a day-off. Phones would be diverted to an answering service and directors' mobiles would be on for critical communications.

The staff, though grateful for the bonus, were sceptical about going to a place called "Let's Play in the Woods", an outdoors pursuits venue. There was such a luke-warm response to the event that Dougal had been forced to sugar-coat it as a barbecue with team games and a free bar. The event started at 10.30am with coffee and bacon rolls in a wooden lodge on a farm, twenty minutes' drive from Cardiff. The Creative Juices staff began to arrive from about 10 am, dressed in trainers, old jeans or shorts and t-shirts, as instructed. The studio arrived in a taxi, laden with bags of wine, gin and beer. On spotting this, Neil Jones, the owner of Let's Play in the Woods, beckoned Dougal to warn him that no-one was to consume alcohol before the events. Dougal nodded sympathetically and shrugged in disbelief as if to ask what sort of fuck-wits would drink gin before getting on a quad-bike. It was partly his fault, of course. The sugar-coating of the event had kept the detail loose and it had not been mentioned that the free bar was to be at the end of the day and for one hour only. Dougal strode towards Wendy to confront her about the booze situation. He suspected that he was already too late as they had all probably been drinking in the taxi, but chose to put this out of his mind.

The group were split into four teams, each of which would rotate around four events - called the "four by four challenge". Dougal had a quiet word with Neil Jones to make sure that the teams were picked randomly, so that directors were separated and the studio were dispersed. The groups rotated through the activities - quad biking, archery, paint-balling and blindfold driving. The blindfold driving was really popular. As the teams passed each other briefly during switch-overs, their facial expressions transmitted ratings scores for the activity they had just completed. Without exception everyone coming off the blindfold driving seemed to be punching out 10/10s.

Wendy's team were next. They were split into pairs. One was to be the sighted navigator, the other, the blindfolded driver. Wendy was paired with copywriter, Tim Hughes. It seemed that each pair very naturally chose their respective roles based on personality. Tim - sensible and thoughtful - was a natural navigator. Wendy -

creative, wild and already slightly pissed - was alarmingly the better choice of blind-folded driver. Fortunately, the course was self-contained and in the middle of the country so relatively little damage could be done, it seemed. The route demanded a navigation of trees through a sparse woodland, the crossing of a large brook and the mounting of steep banks.

"Straight on, Wendy." said Tim. "There's a big tree in about thirty metres. Left hand down a bit now." he guided.

"What the fuck does that mean?" squawked Wendy. "Down on the gear stick?"

"No - don't touch that - down on the steering wheel!"

Wendy slid her hand down the cold metal circle, leaving the steering wheel in the same position.

"No! Move the fucking..." THWACK.

"Fuck, fuck - we've hit the fucking tree!" shouted Tim, in disbelief as the car glanced off the side of the trunk. Had they not been in the obligatory low gear it might have been a lot worse. Wendy was howling laughing now and Tim considered taking over the vehicle, then realising that Wendy was, in effect, his superior.

Rather than give in, Wendy ploughed on, foot to the floor and reached for the gear box to change up.

"Wendy no - we have to stay slow - Neil said! For fuck sake..."

The 4x4 careered through a clearing broke through a wooden fence and emerged at 30 mph in a field full of archers. Wendy, oblivious, cackled and screamed as terrified Tim could only look on and perform his now redundant explanatory narrative.

"We've broken the fence, fuck we're in a fucking field full of fucking archers! Stop, Wendy." Tim began to suspect that Wendy had not only been drinking but smoking something as well, as her current state of mind couldn't possibly have been rendered by a gin or two in the taxi. The archery group looked on in disbelief as the car broke through the fence. Bow in hand, Morris's jaw dropped.

"It's Wendy! Jesus. And Tim. Why doesn't he tell her to stop?" he shouted as the archery crowd fled for cover, bows in hand. The 4x4 ploughed on with Tim trying to wrestle control of the wheel. It came to an abrupt crunching stop as it knocked a Portaloo into a fence and then mounted it. Tim threw himself across Wendy's lap, grabbed the ignition keys, twisted them to the off position and then retracted back to his seat like a spring resetting itself. They were soon surrounded by the archers, event staff and other onlookers who appeared to have come from no-where to look in amazement at a Land Rover atop a Portaloo, astride a fence. Wendy was coming down and began to realise that there may be repercussions for the fun she had been enjoying. She tried to think of something witty to say as she gazed down at the onlookers.

"Thanks very much and I hope we've passed the audition!" she shouted in reference to John Lennon's farewell comment at a final rooftop Beatles gig. Hardly anybody got it.

Peter had reluctantly participated in the event and had even begun to enjoy until the Wendy incident had brought the need for directors to be directors and removed the egalitarian feel about the event. He and Dougal were discussing what to do about Wendy just before the end of the day's awards ceremony. Morris joined them and at the same time Peter's mobile went off. Glancing down, he hoped it was Paula, but the number was not familiar. A Welsh voice. It was one of Piers Jackman's assistants. Apparently, Alistair McFadden's team had responded to Jack-man's request to meet with McFadden by way of exploring opportunities. McFadden had thought on receiving the original email that the opportunities would probably be a little one-sided as Scotland already had independence, but had decided to comply anyway. If Wales became its own state then Jackman and his cronies could become useful contacts. Jackman's assistant explained to Peter that he would be welcome in Edinburgh as a guest of Jackman and that suggestions of possible dates would be sent over email shortly. Peter smiled and returned to Morris and Dougal who were agreeing that today's incident could perhaps be let off with a verbal warning. It actually merited instant dismissal, according to the staff handbook. Instant dismissal was appropriate for acts such as blindfold drink-driving, crashing a Land Rover into a Portaloo, destroying property and terrifying a field of archers. Well, actually the staff handbook didn't say all that it just specified "gross misconduct". Morris and Dougal hadn't taken too long to agree that Wendy's actions fitted the bill, though it may be wise as she was an essential member of staff to let her off with a warning for the time being.

***

Peter stopped for a drink on the way home, buying time to mull over his idea of inviting Paula to Scotland. The meetings were only likely to last a day or so but extending the stay by a further day or so was very possible and wouldn't necessarily arouse suspicion with Justine. But then there was time off work - surely again, no-one at Creative Juices would bat an eyelid at a couple of days with a delegation in Scotland. Paula could fly up separately, enjoy some shopping, they could meet in the evening at the hotel and then enjoy a day or so afterwards exploring Edinburgh.

Peter suddenly came to his senses. The risk outweighed the benefit. Things were working out well with Paula in Cardiff. Why risk anything more? And there was still a tiny element of suspicion about her relationship with the NO campaign. Peter suddenly realised that all in all it had been a stupid idea. Maybe that's what a day's outdoor pursuits do to you, he thought. Justine had texted to say that David had turned up for a coffee unexpectedly and when would his father be home? David had been on the winning team today so no doubt he would be coming to gloat and gossip about the day. Peter headed home.

Although David was happy to talk about the day, he was in fact at his parents to tell them about the wedding that he and Alicia had chosen and planned to book. They had agreed that parents should be asked first and dates checked before any bookings took place. They had chosen to go to Antigua, in the Caribbean for a beach wedding. Because the hurricane season started in June and went on until November, May was the window for this year assuming they didn't want to get married at Christmas-time. So, after June the window effectively shut until the following year. They had both impulsively decided to plump for May, which was only twelve weeks away. Justine's parents - both Civil Servants - could quickly make holiday arrangements and always had plenty spare from their generous 38 days a year. Peter was flexible and looking forward to it. Justine though was swamped with divorce cases that stemmed back to the post-Christmas divorce boom that happened every year. Many of them were now at a critical time and she wasn't sure that leaving for ten days was wise. Peter wished he could just bring in Paula as a reserve, but of course that wasn't possible.

The wedding was to be on the beach. The provisional arrangements were that it would take place at 10am, before the day became too humid and hot. The other options were at the end of the afternoon or early evening, but Alicia had become concerned that people might be getting a bit tipsy by then. The small wedding party would then change clothes pick up a bag or two and then be driven in an air-conditioned limousine to the harbour. Here they would board a boat, bound for an atoll, ten miles off the coast of the main island. On the way they would be served drinks - tropical rum-based cocktails - before arriving at the island and enjoying a swim and a barbecue with the other newly-weds. The boat took the long way back to Antigua so the guests could enjoy the live music and bar on board, not to mention the spectacular views or the pristine green and blue ocean.

"Of course, if you can't make it mum, I'm sure dad can find someone else." said David, jokingly, nearly causing Peter to drop the glass he was drinking from. He recovered and realised he needed to play along so as, ironically, not to give the game away.

"Yes, I've got reserves. They'll be happy to oblige. They'll have to pay for themselves though!" he quipped.

"God, how many are you bringing, Dad? laughed David.

Peter was becoming anxious to change the subject.

"What about your stag do, David? he said.

"Well, what about Alicia's dress? Does she want a hand in choosing one? I'd be happy to help." offered Justine.

David hadn't thought about a stag do. It didn't really appeal to him but he didn't want to let anyone down either. The idea of getting so drunk he woke up tied to a lamp-post didn't really appeal and anyway those types of stag dos were becoming less popular.

"What about that place we went today?" said David. "That'd make a nice afternoon out for a bunch of us - and we'd have a few beers at the bar after?"

"Just because you won today!" jibed Peter, laughing.

But David was keen and decided to speak to Neil Jones the following day, if indeed Neil would permit anybody from today's event to return to the facility after Wendy's run-in with the Porta-loo and fence.

It turned out that Neil was fine about the whole thing. David called and apologetically announced that he was one of the visitors from yesterday, but Neil just laughed.

"No, of course I don't mind taking your money. If you were that Wendy woman, I might think twice. But this world is full of nutters and drinkers and we have our fair share of them coming here too. If I focused on morals, I wouldn't have a business!" Now why don't you pop round for a coffee in the next week and we can look at some options for you. What about a pig on a stick? That's popular..."

"Pig on a stick?" quizzed David.

"Yes - suckling roast pig on a rotating spit roast." replied Neil.

"Ah - yes - well, some of them are probably gonna be veggies, so I don't know...?"

"Well they don't have to have it!" Neil jumped in, missing the whole point. David headed the conversation off by agreeing to meet Neil and discuss the detail - including a potential vegetarian option - later that week.

Chapter 10: Pikelets

The news channel announced that the deadly virus that had killed thousands of people in China had apparently arrived in Europe. It had been suspected a few weeks ago, but it was now confirmed as two people had died and a further thirty had been hospitalised, in Italy.

McFadden grimaced, staring out at the grey Edinburgh skies. They might have won the battle by achieving independence, but winning the war and persuading the Scottish people to join Europe, against a backdrop of the European infections and deaths, was going to be tough. He also felt uneasy about the virus. Would it be another Avian Flu or Foot and Mouth disease? Or something far more far-reaching? He felt a pang of concern for his own family and friends, then reassured himself he was worrying unnecessarily. He called de Malo's office in Brussels to speak with him, only to find out he was in a meeting which might last all day. But Sophie, one of his assistants who remembered McFadden from his visit would be happy to help.

"Hi Sophie, comment ça va?" McFadden ventured, testing his newly acquired basic French from a series of weekly lessons he was taking - in work time.

"Thank you, Monsieur McFadden, I am good, and you are too?"

"Yes, indeed, thank you, but little concerned about the virus in Europe?"

"Yes, the Coronavirus. It is of concern to us very much too and we have a new unit set up to monitor it from both a public health and economic perspective." Sophie spoke excellent English and McFadden could almost picture her in the Brussels office with her fitted skirts, bright earrings and knee length boots. And the smell of garlic. He had mused at the time that it was a shame that such an attractive girl should have to smell so strongly of garlic.

"Why economic?" he asked, thinking that it was very early in the day to be concerned about economic impact and wondering whether he was getting the whole truth about the level of infections and deaths.

"China has suffered the virus and as well as the death toll, there has been a significant impact on their economy, as you will of course know, Monsieur McFadden." she said, being careful not to patronise him.

"Indeed. Well let's hope things don't escalate. The European campaign is about to launch here as you know. Do we still have the agreed response in place from you in Brussels?" asked McFadden.

"Yes, and we think it is critical that you go to the polls quickly on the application to join the EU. As agreed, we will cite the mess that the UK created by, how you say, dithering, about Brexit from 2016 to 2020. We will issue a statement to say that Scotland would be welcome to apply for membership but we respectfully request that the process is executed swiftly so as not to cause a long drawn out process with the debate and uncertainty that goes with it. No reference to the UK of course." said Sophie. "But the journalists will pick that up for us."

***

As the plane touched down in Edinburgh, the pilot gave the usual thanks to the cabin crew, congratulated himself on an early arrival and informed the passengers that it was raining in Edinburgh today. No-one looked surprised. The plane taxied towards the airport building. Jackman and Quickly turned Airplane Mode off on their mobiles and watched the counter in the middle of the email, Whatsapp and message icons begin to increase.

Jackman looked down, matter of factly and made a face that said he was used to this. But his expression changed suddenly to one of alarm and he began speed reading whatever had caused the reaction. He turned to Peter.

"It's in the UK. The Coronavirus. The Chinese thing. Someone's died in London. And my guess is we're not being told the full truth. I'll get our people on it through our private channels." said Jackman, now animated.

Peter Quickly's analytical mind was processing the information. What were the implications? Was it a one-off? Could it affect his family? What about the YES campaign? Had the deceased been to mainland Europe?"

The answer came from Jackman when they were at the baggage carousel. A message from his office. Yes, the deceased had just returned from Italy. Yes, there were more cases - another four possible deaths due to the virus but the government was "awaiting confirmation of the facts" before releasing that to the general public. Jackman knew this was bullshit and that central government had just been caught off guard and were buying time. The message closed with the fact that there had also been eighteen hospital admissions due, possibly, to Coronavirus.

Scotland had always had devolved powers when it came to health and with the independence it was completely outside of the UK statistics picture. Wales had devolved powers when it came to health, but as it remained in the UK, it was obliged to submit its figures to Whitehall so they could form part of the national overview. At this point, no mention had been made of Scotland in the media, but Jackman was more than aware that one single death of a Scot that could be traced back to Italy could end the hopes of Scotland joining the EU altogether. Although there was no real common-sense link between being part of a trading community with supranational laws and the spread of a virus, the general public had a tendency to oversimplify things. And if they didn't, the media did it for them.

The initial meeting with Mc Fadden was at 2pm, but Quickly and Jackman had taken the crack of dawn flight - known as the "red-eye" - to Edinburgh, in case of delays. Having checked into the hotel, they spent the rest of the morning in the lobby, fixated on their laptops, researching Coronavirus and its very recent but devastating effect on other countries. The respiratory illness had spread from China to seven other countries including the UK in a matter of weeks. Whilst many countries around the world were taking harsh measures, locking down borders and ordering their citizens to stay at home, the UK Prime Minister had taken what he called "a pragmatic approach" to the situation. The opposite benches in the House of Commons would simply accuse him of doing too little, too late in the weeks that followed.

McFadden greeted the men with a handshake as Alison showed them in to the oak-panelled room adorned with portraits of famous Scots. Jackman was anxious to bring up the Coronavirus situation.

"Handshakes may become a thing of the past, if what I read about Coronavirus in other countries is true." ventured Jackman.

"Please sit down, gentlemen." said McFadden in a very serious tone, leaving his guests wondering whether he was about to change the subject or elaborate on it. He then gave a five-minute monologue about the independence win, the European opportunity and finally Coronavirus. Most of the way through the speech, nothing new surfaced, it being a mix of self-praise, nationalism and opportunist narrative. But as he spoke about Coronavirus, the tragedies, the losses, the possible economic implications, McFadden's tone changed.

He lowered his voice and spoke in a conspiratorial fashion.

"The virus has far reaching public health implications, possible mass loss of life and potentially huge damage to the economies of Scotland, Wales, England and for that matter, Northern Ireland. For that reason, we feel it is important that the public are not unduly alarmed before we risk-assess the situation, make provisional contingency plans and assemble working teams of epidemiology experts, public health officials and the relevant politicians. That is what we are doing here in Scotland. I would imagine that England are doing similar."

McFadden's words hung in the air. Was he asking about Welsh plans for the Coronavirus outbreak? Jackman knew of a committee that had been set up to monitor progress of the disease but there was nothing as sophisticated as what McFadden spoke of planned for Wales. Peter's analytical mind was working fast. The reason that Wales wasn't prepared was because there had been no deaths, or infections. Jackman had alluded earlier to the possibility that England were only revealing the tip of the iceberg and only if the problem were much bigger would such considerable plans be so advanced. After all, he and Jackman had only heard the news this morning. In turn, Peter concluded, Scotland must have had possible cases or even deaths to be as advanced as they already clearly were in terms of preparations. Jackman had figured it out too.

"How many deaths so far in Scotland, Alistair?" he asked, point blank.

McFadden paused, but didn't look surprised.

"Two." he replied, adding "Not confirmed Coronavirus, though. Both had underlying health conditions and were elderly. Hence the need to be guarded about communicating these things until we are sure."

"Or indeed until after the European referendum?" asked Jackman gently, raising his eyebrows.

Jackman didn't answer directly.

"Our countries are in similar positions, gentlemen. Though you have yet to secure your independence, both of us desire membership of the EU. And the virus could make this much harder for us both. This could deprive our people of a huge opportunity, so we must act responsibly." said McFadden, sugar-coating the cover-up of the deaths as political responsibility.

Jackman and Quickly nodded diplomatically.

"Speed, therefore, is of the essence." McFadden continued. "We will go to the polls in four weeks. This will be announced this afternoon."

It was Jackman's turn to give a discourse of a few minutes, concluding with the confidential information that London had already agreed a provisional independence referendum just yesterday, subject to an agreed set of messaging and final administrative sign-off. Jackman omitted to explain that Scotland would be cited as the precedent by London that had left them no choice as to allow Wales the same powers, albeit hoping that the Welsh would surely hold dear the benefits of strength in numbers, security, defence and respect. So, Wales was also only a matter of weeks away from a referendum on independence, with hopefully another one concerning membership of the EU to follow shortly afterwards.

The three men discussed the politics of both countries, the potential problems, the power of working together as newly independent countries. The allotted time for the meeting was approaching, as Alison signalled by interrupting to remind McFadden of his 4pm call. To add a lighter finishing note to what had been a heavy meeting, McFadden spoke of Wales' rugby win over England.

"Hopefully this will have fuelled your national

pride!" he said encouragingly.

"Yes, indeed, Alistair. And perhaps our draw with Scotland was also a sign of our countries being on an even keel with each other?" said Jackman, glad that Wales hadn't won that match.

Both Peter and Piers were silent in the taxi on the way back to the hotel, digesting the information from the meeting and taking great precautions with confidentiality. The flight wasn't until later, so there were a couple of hours to kill before they needed to get a taxi to the airport. The hotel was too busy to discuss confidential information in, so they took a taxi to Rose Street, packed with pubs and also people on the weekend, but quieter mid-week. Cases trundling noisily and laptops shoulder-slung, they rattled up Rose Street, until they spotted a large pub with just a few people visible at the bar through the window. Having ordered their drinks, Jackman and Quickly took the table the farthest away from the bar tucked away between the toilets and a pool table.

They looked at each other and nodded as if to confirm they were thinking the same thing. Time was running out. The Coronavirus cover-up would only go on for so long before it leaked and then it was traced back to mainland Europe. In four weeks, Scotland was going to the polls for the people to decide whether they wanted to join the EU. It seemed, from news received via Whatsapp in the taxi from Cardiff, the Welsh Independence referendum was to take place at roughly the same time.

Within two days, campaigns for both sides of independence had upped a gear following the announcement of an actual referendum. Both YES and NO camps now had a time-line and a rallying call, rather than just rhetoric. Haines and Jones-Evans went head to head in a televised debate two weeks before referendum day. Creative Juices worked around the clock. Coronavirus unease began to surface, largely nudged on by the media who saw it as their job to keep the public informed. UK politicians delayed on confirming the Coronavirus deaths for as long as possible and when they did no mention was given to how the virus may have been contracted.

On the day of the referendum Coronavirus worries were eclipsed by a day of huge national significance. People were still British-sceptical about Coronavirus as being anything but a flu-variant that effected only the elderly or those abroad.

The streets of Wales were alive with red and white bunting, displaying the national flag. Cardiff, Swansea, Newport and other smaller municipalities came alive with displays of Welsh heritage. It had taken months of planning by Creative Juices, whose turnover had quadrupled in the last year. It seemed that on every public place there was either a display of traditional Welsh folk dancing, a harpist or an actor reading extracts Dylan Thomas's 'Under Milk Wood.' When Dougal, Morris and Peter had first seen the proposed plans from Wendy's team they had been sceptical.

"Fuck me - it's a bit over the top isn't it?" Morris had said. "Folk dancing, harpists, daffodil t-shirts, giant leeks, Dylan Thomas, Max Boyce, male voice choirs, giant helium-filled dragons hovering over every city..."

"I hope she's not stoned again." Peter had said, in a more serious tone.

"Of course, she's fucking stoned. I mean it's completely over the top. What next? Ruth Jones abseiling down the front of the Senedd with Rob Brydon in her arms, acting out scenes from

Gavin and Stacey?" Morris had replied, dumb-founded and exasperated.

"I'd like to see that one." Dougal had chipped in, deliberately lightening the tone and releasing the tension of the meeting. But actually, the YES campaign lapped up most of the ideas and had the money to make them happen. Agencies were used to presenting a series of ideas to clients spanning what they euphemistically called a "range of risk tolerances", only to find that the client picked the safest, most boring one. At one end of the spectrum was a dull, predictable set of ideas that largely copied currents trends. At the other end was something that Wendy had concocted after a few gins and a good smoke. Because clients often lacked imagination, they typically gravitated towards the concepts that they were familiar with - aspirational ones that emulated what their better competition was doing. Despite being urged to break new ground and live dangerously, few did. But YES was one of the small group of clients who had effectively taken the view that they were hiring experts, so it would be foolish to ignore their advice.

So, the seven days run up to referendum day had seen a crescendo of Welshness. Savvy businesses had been nudged months before to prepare for it and those who supported independence and indeed those who didn't, saw a money-making opportunity. Brewers launched special ales. One quirky Newport-based brewer launched three craft beers: One called "YES", one named "NO" and the other "DON'T CARE".

Another brewer from Swansea created "Independence Daze". Cafes and takeaways upped the Welshness, with some displaying posters in their windows offering Welsh cakes, Glamorgan sausages and Pikelets.

After a meeting in the city centre with Dougal and a client, Peter - an Englishman - had observed this and spluttered.

"What the fuck is a pikelet? "

"You probably know it as a bake-stone or a drop-scone." replied Dougal.

"And Glamorgan sausages?" Peter queried.

"Cheesey oniony things with breadcrumbs." answered Dougal.

"Oh - and Welsh cakes, are those ones with the currants and sugar?" asked Peter

"Yep" said Dougal.

The wave of nationalism had also spawned a groundswell of support for applying to join the EU, pre-empting what was planned. Some streets were adorned with green, red and white Welsh bunting and blue and yellow European flags. A shop in one of Cardiff's famous arcades was selling toilet paper with the St. Georges cross - the English flag - emblazoned on it. They sold out fast.

Gethin Jones-Evans went head to head with Alan Haines in a live TV debate one week ahead of polling. Haines - not a natural speaker - had tried to remain out of the limelight and concentrate on using his leadership skills to steer the NO campaign to victory. Three of his colleagues were fielded for media consumption, on the premise that there would be someone for everyone and that individuals would connect with one of the three differing personalities. It turned out to be a very bad move, which weakened the connection with the Welsh electorate who were now engaged with the lilting Welsh voice of Gethin Jones Evans and the tones of trust, common sense and optimism it imbued. The people were now beginning to decide which way to vote with their hearts and not their heads. It wasn't about economics or politics, it was about gut-feel, likeability and trust.

It seemed likely from the polls that independence would win, but the YES campaign was relentless until the end, backed by a fatigued Creative Juices who were managing media relations throughout. Nobody could have forecast the huge margin by which independence won, taking 79% of the vote.

It was in the bag. Wales was an independent nation state. YES had won. Gethin Jones-Evans had won. Creative Juices had won. Or at least won the first part, as Dougal made clear in his speech to the agency on the Thursday lunchtime that the results were announced.

"Congratulations to all for your unwavering support, your hard work, ingenuity, creativity and tenacity. Ladies and gentlemen in case anybody has been asleep for the past hour... OUR CAMPAIGN HAS WON! THE YES CAMPAIGN HAS SECURED 79 PERCENT OF THE VOTE! WALES WILL

BE AN INDEPENDENT NATION THANKS TO CREATIVE JUICES AND THAT MEANS YOU!" Dougal was practically shouting with excitement and had probably gone a little over the top considering that not every staff member supported independence. But the announcement of a paid for-party with free booze and buffet seemed to strike the right note across the board.

Peter hadn't spoken to Paula since the day before, his official duties keeping him very visible. He was a little surprised not have had a text or two and had been paranoid that she was spending time with her ex in the run-up to the election. Grabbing a plastic beaker and filling it with white wine, he extricated himself from the festivities to seek privacy to call Paula. She answered, simply.

"Paula speaking." Odd. She hadn't recognised his number.

"Paula - it's Pete." he said.

"I was beginning to think you weren't bothered for me anymore!" she answered.

"Explain?" said Peter

"Well you haven't replied to my texts!"

"I haven't had any texts." replied Peter, confused.

"You've been on at me to use the pay as you go phone number, not your main work one, so that's what I did. I deleted your main one from my phone - and just wrote it down - so I wouldn't call or text the wrong phone unnecessarily!" she said proudly.

"I stopped carrying the phone around as you never bloody used it!" Peter said, annoyed.

"Anyway, congratulations on the win." said Paula, ignoring his tone. Peter mellowed.

"Time for a celebration?" he asked gently.

"I've got viewings now but after work I'm OK. Fiveish?" she said.

"Where?" said Peter.

"Mine?" replied Paula.

"OK" Peter finished. There was a pause of anticipation and sexual tension before Peter was interrupted by Morris barging in to the room looking for more pistachio nuts to replenish the party's drinks table.

"Seen the nuts, mate?" he enquired, oblivious to the private conversation.

"Gotta go." said Peter to Paula and hung up.

Celebrations abounded in Wales from Thursday to Sunday. Harpists were ubiquitous, and by now presumably very wealthy, after the recent surge in Welshness. Veteran nationalistic Welsh comic, singer and poet Max Boyce wrote a song about independence that went viral within a day of being launched. Every cleverly penned verse ended with the phrase:

I'll know, I had my way,

I'm proud to say,

On Independence Day.

The slogan became widely used, appearing on t-shirts and posters as well as the interim messaging on social media by the YES campaign. It was important to keep the momentum going, the YES team believed, to lead the pathway to the next vote. Creative Juices contacted Max Boyce's agent and before long a celebratory concert was planned in the Principality Stadium, featuring a spectrum of Welsh stars, or indeed those who supported independence, which actually, was most of them. The concert plan was a way of prolonging the excitement so that the campaign to back EU membership could ride in the slipstream of national pride and self-importance.

The momentum of Welshness seem to grow exponentially as the days passed. Creative Juices began to worry that the Welsh people had gone independence-mad and would be less enthusiastic about surrendering their perceived sovereignty to Brussels, so soon after winning independence from London. The Scottish referendum on EU membership was scheduled for a week after the Welsh Independence referendum. The PR team at Creative Juices shifted emphasis from Welshness to exploring the powers that independence brings, citing Scotland's example of applying for membership of the EU. This messaging was followed by more, much borrowed from McFadden's team, about the benefits that Scotland would enjoy as a small nation being part of an international economic infrastructure.

Wales was slow to jump on the bandwagon. A cautious nation on the whole, for the Welsh there was a sense of huge collective achievement at their independence win. But like the lucky occasional punter who wins big, the fear was of throwing it all away too quickly by surrendering control to Brussels. The implications were discussed at a hastily arranged four-hour meeting between Creative Juices and YES. The conclusions pointed broadly in the direction of focusing on Scotland as a role model. The trouble was, that if the Scottish people voted not to apply to join the EU then the YES campaign in Wales would have backed a loser. So, a sub-set of messaging was developed quickly looking at how certain countries' economies had blossomed under EU membership. Ireland was chosen as a prime example, for many reasons. Firstly, it was close to home geographically. Secondly, like Wales now, before joining the EU, Ireland had struggled economically. In

1973, 83% of the Irish population had given the thumbs up to EU membership and the outcome in the years that followed had been significant.

Happily for Creative Juices and the YES campaign, there was no shortage of Irish people happy to talk to the Welsh media about how EU membership had brought major improvements to employment, education and training, agriculture, travel, the environment, research and innovation. Oh, and the economy, of course. Nearly forgot that one. No country wants to cite their reason for joining the EU was the prospect of propping up a dwindling economy with an injection of bundles of Euro-cash. But that was usually the reality, no matter how it was veiled. The EU looked at it more pragmatically, their aim was to realise the long-term potential of applicants for the subsequent benefit of all member states. Ireland was now a net contributor to the EU budget - giving more than it got. But before that, from 1973 up to 2018, the country had received a net benefit of over €40 billion. And in truth the only reason the UK had joined the EU in 1973 was because its economy had been in steady decline. But that was a harder story to tell, so Ireland was chosen as the reference point.

The media ran with it, after a nudge from the

PR community, not that they would admit it. They were feasting on an oversupply of juicy stories in recent months from Scottish and Welsh independence to First Minister's scandal and resignation. Then there was the campaign to abolish the Welsh language and now Scotland and possibly Wales could go European, with Ireland as a role model. Journalists were exhausted from the onslaught of potential, their appetites being sated on a daily basis, leaving them news-bloated and weary, but driven on by hungry editors keen to make a name for themselves and publishers who were watching the advertising revenues soar as news was consumed more voraciously than it had been for years.

Scotland went to the polls on a drizzly Wednesday in early May. McFadden had tried to piggyback the Welsh angle on Ireland in the week that preceded polling day, after a conversation with Jackman over the phone. Truthfully, he was irritated that one of his team hadn't come up with the angle earlier. With two days to go it had limited legs, but Jackman and Creative Juices had been happy to help McFadden use the Irish role model story as it only helped them and added to the media coverage.

Scottish enthusiasm for EU membership was

more muted than Welsh. A richer country, it needed to be persuaded of the real economic benefits of membership and that they would outweigh the advantages of being able to strike free trade agreements elsewhere in the world. This had become clear in the weeks that preceded the election as McFadden's team had analysed the weekly research report. This distillation of the various polls and qualitative information that gave a litmus test of the likely outcome of the EU referendum and it looked pretty close. Too close to call, in fact at 49% against and 51% for. But the Ireland story and maybe other factors too seem to be nudging the dial in the direction of YES, as each daily poll came in. It was minuscule, but the Irish story seemed to be making an impact.

Polling day and night had the politicians on tender-hooks. With no YES and NO groups to hide behind the Scottish politicians could not distance their views and had already established themselves in either camp. Dunbar's Scottish Nationalist Party and its Labour coalition partners were in favour of EU membership, the Scottish Conservatives were not. Dunbar had once again prepared two speeches to cover both outcomes.

When the news came that the Scottish voted in favour of applying to join the EU, Cameron

Dunbar was surrounded by a dozen colleagues a room full of TV screens. The result had been 51% in favour and 49% against. But they had won. The whoops and cheers drowned out the post-mortem of the results on the TV channel playing the audio. Then everyone in the room turned to the First Minister, looking for a reaction. Cameron Dunbar was not given to displays of feelings, least of all enthusiasm or celebration. Like his oratory capability, his emotional signaller was not great, despite efforts to change it for political gain. He had developed a way of using a short pithy phrase in substitute for an emotional reaction. So, when his colleagues turned to him, they knew not to expect an emotional outburst of joy. Instead, he waited for quiet and simply said.

"I think a wee dram of malt might be in order." referring to one of Scotland's hugely successful exports a third of which was consumed in EU countries. With closer ties that had a good possibility of increasing to between 40% and 50%. The Scotch whisky arrived on a trolley with a dozen or so glasses and as many bottles, plus ice and a jug of water. There were hundreds of whisky distilleries in Scotland and Dunbar was careful not to favour one over the other, so there was always a wide choice on offer from peaty to non-peaty and highlands to islands. Dunbar allowed himself a rare moment or pride and smiled as he sipped his shot of Talisker, from the Isle of Skye, his eyes tracking the single ice cube sliding as he moved the glass. He was deep in thought, watching the "legs" of alcohol blur the sides of the glass. There was much to do. His reverie was suddenly interrupted.

"First Minister, The President of the EU is on line one, and wishes to speak with you briefly to offer his congratulations." said an aide, obsequiously.

The conversation was formal as Dunbar would have expected, but the existence and timing of the call was symbolic. McFadden smiled at Dunbar. Then it was his turn to be called to the phone. It was Jean de Malo, full of congratulations. When the bonhomie had subsided, de Malo announced that the call also had formal purpose and he was giving authority on behalf of the EU for Scotland to apply to become a member state. Of course, many people had taken this for granted but again it was an important milestone along the yellow brick road to Europe. Within days the application had been made, the preparatory work having been done some time ago by a working party of civil servants who had been put in touch with de Malo's office. The decision as to whether Scotland would be accepted into the EU now rested in the hands of the twenty-seven member states who had to ponder the application to express their preference. In the event of an approval of less than 80%, a debate would be triggered which could delay the outcome for months.

Chapter 11: Swede

With the backing of the Scottish nation for EU membership, Wales had the advantage of a precedent. The PR teams gradually moved the compass of media focus from Ireland's economic success to Scotland's independence and pending membership of the EU. The polls seemed to suggest this was working, as the percentage of those in favour of applying to join the EU increased week on week. The judgement call was on when to hold the referendum. The minimum period of notice was six weeks, an amendment that had been brought in comparatively recently. In reality, six weeks didn't give adequate time for the logistics involved with holding a referendum, but it did concentrate a debate into a shorter time, though as many argued, it worked in favour of the mood of the nation at a given point. If the run-up period were longer, the barometer of the nation's mood had time to shift and eventually settle on a reasonable average. Short-term reactions, on the other hand, tended to be more knee-jerk and emotional. But the legislation had been in place for two years, so a debate over timing was not going to happen. It worked in favour of the YES movement and the Welsh Government who both wanted to capitalise on the growing appetite for EU membership, no doubt fuelled by stories in broadcast, printed, online and social media.

Justine had been distant since Peter had returned from Scotland. She worked late, rose early and met friends more often than normal on the weekend. When Peter quizzed her, she replied that she was simply deluged with work because of a recent and unexplained divorce boom. Post-Christmas was a normal peak and it wasn't unusual to have other smaller peaks throughout the year but the current one was bigger than most January's. Justine apologised and explained that the occasional Friday-nighters were with other lawyers and Peter was most welcome to come if he desired. He didn't. The chill between them thawed slightly for a few days and then froze over again but with a pre-registered work explanation already in place, stalemate, not confrontation, was the result.

The YES campaign's messaging needed to be changed. No longer did the "YES" stand for Welsh independence from the UK. Now that had been achieved, "YES" now signalled a tick in the box for membership of the EU. Creative Juices had been careful to mitigate issues of confusion that may have arisen from wanting independence one day and then seemingly giving it up the next. The messaging still had a core of Welsh independence but focused on opportunity and used the word " valuable membership" when referring to the EU, as if it were a store card that totted up points whenever you traded with other member states.

The clock was ticking for the YES campaign. Pubic concern was growing over Coronavirus. The government had contained the information about the early deaths "as a matter of public interest and until there was absolute certainty", but the virus was now gathering pace destroying lives in its path, as it went from person to person. It was very much in the public domain now and a matter of huge national focus. Early infections were from Italy, part of which had now imposed a lockdown, so that members of the public were severely restricted in their movements. Cases in Spain began to grow. Next, it arrived in the U.S. Then other countries. The world was gripped by a deadly virus that preyed on the elderly, the weak and those with pre-existing conditions, it seemed. Within six weeks the virus had gone from an isolated but severe problem for a couple of nations to a worldwide pandemic, triggering international red-alerts. The global death toll rose by thousands every day. Conspiracy theories abounded around the source of the virus. Most of them focused around Chinese or Russian malevolence, biological warfare and even 5G - the new technology standard for mobile networks.

Wales had suffered casualties too. Initially, it appeared to have been comparatively un-scathed, but an East to West trend began to emerge as the virus swept the UK, eventually reaching Wales. The imminent EU referendum had been eclipsed in terms of media coverage of the Coronavirus. The situation was debated consistently at Creative Juices, Welsh Government and the YES campaign. It was an extremely sensitive time and focus had to be in public health, but there was still a job to do in terms of the referendum. It was agreed that from a PR per-spective the window of concern over the virus coming to the UK from mainland Europe had now closed. Coronavirus was truly global so it no longer mattered. This played into the hands of the YES campaign, though they were sensitive about admitting it.

The UK government had taken the lead on tack-ling the virus. Even though health was tech-nically a devolved power, it was arguable the national public health was matter for the UK government. With a Conservative UK govern-ment and Welsh Labour government, harmony was never going to be possible. Wales felt it was belittled and frequently made statements and issued directives that contradicted the UK government approach in the months that followed.

Posters appeared everywhere instructing the public to wash their hands regularly throughout the day. Hand sanitisers went from being cheap and plentiful to something that a burglar might prioritise over a TV or jewellery. In shops, staff became so weary of explaining that there was no hand sanitiser left, they put up signs around the store communicating the message to shoppers, to stop them bothering the staff. Supermarket workers occasionally got short tempered. One woman in London reportedly swore at a young man who had simply been the thirty-seventh person that day who had asked her where to find the hand sanitiser. She had exploded under the pressure of long hours, having two young children and endless requests for hand sanitiser.

"Read the fucking signs! No fucking sanitiser! Buy some fucking soap instead and fuck off!" she had said and felt momentary relief until she realised that she would probably lose her job. And if that wasn't enough, the national press had got hold of it and made it worse. If indeed you can call writing about it in a tabloid, worse than telling a customer to fuck off.

Talk of food shortages and stockpiling only added to the frustration of the already weary supermarket staff. Despite assurances from the UK government that stocks would not run low, trolleys creaked under the weight of store cupboard ingredients, booze and toilet paper. With stockpiling stigma in place, customers began to explain themselves unnecessarily.

"Family coming round!" was a common one, usually followed by a look that said "Otherwise, I'd just have my usual small basket of fruit and low-fat meals." Really? Family? How long are they coming for then, a decade?"

The media announced that on the previous day UK Coronavirus cases made their biggest leap - a jump of 83 - to a total of 456. Communication with Creative Juices and YES from Welsh Government became less frequent as the administration's priority shifted towards tackling the crisis. Emails went unanswered for four consecutive days. Jackman eventually called Peter at 6pm on Friday, as Peter pulled into his driveway.

"Piers! I thought you'd lost my number." said

Peter, trying to hide his annoyance at being snubbed.

"Peter. We need to talk. Coronavirus - I don' think the referendum will be able to happen." Jackman cut in.

"I see." said Peter, caught a little off guard and trying to manage the transition from car-phone to hand-held as he switched off the ignition, absentmindedly.

"This is extremely confidential, Pete." Jackman had taken to calling Peter "Pete" since their time in Edinburgh. Peter had supposed that it was an indication that they got along, until he realised that Jackman had recently begun abbreviating the names of everybody he met more than once. Perhaps he's been on some sort of geniality course - thought Peter. Probably the latest in a long line of useless but expensive courses that the Welsh Government had made obligatory for their staff.

"Being Genial: How to be perceived as a nicer person than you are. Don't let people think you're a wanker, just because you are a manager. After this course you will command the respect of all your reports, be more productive, better focused and enjoy a deeper night's sleep." the course literature would have said. Peter's concentration had wandered - and bizarrely. Jackman continued.

"Peter - listen. Public places are likely to be closed in a few days. Shops, pubs, restaurants - all of them. It's not official yet but believe me the announcement is imminent. Looking at what's happened in other countries, some sort or curfew or lockdown could follow. We can't see how the referendum can take place under these circumstances, at least not in the usual way. And we are also concerned over timing. The virus is unpredictable and people's reactions to it are also hard to judge. We don't know how they will view the vote now. As you know from the last seven days the market research has shown erratic results." Jackman said pessimistically.

"What about online? Can we do it - the referendum - online?" asked Peter, looking for solutions.

"We are looking into it, Peter, but we need more time. The digital infrastructure is not yet in place for that scale of public involvement. The cyber-security element alone would be significant." Jackman said, as if the decision had already been made.

It was agreed that Peter would communicate this back to the team and that more news would follow in the days that followed about the viability of an online election. Peter telephoned Dougal immediately to inform him of the news. Dougal was out stockpiling food and booze, which was probably just as well, given the news that Peter was about to impart. Dougal took in what he could in the middle of a busy store and agreed to meet Peter first thing in the morning. He paid for his trolley-load of goods, packed them into his car then returned to fill another trolley, based on Peter's news of things to come.

Peter clicked his key fob, the wing mirrors retracted and whirred as he headed for the front door, ready to unburden the news from Welsh Government and seek Justine's opinion. Justine could always be relied upon to give a balanced view and foresee implications which had often not occurred to Peter. He walked in clicking the door shut behind him and dropping his car keys in a ceramic pot on the console table in the hall.

"I'm home!" he said loudly.

No answer. He proceeded to the lounge, wondering if Justine was in the garden. Laptop in hand, he toed the door open. She was sat in the armchair at the far end of the room, facing him, wearing her smart, chic, work attire and holding a large glass of wine. There was silence. She must have heard him announce his arrival. She wore an odd expression, an odd mixture of sadness, tiredness and triumph. He was confused. Before he could utter a word, she spoke in a loud but very controlled voice.

"Bastard."

"I'm sorry darling?" he answered, as if she'd asked him to pass the salt.

"You heard. You're having an affair. And don't try to deny it." she spat.

Was it a bluff? Their relationship had grown strained in recent weeks and months. If she had a slight suspicion of an affair, she might try to get him to admit it even though she had no real evidence.

So, he did what he thought was best and denied it outright. She watched, biding her time, as he performed a one-minute denial charade, feigning shock, incredulity, hurt and self-pity. It was quite display. Peter was proud of it and hoped it was enough to convince a mildly suspicious Justine that there was no other woman. He closed his eyes as if he were a stage actor closing a brilliant scene and waiting for the audience to applaud.

"That's all bollocks, and you know it Peter." said Justine, staring straight at him.

"Does the name Paula Haines mean anything to you?" she said in a mocking tone. Peter was suddenly swamped with the realisation that she knew something, but how much? He was nervous, wary and unsure what to do next. So, he decided to buy himself time and put his laptop in the far corner of the room.

"So. Paula Haines?" asked Justine, cocking her head and smiling with menace. Peter pretended to occupy himself with a stray leaf on a nearby plant.

"Save us all from another performance of 'I am an Innocent Man" she said in a calculated voice, quoting a Billy Joel song Peter liked, as she did. "

"I have all the information I want. Recordings of the voicemails she left you. Photographs of the two of you having lunch..."

Peter butted in "Lunch isn't an affair!" he protested. Justine ignored him and continued as if she was arguing a case for a client.

"You screw her twice a week, either lunchtime or late afternoon. You prefer lunchtime and usually bring food, which you typically get from Marks & Spencer. She is recently divorced from one Alan Haines - who I am sure you know, is head of the NO campaign - and she lives at the following address: 59 Meadow Gr..."

"OK, OK, stop. Where does this information come from?" asked Peter angrily aiming to fight fire with fire and being careful not to incriminate himself, though that might have been closing the stable door after the horse had bolted, he thought, on quick reflection, his mind oscillating from guilt to defence.

"I don't have to tell you that Peter." she said formally. "But I will." She paused. "I began suspecting you two or three months ago. I tried to put it out of my mind and make things work with you." Her mood changed from one of icy divorce solicitor to devastated, betrayed spouse. He saw a tear. She wiped it away quickly.

"Then I found the phone, which I guessed was a secret one for just you and her. I see it all the time in work, so you'll have to be cleverer than that. It was then that I engaged one of our favourite private detectives to pursue you. He's brilliant!" she said, gloating now. Gee, this was the full spectrum of emotions in ten minutes, thought Peter.

"And he's gorgeous." she continued leaving Peter wondering where this was going. "I could have let him shag me, but I didn't." she said, now coy and wounded. Peter realised for the first time that Justine had been drinking, her non-sequitur and rapid mood changes giving her away. She wasn't anywhere near slurred speech, though. She was too clever for that. It had been a couple of drinks and maybe one too many to give her a little Dutch courage, but it was showing, as she flipped between the two personas - lawyer and wife.

"He tracked your phone, followed you, took pictures and audio. Peter - it's all there!" she said dramatically and swung her arm around to point at a large envelope next to a pile of law books on a table near a shelving unit.

"So, it's over." she said. "I suggest that you pack your bags and go and seek refuge at Mrs Haines' house." she concluded, now weeping.

"What, that's it? No discussion?" said Peter.

"What is there to discuss? You have made your choice."

Peter needed time.

"It's not over!" he protested. "And I'm not going. Let me take some time to let this sink in and then let's talk. I want this to work. Please, hear me out tonight. I need to go for a walk. I'll be back in an hour or so." Time, he needed time to think. To think of what to do next.

***

Peter met Dougal at 8 o'clock the following morning. Morris joined them a few minutes late. Dougal eyed Peter, thinking he looked a bit off-peak, but Morris, ever the extrovert, just came right out with it.

"Peter, you look like shit. You alright mate?" he said, grabbing a biscuit to go with the logoed coffee-to-go he had arrived with.

"Long story, Morris. Trouble with the wife." he said in low tones, then realised he had brought his personal life into work and invited sympathy, which was never good. So, he attempted to lighten the tone.

"Yes, trouble with the wife. And indeed someone else's wife!" he attempted a grin, which didn't really work.

"Well, if we can help..." interjected Dougal.

"It's fine. Let's press on. There is much to discuss."

Peter regained control and his voice altered accordingly.

Relaying the whole telephone conversation with Jackman for Morris's benefit, he focused on the possibility of an online referendum and how - even though it had not been anywhere near confirmed yet - Creative Juices should prepare for it.

"I have asked Rupert to join us at eight-thirty. We are going to need some technical expertise and I think, depending on what he has to say, he needs to be very involved with this project." said Dougal.

As Dougal finished his sentence there was a knock at the boardroom door. Rupert had arrived, on cue, almost as if he'd waited for Dougal's introduction on his iPhone, having bugged the room. Talking to the board didn't faze him. He was confident, to the point of cocky. Typical Rupert. But they needed him. Dressed in jeans and a Google sweatshirt, he began without introduction or greeting or smile.

"You'll forgive me if I quote other sources. But I seek to inform you about online elections and whilst I am happy to give you my opinion, I believe you may better trust a sample of other viewpoints. I stress this just a sample - but it is representative of the overall picture." he said.

"Let me start by quoting a piece from I-News, dated 12th December last year.

"Online voting has been trialled around the world including in the UK for local elections in 2002, 2003 and 2007. Estonia famously became the first country to offer online voting in 2005, and in 2007 it was used to elect its parliament. It has since been used for government elections and referendums in Switzerland as well as municipal elections in Canada and party primary elections in the United States and France. Electronic voting machines are also used in Brazil and India.

Experts also say that security and anonymity concerns make it difficult to implement an online voting system. Jim Killock, executive director of the Open Rights Group, told the Guardian: "There's a fundamental conflict between verification and keeping votes anonymous."

Dougal, Peter and Morris nodded, taking in the

information. Dougal was impressed that this had been prepared at short notice, as he had not called Rupert until 8 o'clock the night before.

"Let me continue with a paper from an organisation called the Brennan Center. They are American, but in the digital world, if you want to see the future, you either look a long way East or a long way West - across the pond." said Rupert, as if imparting the knowledge of the young to the old.

"Anyway, The Brennan Center for Justice describe themselves as a nonpartisan law and policy institute. They published a paper entitled: 'Why Online Voting Isn't the Answer to Running Elections During Covid-19'. It goes without saying that COVID-19 is the name given to the disease cause by Coronavirus and is made up of components of the words corona, virus, disease and 2019." Rupert looked up and saw expectant and surprised expressions. He continued.

"I am going to quote this verbatim. I have also emailed each of you a link to this text. You will receive the emails at exactly 9 o'clock this morning." He cleared his throat before reading the entire text from his iPad.

"There has been growing buzz around the potential for internet voting as states struggle with preparing to conduct safe and fair elections during the Covid-19 pandemic. Companies selling online voting systems promise a "silver bullet" to deal with voting during the pandemic: a new technology that will allow people to vote from their homes, a safe distance from others.

Unfortunately, there is no magical solution for running elections during a pandemic. Ensuring voters and election workers can be safe will require money, work, and time. States and localities need substantial resources to ensure they can handle more mail balloting and keep polling places safe.

Indeed, given all the other changes election officials and voters are facing this year, there couldn't be a worse time to try to add a risky, unproven technology like internet voting into our elections, particularly when we know that hostile actors have not given up on disrupting our democracy.

Leading experts in cybersecurity, computer science, and election infrastructure agree that current technology cannot guarantee secure and reliable voting online. Many states, along with the Department of Defence for service members overseas, have experimented with internet-based voting platforms only to have abandoned them due to security vulnerabilities and ballooning implementation costs.

During the best of times, implementing fundamental security practices for election system technologies continues to be a challenge. Amid a pandemic, a presidential election is not the time to try out this unproven technology."

Rupert looked up. "As I say, the words of the American think-tank - not mine."

The three directors looked solemn.

"From what you say, an online referendum could be unlikely, unless it is implemented with sufficient due diligence. The alternative, one would assume, is that the referendum on membership of the EU is simply postponed. Until when, will depend on the virus." said Peter, employing his ability to summarise a situation succinctly. The others nodded.

"Will that be all?" asked Rupert.

"For now, yes, but thank you. And thank you for stepping up with virtually no notice. It is appreciated." Rupert left, expressionless.

Dougal and the others agreed that the ball was in the court of the Welsh Government. It wasn't in their interest to impart negative information about online elections, presumably the Welsh Government knew this and would either choose to act on it, commission a feasibility study on it or ignore it and make a quicker decision or proceed with it based on a "force majeure" - the unusual mitigating circumstances, which - as Peter explained with his inside knowledge - could be a loophole. Although "force majeure" was usually a term used in contractual disputes, recent governments had introduced it as part of their language in terms of political mandates.

"It's not a question of what's right or wrong for them. It's about covering their arses. As long as a reasonable and robust justification is in place for doing something if it flops, it doesn't matter, as long as there is an audit trail back to the decisions and why they were made. Force majeure would be a reasonable justification for acting on limited information. The broader issue is of cyber-security and implementation and how long it could all take. I need to talk to Piers and seek clarification diplomatically." he concluded.

Meanwhile, Scotland had received approval for membership of the EU from all member states. There was now the administration of transition of laws, the discussion over currency - if and when the Euro would be adopted – as well as a huge number of other projects. Scotland did not want to adopt the Euro but had fudged the issue as much as possible in the run up to the election. The EU directive in place dictated that all member states would adopt the currency by 2022, but certain countries already had a pre-negotiated exemption from this. Scotland had communicated an open-mindedness when it came to the Euro, which many read as political sitting on the fence.

***

David and Alicia were having lunch in a Wetherspoons pub. It was a chilly but sunny Saturday in March and they were out shopping for a coffee table, light bulbs, potatoes, swede and carpet.

It was turning out to be a long day, so David was glad of the lunch break en-route from carpet shop to supermarket. Wetherspoons pubs were always full. The hugely successful formula of cheap drinks and food in quirky buildings certainly pulled the punters. David and Alicia weaved through the large dining hall packed with diners and drinkers, struggling to find an empty table. Alicia suddenly shot ahead as if a turbo switch had been flicked and nabbed a table that no-one else had yet spotted. She had a knack of doing that. He would tease her that she could spot things normally not visible to the human eye. Squeezed between two pillars and overlooked by a huge TV, the table wasn't ideal, which is perhaps why it had been rejected by others. David went to the bar to peruse the enormous selection of cask beers, while Alicia tidied the table and laid out the menus. As David turned from the bar, he saw that Alicia was fixated on the TV screen. She wasn't alone - a small crowd was gathering. She looked around for David, peering to the side of the crowd. Their eyes met and she beckoned him to come quickly. He did his best, given the crowd and the two full glasses, which he slopped and spilled like an incompetent child in an egg and spoon race.

"They're shutting stuff. Pubs, leisure centres, cafes - everything." she said, clearly stunned. "On

Monday!"

It was true. Coronavirus escalation meant the government had called time on pubs, closed cafes, locked down leisure centres and probably ruined retail for good - the tabloids would write the next day. The high street had been dying for years as online shopping and delivery services got better and better. A sector in such a brittle state would be unlikely to survive sustained closures without major casualties. David and Alicia became animated, as did everyone in the pub, discussing implications, making plans, speculating on what the government would do next and lining up some serious stockpiling.

Alicia looked up at the screen again. News reporters were helping to turn up the dial of public speculation and worry by suggesting what could happen next. News-anchors were cranking it further by asking questions like

"How bad could it get?" and "Will food run out?"

To add a sprinkling of reality, circumstances in other countries were discussed. David and Alicia were glued to the screen. Many joined them, keen to know what they were in for. Others had heard enough. If the pubs were closing on Monday, they needed to make the most of today.

"The wedding!" Alicia slapped her hand on the table as it dawned on her that their wedding as unlikely to take place.

"The referendum!" said David, probably too quickly.

Lunch - when they eventually got around to ordering it - came quickly, was eaten hungrily and in deep thought. The silence was interrupted only by facial expressions that suggested that they hadn't really seen this coming and didn't know what was going to happen next.

They suddenly both looked up from their respective meals, having arrived at the same mental destination via separate routes.

"Stag and hen?" asked David, checking that Alicia's thoughts matched his. She nodded, still chewing.

Their stag and hen parties were only a fortnight

away. Alicia's was a spa day. David had succeeded in persuading Neil, the owner of Let's Play In The Woods, to accept a couple of thousand pounds worth of business. He had had to promise humourless Neil that there would be no drunken quad bike jaunts and no-one would mount a Portaloo or break a fence. David had begun to think he was going to be asked to sign something to that effect. After all, although what Wendy had done was serious, it had nothing to do with him at all. They had just unfortunately been on the same away-day. The deal-clincher with Neil had been the fact that - as David explained - he didn't work for the same company as Wendy. He worked for Juice-TV, and Wendy worked for Creative Juices. Neil, a suspicious, wary farmer, had eyed him menacingly as if to suggest David was taking the piss out of him with these juice-variant companies. His look had turned to disdain with an expression that said "Office bound wankers - they don't know the meaning of work". Just as David had been wondering what to do next, Neil's expression had changed to one of interest. David hadn't foreseen that.

"What do you do? the TV thing?" Neil had asked, lowering the temperature of the conversation as he did.

David had explained about how Juice-TV made quirky promotional videos for companies and organisations.

"Could you do one for me?" Neil had asked, immediately suggesting some sort of contra-deal with the stag-do.

Typical tight-fisted farmer, David had thought. But Neil's interest had been genuine. After a few weeks of discussions and quotes, a contract - for real money - had been agreed. Conveniently, David's stag guests were also to be the stars of the show.

"Oh - you've been really looking forward to your spa day with the girls." said David sympathetically and diplomatically. She nodded.

"But yours is a work-thing too, isn't it? Is that going to go? Will you lose that contract? Alicia replied thoughtfully. David's musings hadn't gone that far.

"Who knows?" he said casually. "Let's wait and see. I'll call Neil now and you'd better phone the spa. I'm guessing they'll be shutting, as hotels are on the list of businesses to close."

"Shall we go? I'm done." said Alicia, keen to get on the phone to the hotel, holding out the rather optimistic hope that they would be an exception to the new rule and be able to stay open.

David was more realistic. His opening remark to Neil was

"Seen the news, Neil? Looks like we're postponing then?

Neil hadn't seen the news, on account of the fact that he'd been in a field for last two hours marking out a new sword-fencing area. Reluctantly, David explained the government bulletin to Neil, who seemed to blame David for it, firing questions at him as he finished.

"Hey, Neil... I'm just the messenger. Look it up on the web!" said David. "Then let's talk Monday."

Chapter 12: Baileys

Peter answered his mobile, surprised to see a call from Dougal on a Saturday.

"Looks like Jackman was right." said Dougal briskly. Peter paused before replying.

"Well, they know. They know more than we do. And they know more than they let on. I know - I was one." replied Peter, who had taken up temporary lodging at a Premier Inn hotel, a few miles from what Justine now referred to as "the former matrimonial home". It was brutal, clinical lawyer-speak, but it probably hid the emotional fractures he had caused her by having an affair with Paula.

After returning from his brief walk following Justine's confrontation, Peter realised that he had wasted the time he had bought to reflect on how to react. He had spent it in a sort of dilemma-stupor, feeling like a rabbit in the headlights, frozen and unable to think which way to jump. She, on the other hand, knew what she wanted and when he returned and stumbled his way through an ill-thought out justification for the affair, she proposed that he pack his bags and go. He felt relieved to be granted more thinking time but made it clear that this was to be a temporary arrangement for a few days, to give them both space to think. He confirmed this in an email to her the following in day, having taken advice from a solicitor friend.

Peter packed a suitcase and suit carrier, unsure what would be necessary for what would happen next. His old-fashioned CD alarm clock went in, even though he hated it. Familiar things would give him a sense of history, of belonging. Then a comb, a wash bag and a phone charger. As he piled items into his case, he noticed in an odd moment how many labels read 'made in China'. He muttered something about how British-made was always better and carried on with his random packing, hastily grabbing a bottle of Baileys Irish Cream Liqueur from a kitchen cabinet. Peter didn't really care for Baileys, but had simply figured alcohol might be needed in the next couple of days. His mind seemed unable to concentrate properly, thoughts and possible implications spinning away with no direction. Perhaps the Baileys would help. His old acoustic guitar went in the car too. Why these random things? he had muttered. It wasn't as if he was going to grow his hair long, run away with a folk ensemble and drink a thick creamy liqueur after every gig. Apart from work clothes, his choice of garments had been poor - smart-casual shirts and trousers. Not ideal for hanging out in your room at a Premier Inn.

"It comes down to what will happen next, Dougal." Peter continued, trying to block out his current problems. "My sources tell me that businesses may have to tell their staff to work from home. We need to prepare for that." Peter's ego swelled whenever he used the words "my sources". It quickly deflated again when he took stock of his situation, holed up in a purple hotel room wearing boxer shorts and one of Justine's baggy sweatshirts he had mistaken for his own. The sweatshirt was quite tight on him. It bore the slogan "Girls Rule", making him glad that Dougal hadn't Face-timed him. He couldn't help but muse that on a deeper level, that the slogan was oddly appropriate for a man having problems with two different women. Dressed in his "Girls Rule" sweatshirt, drinking Baileys Irish Cream Liqueur from a plastic tumbler, sitting cross-legged in the middle of an overwhelmingly purple room in a downtown hotel, he began to feel, once again, that life was mocking him.

He deliberately hadn't gone to Paula's. An evening in a hotel, a long walk, a beer, food and a sleep had helped him awaken his analytical mind to get to work on the problem. He waited until the morning before texting Paula, so that he was absolutely clear about what he wanted. The text read: "Justine has found out about us. Need to talk. x"

Peter wanted to make things work with Justine. After all, they weren't at all bad really. But Paula had given him attention at a time when Justine had been tired, overworked and providing box-ticking sex, or not, as the case had often been. This was what he'd tried to explain to Justine, but he had stumbled over the sex bit, making things worse.

Paula called Peter immediately after she saw his text. Neither of them had yet gone to work, it was 7.45am. She was angry and accusatory, as-suming that Peter had volunteered the informa-tion about their affair.

"Why didn't you come straight here? Or ring me?" she hissed. Peter decided that Paula needed some time to calm down and think and simply told her he would be away for a few days with work in Scotland and that he would keep in touch with her. More lies. Now he was drown-ing in them. And there was the risk of Paula spotting him somewhere. Damn - what a stupid idea. But he had bought time and not ended up in bed with her - which was an extremely tempt-ing alternative to drinking Baileys from a plastic beaker in a Premier Inn. And he could now con-centrate on winning back Justine.

After work, back in his hotel room, he called Justine, explaining that he was ready to talk and that he wanted to reconcile, if she would forgive him. She slammed the phone down. He collapsed on the purple bed, exhausted from the mental stress and a difficult day. Oddly, he'd grown rather fond of the Baileys and as the half-empty bottle he had half-inched from the former matrimonial home was empty, he had invested in a replacement. He sat up on the bed, trying to stop himself from sleeping and telling himself that fresh air would be better. He poured himself a small beaker of Baileys and headed for the bathroom to wash and shave. His mobile rang. It was Paula. Her tone had completely changed from furious to flirty. He knew the voice - the one she used - as soon as he heard it. It wasn't the voice of someone who wanted to talk about wives, divorces or private investigators. It was her coy, dry, coquettish tone and it was already working on him. She skipped briefly through how his day had been and quickly cut to the chase, describing her memories of what they had done together and what she had worn the previous Friday lunchtime.

***

David and Alicia woke to a drizzly Spring Sunday. They were both on pre-wedding fitness regimes and a bike ride had been planned for the morning. David's enthusiasm was dwindling as he watched the sheets of rain fall.

"It's really wet rain." said Alicia.

"Well, isn't all rain the same? One isn't wetter than the other?" answered David, suspecting that this was one of Alicia's long-harboured, idiosyncratic beliefs.

"No, it's true. My grandmother always said this sort of rain gets you wetter than the normal, proper rain." Alicia replied.

"Oh? What did she call it?" asked David, playing along, as he had learned to.

"Wet rain." Alicia replied. There was a pause.

"I'm not sure it'll be great for cycling then?" said David, spotting an opportunity to swap a quick yoghurt and a rainy ride for a lazy morning and a bacon sandwich.

"And the wedding..." his words hung in the air.

He was about to ask whether the fitness drive was still necessary now that their overseas wedding was likely to be called off. Then he realised that Alicia had deep emotional connections with both the concept and the event of marriage. She had probably been planning their wedding day long before they had met. David, on the other hand, saw it as a logical progression, a step up in terms of status and a security blanket to cover their relationship, making it fixed and permanent. A minor row ensued, after which David agreed that the wedding had not been cancelled yet and even if they couldn't go abroad, the wedding would be "postponed" rather than "cancelled". An important difference, apparently.

Twenty minutes and two yoghurts later David and Alicia set off into the wet rain to make themselves more attractive for the wedding that was almost cancelled. Sorry - postponed. Not cancelled! Postponed. Their bikes were new ones - hybrid bikes - a sort of cross between serious drop handle bar road bikes and mountain bikes. They were - the salesman told them - perfect for casual biking. David asked him if that was just a nice way of saying they were great for fat people. Alicia cringed and the salesman had stumbled through an answer.

"Well, fat, thin...." his words were drying up and the silence engulfed him. He soldiered on.

"Blacks, whites, Asians, pensioners, gays, lesbians, cross-dressers - yes, anyone can enjoy this bike!" He smiled triumphantly as he came to the end of what he thought had been a very balanced answer. Good job he'd attended a diversity and inclusion course the week before, he had thought smugly, blissfully unaware that he might have missed the mark slightly. But the bikes fitted the bill and they were duly purchased along with a gamut of accessories which cost nearly as much as the bikes.

David and Alicia felt awkward in Lycra shorts. They both had reasonable figures, Alicia in particular, was curvaceous and well-proportioned. But they felt like imposters. "All the gear and no idea", newbies, city-types playing at country life. To make it worse, the drop handle bar roadbikers shot past them at lightning-quick speed, leaving them wondering if they could somehow catch a quicker ride in their slipstream. The road bikers were, without exception, wiry types, fully clad in Lycra and with no apparent belongings other than what looked like a mobile phone in an oddly placed pocket on the back of their Lycra tops, which often bore the moniker of a cycling club - Swansea Speedsters, Taff Valley Tearaways. By contrast, David and Alicia, although sporting the Lycra shorts, adorned their upper bodies with more traditional t-shirts and sweatshirts. And they both carried small backpacks, with water, some food and other apparent necessities for a bike ride. Alicia had a book, food, napkins and knives and forks, in case they stopped for a picnic. David's bag contained a plastic sheet, two chocolate bars and enough water to satisfy all the riders in the Tour de France for a day.

Alicia struggled on the first hill, a little.

"Just getting going!" she puffed - sucking in the cold, wet rain.

"Let's get off and push for this one?" shouted David, who was having some issues with his chain, which had somehow disengaged itself from the bike when he had attempted to change gear to one that would make him pedal fast but proceed slowly uphill, though with little strain. Walking next to each other they pushed the bikes up the hill to a lay-by that David had ear-marked for fixing the chain. Or trying to. The rain machine turned itself up.

"I think we might have been better to leave the picnic stuff at home!" he said. "I can't see you reading a book or lying by a river in this wet rain. And we could do without the weight!" he added, directing the remark at her, as she had been the one who had initiated the whole picnic thing, claiming that the weather would get better. The bike ride was aborted ten minutes later when it was mutually agreed that it would be more beneficial to be warm and dry, especially with mystery respiratory viruses lurking.

After a shower, they spent the rest of the morning catching up on household chores. David's first job was to re-clingfilm the sandwiches that had somehow escaped from their wrapping in Alicia's bag. In their bid for freedom, the sandwiches had killed off their clingfilm, leaving it shrivelled and useless, so David had to use another lot. He took the roll from its place in the cupboard. No end though. It looks simple enough, but it isn't, thought David. He hacked away at it, only succeeding in tempting small shards of film from the main ballast. When he thought he'd done better he only got to halfway across, then, figuring speed would be the answer stripped half a metre of it away quickly hoping the full width would present itself soon. Instead, he was left, by the time he tried it again, with nearly a metre of wasted film plus a few shards on the floor, remnants of his initial tactic.

He rolled his eyes. There was a list of things he struggled with and knew it. Clingfilm was one. Duvets were another - and they highlighted two of his inefficiencies. Firstly, when he and Alicia made a new bed together and began fixing the popper-fasteners at opposite ends of the duvet cover, David always started wrong and arrived to meet Alicia in the middle, late, incorrect and pissed off. The second problem in the duvet department was a new one, only discovered the previous weekend. They had been taking off some new bedding that Alicia had bought and, inexplicably to David, washed and ironed before they had put it on, a week or so ago. Whilst David wasn't good at the fastening of the poppers, he loved trying to pull them all apart at once, enjoying the rapid clicking sound and the lack of hard work involved in exposing the duvet.

So that's what he did. With gusto, as well. The trouble was that the new duvet cover did not feature the popper-fastener method, preferring instead traditional buttons. Most of these ended up elsewhere in the room or hanging by a thread. It hadn't been his finest hour. But, as he had explained to her, 'you can't be good at everything'.

***

Although Peter kept chasing his contacts at the Welsh Government, there was no news of progress on what was going to happen with the referendum. The campaigns were battling it out on multiple media channels, one extolling the virtues of a wonderfully independent Wales, the other promoting membership of a huge trading community which would afford great opportunity. And grants, probably. The Welsh Government - or the WAG (Welsh Assembly Government) - as it was previously known, was utterly preoccupied with Coronavirus matters. Dougal was worried that the YES campaign would go off the boil as the public's attention turned to the great priority of dealing with the virus and the seemingly huge implications it may imminently have on everyday life, work and public health.

The pace of life slowed momentarily at Creative Juices. The YES campaign work was up to date with the next phases of messaging in place, ads booked with traditional media or scheduled on digital media. All that was left was basic administration and sporadic interaction between Glenn Tilley, Creative Juice's PR manager, the YES campaign and Welsh Government. Glenn had been brought in full-time recently having previously been the occasional face of a freelancer, drafted in when a press release or two was needed. The ex-journalist had worked for a number of national and trade titles before coming back to Cardiff to enjoy a quieter life writing for the local paper, which soon became part of a larger, national group. He jumped ship after six months, for no other reason than things were all getting too digital for him. He was old school and the demands for content in a digital world in his view meant that great journalism had become dumbed down, become a rare species, existing only in a select number of broadcast media and printed titles. That was his view, of course. Most of the younger staff knew no better and relished the fact that user-interest could be measured via a heatmap which showed how far into an article people read before their interest tailed off and they left the page. But unlike Glenn, they couldn't take shorthand notes. The generation gap was clearly evident.

The acquisition of the YES campaign account had involved bolstering the PR function at Creative Juices, even though YES had their own PR man and the Welsh Government had PR department. So, Glenn was new. He enjoyed the work. Feeding hungry, overworked journalists ready-packaged stories they could simply check over and run was a joy. A fifty-five-year old, grey haired bespectacled man, Glenn looked older than his years, though he cycled daily to and from the office, using taxis or trains when he needed to attend meetings elsewhere.

Biking the six miles in one morning he had reflected on how this was probably the job he had enjoyed the most in his career, which had started in a publishing house in London in the 1980s. Back then he had been a rookie - with only a degree, a journalism post-grad and a small suitcase to his name. He had been recruited to work on a magazine about tunnels. The publishing house produced over forty titles and Glenn had hoped for something in computing or catering. Computers were just getting popular and catering had sounded like fun. But, no, Glenn had been offered tunnelling. After a brief exploration of Glenn's journalistic abilities, the weary interviewer had asked if he knew much about tunnelling. Glenn was generally good on his feet and an adept improviser, but this question had stumped him. He had never even heard of the tunnelling magazine. So, searching his mind for anything tunnel-related he had blurted out the words 'Channel Tunnel'. At that time, the Channel Tunnel between England and France had not been created, but the public were aware of its potential imminence. The interviewer had been surprisingly impressed at the Channel Tunnel remark. Glenn had pressed on, suggesting that not since Isambard Kingdom Brunel's day, would tunnelling have been put under the microscope to such a degree as it would be today with the creation of the Channel Tunnel. The off-the-cuff observation had been enough to win him a job and kick-start his career in journalism.

Glenn's job at Creative Juices as far as the YES campaign was concerned was to co-ordinate messaging with YES campaign's PR man and working to a schedule, to manage the effective dissemination and follow up of media releases to various key papers, TV channels and radio stations. There was online to do as well and Rupert had been assigned to help Glenn in that direction.

***

Peter and Paula had ended up in bed together shortly after the telephone call. The hotel room was a perfect safe-haven and avoided any possible clashes with Paula's son's timetable. Peter had attempted to dissuade Paula from coming to the hotel to see him, trying hard to hold his resolve to reconcile with Justine. But although the words came out, the conviction did not and Paula simply ignored them and arrived at his hotel half an hour later. She wore a short back dress. Her hair was freshly washed and worn down, bouncing gently off her shoulders as she moved. She may have worn the dress for work that day, but it looked shorter and tighter than Peter remembered her typical work clothes.

The Premier Inn sessions - as Peter referred to them in his mind, imagining them as a title of some long-lost demo tape of a now-famous band - went on for several days. This did nothing other than provide short-term relief, whilst exacerbating the longer-term problem. Peter was growing closer to Paula. When she wasn't there, he took long walks and tried to talk some sense into himself, but her spell held him paralysed and unable to escape to do the right thing with Justine. He badly wanted to go and see her and talk it out. But Justine would not even answer the phone, let alone let him in. Her refusal to discuss matters did not encourage Peter to break things off with Paula. If Justine would only open the channels of communication, Peter felt he might be able to break the Paula spell and move closer to getting back with Justine. He spoke to his solicitor friend again. James was an old friend from school and a very good divorce lawyer who had frequently gone head-to-head with Justine. His initial advice had been as a mate. Now he needed to charge because he worked for a big firm. Although as a Partner he could do some work without charge and be very 'generous with his time', he did have to start some sort of billing for the matter, he explained.

James ushered Peter into a client room, a euphemism for one of a series of interrogation booths, that made the firm look like some sort of litigation factory.

"She may be having an affair too, Peter." James suggested as they sat down opposite each other, overlooked by framed logos and accreditations of the firm, an attempt by the unimaginative to brighten up the uninspiring. "After all, she is reluctant to talk to you. What has she got to lose? And she knows that will go against her in terms of a settlement. Judges prefer communication these days and indeed mediation. She knows that. She's a divorce lawyer for God's sake!"

Peter scratched his head and shrugged. His analytical mind wasn't being as objective as normal, fuelled by a lack of sleep, worry, an excess of sex and Baileys and concern over the referendum. After his meeting Peter had decided that James was probably right and that Justine's silence signalled guilt. 'Attack is the best form of defence' - James had counselled, expensively. Peter needed little encouragement to follow the natural course of events and, having unsuccessfully tried to call Justine numerous times, he decided to enjoy the Premier Inn sessions, some freedom and a rest. He met David for a coffee to discuss that matter, feeling that his son may have lost respect for him. This wasn't the case at all, though David wanted some sort of explanation as to why his parents had broken up - whether temporarily or not. Peter tactfully explained that it was neither person's fault and these things were complicated and took time. David gave him a look that said "Well, thanks for that but I'm not seven, and you've been shagging someone else." Peter offered to take him out with Alicia for lunch and shopping on Saturday to diffuse the situation.

Paula texted to suggest she and Peter go for dinner that evening, he suspected, as a break from sex in a purple hotel room. He replied and insisted on paying, bizarrely happy to have a rest. The evening was bonding. Paula was still having hassle with Alan over a financial settlement and her legal bills were beginning to look as if they might equal any assets she may get from the split. The shared disdain for solicitors and pain of torn relationships brought them close emotionally, rather than just physically. Peter could feel the balance of favour weighing in favour of Paula. He couldn't move in though and he certainly didn't want to, but the hotel costs were mounting up. His hotel account, having to eat out all the time, coupled with his mounting Baileys bill meant he had to do something about his living arrangements that was less short-term and expensive.

Peter decided to rent a small flat. Of course, Paula was perfectly-placed to help him and advised him that the minimum term was six months. By this time Peter had seen Justine. His solution to unanswered calls had been to turn up at the house unannounced. He had been careful not to be confrontational and asked politely how she was. She had replied in a civil way. He had then explained that, as she clearly wasn't interested in getting back together, he was going to make things easier by moving out. Aware that he would now be paying half the mortgage and his own overheads, he raised the subject with her, politely requesting that she think about how best they could deal with the matter. Justine was surprisingly amenable, only fuelling Peter's belief that she was having an affair. James had suggested having her followed by a private investigator. Peter had felt it was too early and was worried about escalating costs. But he still thought about it. He still wondered.

***

Justine had met Evan Tomkin by accident, not intending or wanting to have an affair. Even though Justine had no idea, Evan was a uni-friend of Paula's ex-husband, Alan Haines. Evan and Alan had always mixed with different circles of friends and their paths had rarely crossed after graduation, until they both became involved with the NO campaign. They were different people. Alan was outgoing and gregarious. Evan - geeky, bright and with a gem of a sense of humour when it was prised out.

Justine had been on Facebook for years but been extremely careful with privacy and posting, largely because of her job. She had always been a two-or-three-times-a-week viewer of her feed, usually before sleep, to catch up on friends' news. But since the split with Peter, she had felt isolated. David came around for dinner or a drink after work about once a week. And, she worked late regularly and went to the gym when she could. But a long evening was a struggle and often she was too tired to go out, so she developed habits to keep her entertained. One was watching old movies - which she typically divided into two parts as time rarely permitted an entire movie in one evening. The other was Facebook. And that was how she and Evan had started.

They had originally met at a charity fundraiser - a garden party in the grounds of a castle. Evan had explained he was on the board of the charity. Justine was attending because the firm had been sent an invitation and it was her turn to attend a "corporate event". A few days later, Evan had sent Justine a friend request on Facebook which she accepted, knowing who he was. That had been two years ago. She had completely forgotten who he was until he began to pop up on her Facebook feed. Justine had now become more active on Facebook adding the occasional sensible and well thought-through post. Evan commented on one, arguing her point. She had come back at him, disagreeing. Then he had privately messaged her to apologise and to ask her if she would like to meet for coffee. She had surprised herself by agreeing, telling herself it was good to be seen to be going out on a date, that it was just a coffee and that it would fill an otherwise potentially lonely evening, if she included a trip to the supermarket while she was out.

Justine had wondered what to wear on the date, then decided to meet Evan after work, thereby depersonalising her choice and retaining her professional force-field and persona, a far stronger one than her personal one at the moment. Evan recognised her immediately as she walked in, but felt embarrassed at how smartly dressed she was in comparison to him. He wore chino shorts and a well-pressed summer shirt, by way of combating the unusual heat of a Spring day. She wore a striking black and red knee-length dress that hugged her contours in a subtle, professional way. Evan decided to make light of the contrast in clothing. They shook hands, as if in a business meeting.

"Well, look at me compared to you. Now everyone's going to think I'm having a no win no fee legal consultation in a Starbucks!" Justine wasn't sure how to react. The pause and associated facial expressions wrong-footed Evan who felt embarrassed as he'd made an awkward start. More words came out before he could stop them.

"No - I didn't mean that in a weird way. It's just with the summer and everything, well, I'll be cooler and you're, so... hot. Well, not in that way... I mean you'll be warmer in work clothes rather than without them..." Shit, now he was suggesting she would be better off taking off her clothes in the middle of Starbucks. Twenty-seven seconds into the date and it was looking as if they might not even make it through the first minute. Change the subject, Evan, he thought.

"So, coffee?" Then, trying to find a link between his bizarre opening and the banal drinks conversation, he added

"I'm having iced coffee - great for a hot day."

"Thanks Evan." Justine was smiling, relieved to be having some company that wasn't work-orientated and mildly amused by Evan's nervous wit.

"I'll have the same, please."

When Evan returned he still seemed a little nervous so Justine asked him what he did for a living by way of an easy start. Evan explained that he was a Technology Consultant, specialising in cyber-security. He had a number of clients that he divided into three groups: Those who had already suffered a security breach and didn't want another one. Then - companies that had been the victim of data theft and ransom demands for a tonne of Bitcoin. Lastly, were companies that had sensitive personal data or those that were nervous, having heard 'the stories'. Evan seemed to have plenty of work. He happily reeled off a list of companies he was helping, making Justine - who was hyper-sensitive about confidentiality - think that for a cyber-cop, he lacked discretion. She was warming to him though. He was clearly intelligent and she sensed with a little push he might be quite entertaining. She asked him about how hackers found information. He replied again without thought for who may be nearby, happily informing half of Starbucks how to infiltrate a computer network. Though in reality they would have needed a lot more information. He explained how passwords were sometimes sold for money - or more usually - Bitcoin.

"Where do they find them? I mean where do they buy them?" Justine asked. Evan looked surprised at such a basic question.

"Well, the Dark Web, of course." he answered. Justine's expression indicated that she was not sure whether he was talking fact or fiction.

"Ah. Let me explain..." said Evan, enjoying the superiority switch and about to entertain Justine with stories of cyber-crime in the part of the web that most people didn't even know existed.

Chapter 13: Hobnobs

With little news of what would happen to the referendum, Creative Juices were in limbo. Ad campaigns were still running but all attention had turned to Coronavirus. The atmosphere in the ad agency was strangely subdued because of the lack of energy that the YES campaign's demands usually created. Other accounts were given more time. Normally, lunches would be booked for all clients, but the closure of the hospitality trade had put a stop to that. A boardroom party was mooted but the general concern over what was going to happen with potential Coronavirus restrictions dampened enthusiasm. David was making sure that Juice TV crammed in as much filming as possible, in case some sort of restriction of movement was introduced, as it had been in other countries - some of which had closed borders too. It seemed bizarre in the cartoon-world of advertising to be talking one minute to a client about floating a gigantic mallow-filled wafer waffle above a factory and in the next discussing the virus that was killing people.

The waffle thing was a new account. Creative Juices hadn't done a great deal of packaging, but their fame - acquired through their work for the

YES campaign - had attracted the attention of a Labour party councillor, whose brother was Operations Director at a confectionery factory in the Rhondda Fawr Valley. Alicia had been excited at the prospect of David working for a sort of Willy Wonka outfit, though disappointed to find out that the name of the company was simply J. Thomas and Sons (Confectionery and Food Service) Limited. Not very Wonka. But it didn't need to be. The company supplied many of the major supermarkets and the brands were own-brand products, the identity of which were often created in collaboration with their client, though they had some of their own brands too. Some of these had suffered in recent times and there was - buyers had warned - a possibility of "de-listing" them. De-listing is a euphemism for not buying any more - a nice way of saying "unleashing the Grim Reaper" on your product. Whilst the majority of the business came from supplying own-brands, the company didn't want to lose their in-house brands.

So, Creative Juices had been brought in to solve the problem and after much research and creative consumption, the Wonder Waffle was born. The Wonder Waffle came with a promotion called "Wonder Where You'll Go?" giving the consumer a chance to win numerous destination-type prizes from foreign holidays to weekends away in the UK. They had to share a Wonder Waffle post on social media to qualify. The waffle itself had originally been, well, waffle-coloured. Creative Juices had asked why. The reply had been that because it had always been that colour. 'What if it were pink?' the creative team had asked, a suggestion that led to creation of the pink (limited edition) Wonder Waffle with a spin off social media campaign "Wonder what colour it'll be next?" with the option to vote for a change in colour for the Christmas edition of the waffle.

***

Peter and Paula had argued. It had been coming for a while, perhaps caused by over-exposure to each other. They were, after all, very different people, even though they had strong chemistry between them. Peter had apparently offended Paula with some offhand remark about where she shopped. Paula had misunderstood, thinking that Peter was inferring she wore cheap clothes. They hadn't spoken for a couple of days. Peter was still holed up in the hotel, having checked out two apartments and rejected both. She broke the silence - which was unusual. Calling him at 10 o'clock one Monday night, she didn't announce herself, knowing that his phone would do that for her. She simply said:

"Your wife is sleeping with the cyber guy - the

hacker - I told you about. The guy who works for Alan. I thought you should know, that's all." she said, without emotion and giving the impression that she was about to hang up. At first, Peter didn't believe it. But Paula was happy to supply full details of Evan Tomkin. Peter saw it as an olive branch and the two agreed to meet after work the following day. Although Peter had been on his way to bed, his mind was now active so he switched on his iPad and began to research Evan Tomkin. Tomkin's LinkedIn profile provided his career history, omitting the alleged stint as a hacker, which Peter was beginning to suspect might just be rumour. LinkedIn also suggested some of Tomkin's contacts of which a number were prominent NO campaigners, including Paula's ex, Alan Haines. He put down the iPad and sat back to concentrate on the situation and new information, activating his analytical mind, even though it had been happy thinking it was on the way to bed.

Why had Paula given the information? Was it just a way of distancing him from Justine in the hope he and Paula would become closer? Was it true? Had Tomkin hacked into the YES campaign's computer system? If so, and if it could be proved that it was on instruction of the NO campaign, it would be a big PR problem for them. But how could it be proved?

Peter called Justine first thing in the morning to ask if she was having an affair with Tomkin. She happily told him she had been on a couple of dates with him and that, as for an affair she and Peter were technically separated, so she did not regard it as such. Peter became angry, suggesting that her affair preceded his and slammed the phone down - or whatever the mobile equivalent is. He made a decision to look with more vigour for an apartment now that the hotel was closing in a few days and he also vowed to enjoy time with Paula. He texted her to offer her an early dinner as a treat, but hinted that he'd want something in return. Paula rolled her eyes and smiled on receipt of the text, thinking she knew what he wanted. But another text came hot on the heels of the first, saying "I thought you'd think I meant that. But I don't. I need some more help with apartments :-)" Paula almost felt disappointed. Then the third text arrived: "And anything else is a bonus." Plus, a smiley face. Then he remembered that all the restaurants were closed. So, they met at his hotel. He had bought some fancy snacks from a supermarket along with some bubbly. She barely touched the smoked salmon blinis and Roquefort and pear crostinis and only sipped politely at her Prosecco.

Over food, she announced that she was going

away on a course for a couple of days in London, then an old school friend from Plymouth was coming to stay for the weekend. She suggested a walk in the Bay as she felt tired. Peter sensed a cooling off, confirmed when the couple parted an hour later with a kiss on the cheek and an apology from Paula that she had a "busy few days" ahead. Car keys jangling in her hand as she walked away, Paula nervously clicked the fob to indicate the location of her car, even though she was not yet near the car park. She seemed preoccupied, walking quickly, the bottom of her long black coat moving from side to side with her pace.

Peter wandered. He was on foot and despite the early Spring chill and dark evening, he meandered around the Mermaid Quay. The dark night didn't usually matter in Mermaid Quay as everything was usually lit up in this part of the Bay by the pubs, clubs, ice cream parlours, cafés, stalls and often markets and events. Not tonight, though. The new rules and closures made the place feel empty and soulless. No cheer, no laughter, no lights - just the sound of metal boat-bits clinking together in the cold breeze. Peter sat on a bench overlooking the boats, watching their hypnotic bobbing and becoming oblivious to the cold wind as he reflected on the evening with Paula.

A xylophone chiming of a text broke the thought-train. Peter reached inside his coat for the mobile. It was Paula. His suspicions were confirmed. She was suggesting they had a break for a few weeks. Work pressure, the course, the weekend with the friend - the list went on and felt like a list of random reasons and excuses rather than a facing up to the truth. Peter felt relieved. He wasn't sure why, but he did. He felt hurt, but then told himself that he had been fun and the fun was over. For now. It would allow him to concentrate on finding a flat. The hotel was allowed to be open for key workers and permanent residents, Peter was generously classified as the latter. But Peter was growing tired of hotel-life, wanted his things near him and also needed to reduce his spend.

He replied to Paula simply saying that he understood and to enjoy her course and her weekend. His text was deliberately curt, so as perhaps to encourage her to have some regret. It was subconscious. He didn't add any kisses to the end of the text as he usually would have. Heading home for a nightcap of Baileys, he couldn't help but think about Justine, their family and the good times they had enjoyed. He was a man between two stages of life, stuck in a transitional vacuum where there was only loneliness, confusion and... well, Baileys. He poured himself one, wondering if he should go back or forward one step in his life.

The following day, Peter used some work time to book appointments with a rival estate agent to Flawless. There were quite a number of suitable apartments on the market for rent. Having been previously limited to what Paula had on offer, he was pleasantly surprised. By seven o'clock that evening he had viewed four and shortlisted two. He needed to agree how he and Justine would deal with belongings before making a decision as, although his favourite had brilliant views over the Bay, it didn't have a lot of space and common sense told him to go for the other one. Work was busy so he mulled things over for a couple of days, even though the estate agent called him with alarming regularity. Gosh - he thought - I've just got rid of one estate agent now I'm being chase by three more!

He agreed to meet Justine at their place that weekend - Saturday 21st March - a date he never forgot as it was his late mother's birthday. Peter arrived at the former matrimonial home at 11am, as agreed. He had prepared himself for diplomatic and reasonable discussions, having been for an early long walk over the Cardiff Bay barrage to Penarth on the other side and then back again. Justine was a respected divorce lawyer so she would doubtless know every trick in

the book when it came to divvying up possessions.

He wasn't, however, prepared for what happened. Justine greeted him warmly and as she
was making coffee, asked how he was and if
he'd seen David recently, outside work. The pair
chatted is if it were old times, nibbling on Hob-
nob biscuits as they did. They both had a weak-
ness for biscuits. Oddly, Peter had never thought
about the naming of Hobnobs before today and
couldn't help but wonder if there was some sort
of sexual connotation to them. He pulled himself together, quickly realising that his thoughts
were both inappropriate and ill-founded, Hob-
nobbing was just an expression about socialis-
ing with the elite and not a reference to a sexual
act. His mind had drifted so he snapped it back
into place quickly, before things got worse.

He felt wary and that he may be being led into a
trap. A quick analysis of the situation provided
him with the answer that he should mirror what
she was doing. So, he asked about her, how she'd
been, how work was - and so on. What may have
initially been a tactical move was oddly turning
out to be a rather pleasant exchange.

"In case you're wondering, I'm no longer seeing
Evan." Justine volunteered.

Peter wasn't sure how to react, torn between wanting to have the upper hand of still having an affair and spotting an opportunity to play a level playing field with Justine, which felt wiser.

"Yes, me neither." he mumbled. "Paula and I have split. I broke it off." Now he was unsure of his territory. If he was levelling with Justine and some sort of mutual accord, a lie wasn't a good place to start. So, he added:

"Well, it's more complicated than that. But I'm on my own now and for the record I deeply regret what I did and I apologise."

"You've never said that." replied Justine.

"I felt I never had chance. I tried to contact you. But I'm not going to explain myself. I was in the wrong." said Peter solemnly. He surprised himself that for someone with a famously analytical mind, his subconscious --- had obviously been working on an alternative plan which it had only now decided to tell his conscious mind about.

Justine stood up and stretched yawning as she did, but also displaying her slender figure and pretty green eyes in the stage spotlight of a shaft of light created by a gap in the blinds on the first day of Spring.

"Long week." she apologised, referring to the yawn. "More coffee?" Justine was buying time, thinking of how to play things. The quickest way to deal with things was to put her lawyer brain into gear and see things objectively. His non-lawyer, emotional brain was just screaming out that they should get back together. The solicitor in her could articulate things better. She walked softly across the kitchen tiles onto the large cream rug in the lounge then onto the wood block floor, making no sound as she moved, gracefully towards Peter. She handed him a large, brightly coloured cup and saucer. Peter instantly wondered why she hadn't simply swilled out the mug that had contained his first drink. She had a matching cup. He looked at them, trying to place their origin. She smiled.

"Italy. Sorrento. You remember? We bought them on the day trip to Capri." she raised her eyebrows as if looking for agreement. They remained there as if they would only retract when Peter gave an affirmative response. Fearing that the eyebrows might remain stuck that high up Justine's face, Peter nodded, relieved to see facial normality resume.

"So, you have a flat to go to. Is that what you want?" asked Justine. Peter shrugged.

"And you're here so that we can make arrangements over the possessions we have amassed over our lives together?" Justine's question seemed to be loaded with emotional bias. There was a long silence.

"It's not what I want at all." replied Peter quietly.

"It's not what I want either. But I still can't forgive you for what you did." answered Justine, knowing that she owed her professional-self the attempt at reconciliation. Or at least that was how she explained it to herself.

"Why don't you stay for lunch and let's talk some more?" offered Justine, almost causally, before adding "Unless you have plans?"

Peter didn't have plans beyond a beach-walk and then home for a movie in the evening. So, he agreed. As if to subliminally encourage their mediation, a text from David popped in simultaneously to both his parents' phones, creating a discordant duet for xylophone and glockenspiel as they did. Justine's mobile glockenspiel was of unknown whereabouts, as was always the case, Peter remembered. He reached into his pocket for his xylophone and read the text from David. He laughed out loud. Justine - reading the same text in the hall on the glockenspiel phone reacted with horror.

"Oh no! This could spell big trouble!" she said, rolling her green eyes and calculating the potential damage and the defence line as she did.

David's text was asking their advice collectively, as mother, father, solicitor and colleague as to what he should do about an incident that had taken place an hour ago at J. Thomas and Sons (Confectionery and Food Service) Limited. The gigantic inflatable wafer had broken loose from its tether, twenty metres above the roof of the factory. A sudden gust must have broken a fixing and now the blimp was enjoying its new-found freedom and heading in the direction of Cardiff. Perhaps it was having a jaunt to the shops. Whatever its intention, the waffle was being helped along by a stiff northerly breeze. It was highly visible on this cold, gold day. The blimp was heading south, obediently following the traffic on the A470 between Pontypridd and Cardiff, providing drive-in cinema showtime for the motorists below stuck in the traffic. They craned their necks out of car windows to watch the waffle, thrusting mobiles out to capture the unusual spectacle of a giant waffle on its commute from the Valleys to Cardiff.

Justine called David. Peter called Dougal.

Justine: "Is it still up there? I hope you've got the paperwork from the Civil Aviation Authority?"

Peter: ".... yes, Dougal - I'm watching it on TV, now. And there are shots of it on Twitter." Although David was technically the "Account Manager" for the factory, Dougal was the Director in charge of it. He replied:

"Yes, Peter, the CAA licence is in place. So, let's not fret. You can't buy this sort of publicity. The trouble will be charging them for it!" he laughed. He was on speaker-phone now that Justine had finished with David and walked over to the sofa where Peter was talking to Dougal and watching the giant Wonder Waffle waft down the valley.

"The problem you are likely to have, Dougal, is how you can prove that it wasn't done on purpose, as some sort of PR stunt." said Justine loudly. Dougal's excitement subsided. Peter chipped in.

"Sorry Dougal, I should have said, you're on speaker-phone. And I'm with Justine" he added, emphasising her name, to avoid what might have happened next.

"Hi Justine!" said Dougal genially and falsely then added "Probably another job for your firm then?"

which changed the context of the situation for Justine, who was now potentially representing the firm and not just dealing with an airborne runaway waffle that her family had somehow let loose. As a divorce lawyer it wouldn't be her matter but, until she passed it over to a colleague, she had to be professional about it.

Dougal fired up again: "Peter. Get hold of David and tell him to get out in the car and get some footage of the bloody thing. Make sure he takes another driver in case he has to do it on the move. There'll be plenty knocking about on social media but we need decent stuff just in case it becomes useful. Oh - and if he gets asked, it's not for publicity it's for potential evidence should we find ourselves in the spotlight."

"Evidence of what, Dougal?" Peter said clinically. "Floating down the A470, there's a thirty-metre waffle which has already appeared on the BBC, Sky, ITV, Twitter, Facebook and probably Instagram. I doubt anyone is going to query whether the event took place."

"OK, OK, just tell him not to make it obvious we're doing it for commercial gain." said Dougal, back-tracking. "I'll call Rupert and get him to monitor the social media coverage. That might be a way we can charge for it." he added greedily.

Peter and Justine discussed the event over lunch and it began to feel as if they were a family again. Divvying up possessions after the last few hours seemed like a non-sequitur. They both knew it. So, Justine broached the subject and suggested Peter move back in, initially to the spare room with a view that they may or may not be able to reconcile. At least time together would give them the opportunity to find out. Peter agreed, feeling instinctively that it was the right thing to do. They called David and Alicia to invite them around for Sunday lunch, briefly explaining the situation and asking that it wasn't referred to the following day.

Peter felt happy. Happy, but still cautious. And happy that his family would be visiting later that morning. He had nipped out early on Sunday to collect his belongings from the hotel, check out and purchase a helium birthday balloon, some sticky tape, small sheets of fluorescent paper and a marker. On return, he spent half an hour creating his masterpiece - a model of David's blimp that would hover over the dining table that Sunday. When Alicia and David entered the dining room it had the desired affect - raucous laughter and disbelief. The proper blimp had come to an unpleasant end, crashing into Caerphilly mountain, to the surprise of the walkers and cyclists, none of whom were harmed. Justine had made a phone call to her colleague and given the CAA licence was in place the outcome didn't look as bad as it could have done, though the firm would inevitably make money preparing damage limitation statements and dealing with any fallout. So, lunch was convivial and pleasant, as if everyone accepted that things were normal again, apart from the elephant in the room, who wasn't convinced yet.

Monday arrived. And everything changed.

There was a sense that something to do with further restrictions was coming for the government, but the severity of them caught Britain off-guard. In an announcement to the UK, the Prime Minister declared a national lockdown. Everyone was to stay indoors and there would be only four exceptions. Shopping for basic necessities, one form of exercise a day, medical needs and travel to work, but only if unable to work from home. Wales and Scotland followed suit within an hour. Both were in discussion with each other and intending to make a similar announcement the following week, but the English directive had forced their hands to put it forward. The concern was that if - even for spurious reasons - the death toll in Scotland and Wales was higher in the gap week or weeks - they could be blamed for arriving too late with the measures. So, they were forced to rely partly on the English science and partly on their own until they could both play catch-up. Unofficially, of course.

In his address the English PM underlined the rules:

"These are the only reasons you should be leaving your home. You should not be meeting friends, you should not be meeting family members who don't live in your home, you should not be shopping except for essentials. If you don't follow the rules, the police have power to enforce them including with fines. We will immediately close all shops selling non-essential goods as well as other premises including libraries and places of worship. We will stop all gatherings of more than two people in public and stop all social events - excluding funerals". he went on.

Peter and Justine - both in work as the announcement was made, but both following it on their mobiles, suddenly realised the implications it had for them. They were locked in lockdown together. This wasn't exactly what they thought they had got themselves into, both envisaging easier get-out options if something went wrong. But it looked as if those escape routes were gone.

The informal co-habitation relationship testing agreement they had dreamt up on Saturday had one serious flaw now. There was no get-out clause. They had previously agreed that either party could call time on the situation if they deemed it wasn't working. They had promised that there would be discussion to resolve differences, unless those differences involved sleeping with other people, Justine's so called "red line". In those cases, they would part immediately, in the case of the relationship simply deteriorating either had the power to call a seven-day truce with a view to making things work. If the relationship broke down in that time then they would separate, ideally amicably and preferably quickly. Draft financial arrangements had been agreed and signed. Justine insisted on the formalities and Peter would have expected nothing less from a divorce solicitor. He didn't stand to lose anything, it just set out their situation and the ground rules.

Both Justine and Peter told themselves, separately, that all was fine. They both wanted to make it work, but neither had expected the added pressure of being under virtual house arrest. The potential for rowing would surely be exacerbated, though on the up-side, it would be difficult to sleep with other people. Both minds decided to resign themselves to the stalemate which would or would not happen in their relationship and turned instead to the practicalities. Justine had already been buying extra food and drink for two weeks but it looked now as if they both needed to do some major shopping on the way home. Peter called Justine and they avoided the bigger issue of joint imprisonment and focused on whether he would buy spring onions or red onions.

***

"What do you mean, you're leaving, Rupert?" said a shocked Dougal, who (was) had assumed that the call was about lockdown procedures and remote-working from home, a project he was managing. Creative Juices had prepared for the eventuality of lockdown after a tip-off from Piers Jackman. Rupert, as the technology whizz-kid was naturally in charge of making it happen, ensuring that everyone would be able to work remotely. This was much harder for the studio, most of whom, needed access to more than just a little laptop at home and worked on Macs, which didn't always like communicating with PC-based systems. There were also consider-ations of how to manage the network, the secur-ity implications and variable broadband speeds.

Dougal, despite his long-running disdain for Rupert, had never got around to thinking about replacing him. So, Rupert had grown more cocky by the week as more as the importance of technology on marketing and everyday life grew exponentially. Now, seemingly out of the blue, Rupert was leaving. He had a staff of one graduate, who might be able to manage some of the existing digital marketing campaigns but nothing much else, Dougal suspected.

"Why are you proposing to leave, Rupert?" asked Dougal, resuming control having recovered from the shock. Rupert explained with cool cockiness that he needed new challenges and when he had been approached by another company, he had only talked to them out of politeness but they had offered him interesting work and more money. Douglas asked about the money, mooted a pay-rise, but Rupert replied that it was about other things too. Resigned to the fact that Rupert was going, Dougal felt uncomfortable about Rupert being involved with the business for the month's notice, and so Rupert quickly found himself a free man at Dougal's expense.

Dougal called in Peter and Morris to brief them. But Peter had just received news of his own which cheered up Dougal a little. Gethin Jones-Evans had called from the YES campaign HQ on Park Place in Cardiff to tell Peter that YES had acquired the support of Gerald Mattison, the internationally famous Welsh multi-millionaire. Mattison had made his fortune in the gaming world. The programmer-turned-businessman had begun writing computer games as a twelve-year-old, progressed quickly and begun selling online, creating some of the world's first gaming communities. It grew quickly into a fully-fledged highly-successful business. Then a joint venture with a US company based in Silicon Valley that designed hardware propelled Mattison to international fame by the time he was twenty-five. What started as a passion of a geeky teenager turned into an international business empire, which included a huge property portfolio.

"What is significant..." said Peter, in a measured way, trying to calm an initially low-key and now animated Dougal "is that Mattison, by all logic, was expected to back the NO campaign. So, this is... and it's hard to overstate it ... a goldmine for YES in terms of endorsement. It is, at the moment, a secret. Gethin wanted us to be the first to know so that we can carefully manage what they see as a huge media coup. Gethin has prepared an outline of how they see Mattison's involvement. I can email it to you. But I mean, really, what he does is up to him." said Peter. Morris looked up for the first time.

"Great, Pete, great. I know we've landed a big one, but it's 2 o'clock and this is gonna be the last day we are properly open so I've got a tonne of work to do. And where the fuck is Rupert? I know we said he could work remotely a bit, but people are asking about which bits of kit they can take and Rupert is supposed to have sorted all of this."

Morris was the director in charge of the transition to remote working. Not because he was the best qualified but because Dougal and Peter had more important things to do and Morris didn't. Morris had leaned heavily on Rupert, who had now drifted away with the knowledge needed to pull it all off. Morris texted Rupert who replied to say he was on his way in and of course he'd be there to sort all the kit – the allocation of which was already documented on a spreadsheet with a bar-coding system in place. Dougal couldn't help wonder why Rupert hadn't talked to him face to face about the resignation if he was coming in anyway. But then, he had never really understood Rupert.

Peter arrived at the former matrimonial home at quarter to six, aware once again that fate had dealt him a strange hand. He was now about to enter an unspecified period of time in confinement with what had nearly been his ex-wife. He had mixed feelings and knew that their agreement specified separate rooms. Perhaps that would be a test of the relationship. Suddenly

Peter wanted to have sex with Justine, picturing her coming home from work dressed smartly and looking chic. He realised with some disappointment that it was going to be a long game and that short-term wins were unlikely. But Justine was worth it. His marriage was surely worth investing in. Apart from anything else - and he knew it was a "bloke thing" - it was the easiest option and Justine was, after all, an attractive woman. His analytical mind reminded him that she may simply be going through the motions of making it work as a tick box on the divorce sheet - some kind of tactical move that she'd seen work with a client, perhaps. He told himself to go into it with an open mind and do his best.

Chapter 14: Breaded Haddock

Caroline and Rupert had only been going out with each other for six weeks. It started when Rupert needed graphic design input for some of the digital campaigns he was working on. So, Caroline was assigned to the project. Rupert began to realise that he was finding excuses to nip down to the studio and see her more often than necessary. She was quiet, but bright, highly talented, but not boastful. Their personality types didn't match, but that seemed to create some sort of chemistry between them that neither had envisaged. She had always thought of him as arrogant, but working with him she began to re-frame it as "highly intelligent and direct". He had always thought of her as the "pretty, quiet girl in the studio." But she was looking different recently, as if she'd turned up the sexiness dial. Her hair was cut short and highlighted. She had also bought two trendy jackets on a trip to Bath. The combination of the minor alterations tipped the scales from "pretty" to "highly desirable" - in Rupert's view. And indeed, in others' too.

He asked her out in a typically Rupert way. She arrived at her desk, fired up her Mac and an animation had somehow taken over the screen. At first, she thought it was a virus. But then there was text:

"It's not a virus. It's me, Rupert. I'm not in the office today otherwise I'd have asked you in person. How about a date? Coffee maybe? Tick one of the boxes below to reply." The boxes made it easy for Caroline to express her views, unsubscribe from similar communications in the future, sign up for the date, or decline, suggesting that the subject matter was not of interest and that he should be potentially reported for spamming her. It was funny. She giggled before pressing to accept. To her surprise, a series of terms and conditions popped up that she had to agree to before the date. They were only fun things - he would pay, she had to have fun, there was no obligation for another date, it wouldn't affect their working relationship. The idea was to emulate the marketing emails that the agency managed on behalf of its clients. She clicked to accept and their courtship was born - in fact with a welcome email.

The relationship blossomed quickly, much to everyone's surprise. Rupert discussed the job offer he had recently received with Caroline, who had very mixed feelings about it. The money was nearly double what Rupert was earning at Creative Juices. But what did he know about the company – Techfix 49? There appeared to be only ten employees, apart from potentially Rupert and one director. Wouldn't he miss the buzz of the agency with thirty staff? They ping-ponged pros and cons for a while but Caroline was diminutive and Rupert was bombastic, so eventually his opinion took the lead.

***

Justine arrived home looking tired, but trying to hide it. Peter knew the expression well. He poured a large glass of wine and placed it on the kitchen table.

"I haven't had chance to get to the supermarket yet. I'll go now." she said wearily.

"No need, Justine. I have bought more than enough and I will go again at seven in the morning to stockpile. I haven't got anything fancy for tonight, just some prawns to start, which I thought I would do in chilli and garlic. Then some fish - pre-packed - the fishmonger was shutting. And a bottle of Chablis - which is currently getting cold in the freezer." he added with enthusiasm. She thanked him and seemed pleasantly surprised, disappearing to shed her work armour and replace it with an old pair of jeans and a faded pink t-shirt.

A bottle of Pinot Grigio later and Peter and Justine were still at the kitchen table, talking. Her day, his day, lockdown, David, Creative Juices, YES, the economy - the list seemed endless, but all lockdown related. There were so many implications. Peter suddenly realised that time was slipping away.

"Bollocks, I haven't even started dinner yet. Oh - and the bloody Chablis is still in the freezer!" he said seriously. Justine laughed and Peter mellowed. There had been a role reversal. She had arrived home stressed and weary to a very laid back and in-control Peter. Now he was fretting about time and wine. And then the fish...

"Where the fuck is the cooking time?" came the muttered rhetorical question. Peter was examining the packet of two breaded haddock fillets, turning it over and moving it closer to his face. He had developed a habit of talking to himself during his time at the hotel. Justine found it amusing, especially after a drink or two. Reverting to his living-alone persona - which was seemingly oblivious to Justine's presence - Peter began to rant quietly but with a gradual Basil Fawlty-esque crescendo of impatience.

"So, I can see everything. Everything apart from how to cook the fuckers. I know the protein and carbohydrate content of the fuckers, where the fuckers come from, how to freeze the fuckers, how long the fuckers will last and even how recyclable the fuckers' packaging is!" The crescendo had reached its peak. Then he spoke in a soft, pleading voice.

"But not the fuckers' cooking time. And where, one wonders, might I find that seemingly trivial piece of information, eh?" He was addressing the packet now, in a bout of effected lunacy. Justine was giggling, partly because of the wine and partly because she rarely saw this side of Peter. He reminded her of her favourite comedian, Rhod Gilbert.

"Ah - here it is!" he exclaimed. "A tiny little sentence in point six size text telling me that to access the cooking instructions I need to peel off the label and they are on the other side. Well, how obvious, how stupid of me not to think of that! No need to put them in pride of place on the front. No, let's leave that coveted position

for the recycling guidelines!" he said sarcastically, attempting to pull the label free of the
packet. The label was having none of it, resist-
ing with stubbornness. Peter fought back determined to win the battle with the product. But
the label tore. Not a neat tear, a horrible mess
that left part of the label in Peter's hand along
with some of the covering of the piece that was
still on the packet, now just an abstract piece of
white backing, still glued to the plastic with the
elusive instructions on its underside.

"And what a great example of packaging genius
this is!" shouted Peter in mock temper, yanking
the fish from their confusingly-messaged plastic
home and lobbing them onto a nearby baking
tray before casting the empty packet away with
mock disgust.

The cooking time was duly estimated, based on
the fact that all fish seems to be cooked in a fan
oven for about 22 minutes on 180 degrees. Peter
and Justine settled down to a prawn starter and
a bottle of Chablis which had initially been too
cold to touch without creating freezer-burn.

"Can I ask why you and the Tomkin broke it off?
asked Peter, suddenly serious. Justine was eating
and took time to chew properly while compos-

ing her answer.

"He was spying on me." she said, almost looking embarrassed. "Well, not literally, I mean on social media, on the web..." she tailed off.

"Go on." encouraged Peter, stabbing a piece of fish with gusto as if to take revenge for its lack of cooking instructions. There was a pause, then Justine spoke.

"He knew things about me that I hadn't told him. He let it slip once when a package arrived for me as we were both having coffee. He knew it was from Amazon and what it was, even before I opened the door to sign for it. I hadn't ever mentioned it. He passed it off as a guess, but a few days later he referred to Fiona - my friend from Inverness - anonymously, calling her "my friend from Scotland". But I had never mentioned her, ever. And here's the big thing - Fiona and I had been exchanging emails over the previous few days - she is splitting up with her ex.

Peter nodded, suspecting he knew what was coming.

"So, I confronted him with the evidence." Justin said proudly. Peter winced, knowing that this would have been done in a clinical, solicitor-like manner, probably with supporting documentation and typed expert-witness statements.

"You'll never believe what the bastard had done, Pete." she said, sounding hurt. Peter played along not wanting to steal the punchline that he had guessed sometime earlier in the story.

"He'd hacked me. He was reading my emails, probably watching me on social media. Who knows, maybe the little bastard even had control of my webcam!" she said angrily.

The conversation continued before finally winding its way back to how life would be different under lockdown. Video conferencing was to be the big thing now, with everyone working from home. Zoom was the platform of choice. Peter couldn't help but think that its owners must have been rubbing their hands with glee at being in the right place at the right time. There had been a number of predecessors that had stumbled and fallen, he thought. Zoom was no better, but now people were ready for it. And right now, they were about to become dependent on it. Peter wondered about security. Was Evan Tomkin still snooping or would he presumably have lost interest now that relationship was over? Did it present a threat to his own confidentiality? He concluded that he didn't know the answers to either question nor would they be easy to obtain. He hadn't told Justine about Mattison and he didn't intend to. He needed to be careful with what he gave away. He and Justine were reconciling, but it might not last and she had also been recently hacked and possibly bugged. The couple turned in by quarter to ten to separate rooms, both keen to make an early start and get to grips with remote working.

The first thing that Peter thought when he woke was that there was no need to shower. A shave - yes. But his 8am call was by video, by Zoom. No need for trousers either, then, thought Peter, lazily, then mischievously wondered if Justine was following a similar thought pattern. He imagined her sitting at her desk, mousey hair up, back straight, fully corporately dressed on her upper body and wearing only a pair of knickers on her lower body. It was enough to propel Peter out of bed, grab a dressing gown and rush headlong into Justine's study-office with the offer of coffee. He was disappointed to see that his rather optimistic and unrealistic fantasy was not playing out. Instead, dressed in thick, warm, old, contour-hiding dressing gown, she simply thrust an empty mug out with an outstretched arm, without taking her eyes off the computer screen.

"Sorry - very busy. Thanks yes, coffee, please. See you tonight." she said quickly, giving some indication of her expectation of contact time during the next nine hours or so.

Peter dutifully brought the coffee in silence and disappeared to the kitchen table to his laptop. He had never used Zoom before so thought it best to start his remote working life by searching You Tube for useful videos and tips. Dougal had told him a story of someone in his wife's company who had given a presentation to thirty or so delegates over Zoom. It hadn't gone as well as she had expected. Then, she had struggled to answer two of the five questions in the Q&A session. As soon as the session had finished, she clicked a button on the screen to end the call and immediately burst into tears, slamming her fist down on the table and for some reason muttering: "Bastards, bastards, bastards!" It made her feel good and the tears started to dry up. So, she said it a few more times until she felt much better. She decided to have one last one crack at using this magical expletive with amazing healing powers. Sitting up straight and grinning at the screen she slowly enunciated the words, exaggerating the movement of her lips and mouth as she did. "Bastards. Bastards. Bastards." She relaxed back into the chair.

Then someone spoke.

"Uh, Jennifer, we can still hear you and see you. I think you need to close the meeting - maybe you've pressed the wrong button?"

***

A strange couple of weeks passed. Lockdown took some getting used to. Every afternoon at five o'clock the English Prime Minister gave an address to the nation, flanked by two top scientists to whom he fielded most of the questions about the virus. Labelled as the greatest threat to the nation since the Second World War, the virus was still spreading fast and the sombre briefings communicated the daily death toll as well as new rules and developments. A 'two metres apart', social distancing rule had been introduced before the lockdown and public business closures. It now meant that if English people had to go out - for exercise, food shopping, health reasons or once-daily exercise, a two-metre distance from anyone else was mandatory. Peter watched the briefings every day, Justine was usually still working.

As an ex-Welsh government employee and someone who was close to Welsh politics, Peter was alarmed at the way that First Minister Tomos Davies, who gave his briefing at six o'clock, seemed to be going out of his way to take a different approach to England on how to tackle the crisis. The situation was complex. Wales was not fully independent yet in terms of infrastructure. Legally it was in transition, signed off, able to request EU membership, but administrative transfer of power was estimated to take six months. So - agonisingly for Davies - Wales was still slightly beholden to the UK government. Health, however had always been a devolved power, so Davies attempted to assume-complete responsibility for it, even though as a public health issue, the draft transitional agreement stated it should fall to the UK 'until the end of the transition period'.

Unlike his predecessor, Tomos was ambitious, confrontational and with the power of being head of a nation state, potentially dangerous.

He was the right man to have taken Wales out of the UK and with any luck into Europe, but his handling of the Coronavirus pandemic began to worry some. Ironically, Scotland - also now independent - made a particular point of how the four nations should work together, liaising closely with Westminster and declaring the virus to be "above politics" and an emergency which 'we will defeat with our neighbour states and banish it from the shores of our islands.' 'Our islands' was the new Scottish phrase for the former UK.

The two approaches reflected an ideological drifting apart of Scotland and Wales. England had very much taken the lead on lockdown. Wales and Scotland had collaborated on scientific work and had similar plans, in terms of timescales. But when England had made the lockdown announcement out of the blue, Wales and Scotland had been caught off guard - expecting the announcement a week later. So, they had been forced to follow suit to avoid retrospective public outcry in the case of rising death tolls in their respective countries. In the period that followed, Scotland took a more conciliatory role with England, criticising Wales for its lack of enthusiasm to participate in a four-nation approach. Wales was bitter about the early English lockdown, felt it was perceived as playing catch up and was behaving like a spoiled child. Plans had been mooted to shut the Welsh border, but civil servants quickly pointed out that this muscle flexing show of independence would be impractical due to the sheer length of the border with England - 160 miles in total.

The Welsh version of the two-metre rule social distancing rule was the 2.5 metre rule. It was, some said, based on flimsy scientific evidence and widely thought to be an egotistical ploy of a man who wanted to go down in the history books as someone who took Wales out of the crisis before England. Supermarkets policed the 2.5 metre rule with various levels of commitment. Some had armies of staff - or colleagues, friends, buddies, whatever they were calling them - others posters and barriers creating a one-way system of traffic around the store.

Peter did the shopping, as Justine was busier than he was. He was also now realising that he was subconsciously making an effort to impress Justine and not just because he wanted her to live out his Zoom fantasy. He shopped daily, usually at seven in the morning. The nations - all four of them - had been advised against panic-buying or stockpiling, with assurances that there was plenty of food in the supply chains.

No-one believed it of course. If a celebrity had told them, perhaps they might have. But people have an inherent mistrust of politicians. As Billy Connolly once said 'The desire to be a politician should prevent you from ever being one'.

Peter's first dawn-raid on the supermarket didn't go well. How hard can it be to buy a lot of stuff? thought Peter. But it turned out he wasn't very good at stockpiling. He chose the smallest trolley, stockpiled more fresh fruit than store cupboard provisions and was a day too late to get paracetamol and sanitiser, which were already cleaned out. If he'd still been working for the government, they would have sent him on a three-day all expenses paid residential course called 'Stockpiling for Beginners', he mused.

The shelves were being stripped bare as Corona-crazy vultures swooped in to stock enough booze and food to see them until the new year. And it was only Spring. Peter wasn't really worried, so his shopping style was more casual than the others. He lacked the look of desperation in his eyes, the worry of no alcohol, chocolate, crisps or doughnuts to see him through a fortnight at home. Not that he knew it would be a fortnight. There had been talk of self-isolation for fourteen days if symptoms were self-diagnosed, but how long the lockdown would go on was anyone's guess. Hence the panic-buying. Or in his case, laid-back mass acquisition of random items based on impulse, rather than necessity.

***

After a lengthy online video meeting on Monday afternoon, Creative Juices and the YES campaign agreed that the news of their new supporter, Gerald Mattison, would be released on Thursday to the media. Speed was of the essence but early week news was very Coronavirus-heavy. For maximum impact, the end of the week may be better, but not a Friday, which could be a little too much like the start of the weekend. OK for a light story, but not right for this. The call finished and Head of PR Glenn Tilley, Dougal and Peter switched to a private Zoom. YES - who had initiated the meeting - had used a different system. It had thrown Peter, who had spent some time getting an appropriate virtual background on Zoom, only to find that the application that YES used did not support virtual backgrounds, leaving his rather untidy kitchen on public display. Now he was on Zoom again he felt happier looking at himself on-screen, with the kitchen removed and a busy office in its place.

Peter was paranoid that - even though he hadn't ever looked at porn on the computer - his looped background video would suddenly morph in the middle of an important client meeting from an office to a scene from a porn movie. Of course, he would initially be unaware of it, because he had turned off his own screen monitor. What had happened would only become apparent by the horrified and amused faces of the other nine people on the video call. Then, he would try to turn it off, fail and be forced to exit the call altogether without explanation. Then, there would be shame of having to email the other participants with some sort of fabricated, unnecessary explanation. Finally, he would live with the lifelong moniker of 'Porno Peter'. Back to reality...

The Creative Juices Zoom was a debrief of the video call with YES. Glenn briefed Peter and Dougal on his intended course of action for re-leasing the story, they rubber-stamped it and the call was over. Monday came and went. Peter shopped early on the Tuesday. The garage was getting full of extra supplies and he now bought a second fridge freezer online which had also taken up residence there. There was no room for a car in there. You couldn't move for towers of baked beans, pallets of beer and wine and drums of hand sanitiser. Peter managed to find some room in the garage for the extras that he had acquired that morning, stacking them neatly in date order, he smiled, proud that he had become good at stockpiling in such a short time.

At 9 o' clock he settled into the kitchen/busy office/porn-set for a day of video meetings and emails. By ten-thirty the course of Peter's day had changed. The news he had received meant he had to cancel the rest of the day's non-critical work. He needed to focus on the shocking and damaging news that he had received just after ten o'clock, when Gethin Jones-Evans from the YES campaign had called him on his mobile. Peter knew straight away something was very wrong by the tones of Gethin's voice.

"Peter - Gethin Jones-Evans. Peter - you obviously haven't seen the breaking news, no matter, it was only minutes ago. I don't understand how this has happened Peter, but NO have got in before us..." he sounded confused and exasperated.

"What do you mean, Gethin" asked Peter, trying to sound calm but frantically searching for the news on his computer, which - as computers do - seemed to be letting him down in his hour of need. Then he saw it - a lead piece in the Wales

news, more prominent than the Coronavirus updates. 'Billionaire Lipstein backs NO campaign'
read the title. Peter was too shocked to read on.

"Jeeze, Gethin - I've just seen it! What on earth...?"
he started before Jones-Evans cut him off.

"Read on, Peter. It gets worse."

Peter skimmed the paragraphs. The gist of the
sub-story was that American Billionaire, Jingo
Lipstein, was to open two sizeable internet call-
centre businesses in Wales, providing employment for up to a thousand people, directly and
indirectly.

"I think someone had inside knowledge, Peter."
said Gethin. "This really takes the wind out of
our sails for tomorrow's big release about Mattison. What do your media people advise? Do we
hold off or go for it? I don't know how we get
to the bottom of the leak, but something funny's
going on. I am going to call in our tech people
and get them on it."

"Right...who could have known?" Peter said in
a hollow voice, knowing deep down that the

answer was probably Evan Tomkin. Proving it, however, would be another matter altogether. Peter got up from his desk and walked towards the office to break the news to Justine. She was shocked, initially defensive - suggesting it wasn't Tomkin - then, when Peter pointed out that Tomkin had snooped her emails, Facebook and other personal details, Justine began to concede. Adding her legal opinion, she finished with:

"You'll have a devil of a job proving it, Peter."

***

Rupert and Caroline weren't supposed to see each other. She lived with her parents and he had a flat of his own. But the lockdown rules stated that travelling to see each other was not classified as 'essential travel'. So, as soon as lockdown had been announced and much to the dismay of Caroline's parent's, she had 'temporarily' moved in with him. The relationship was so new it would just not have happened under normal circumstances. They were still finding out new things about each other every day even though they were living together. He didn't know that her middle name was Laura, only discovering this fact when some official-looking re-directed mail arrived for her addressed to Caroline Laura Davies. She hadn't realised how obsessed with science fiction he was. He subscribed to magazines, spent hours chatting on forums and frequently bought memorabilia via online auctions. She didn't mind, but he was geekier than he had let on. His arrogance was beginning to show through as well. She frequently felt undermined and wondered if he had deliberately turned down the arrogance early in their relationship to woo her. Or perhaps she had been blind to it. Maybe that's what the expression 'love is blind' means, she thought.

Her confidence had grown as well. Facebook friends praised her new look and over half the 140 likes of her new profile picture had been from men. This was new territory for Caroline. She felt more confident because of the attention from others and this diminished the surge the self-worth that Rupert had given her when they had first met and moved in together. He boasted frequently now - about this and that - usually tech things she wasn't really interested in. On balance things were going OK, for a couple that had been thrown together by lockdown, but Caroline began to feel that it wasn't going to be a long-term relationship and accepted in her own mind that she would probably soon be returning to her parents. But until something happened to make her move out, she was happy enough for the time being, especially considering what many people were going through, as emergency hospitals opened across the country to deal with the casualties of the pandemic. When Rupert's self-obsession abated, his sensitivity seemed to kick-in and replace it. He became aware that he had irritated her and then made amends, with shopping, a meal and a more special evening. But by the following day his alter-ego had usually buggered off and persona normalis was back in the driving seat.

Last night had been good initially. Rupert had been ebullient and before long it became apparent why has mood was so upbeat. He almost couldn't wait to tell her but forced himself to pour drinks first and lay the table. The dinner - a five bean veggie casserole - was in the oven. They sat down and he raised his glass.

"To us." he started, but then spoiled the impression he had made on Caroline by adding "But tonight, especially... to me!"

He went on to explain how he and two colleagues had uncovered how the YES campaign were planning a big announcement (on) tomorrow and how by finding this out they had been able to fast-track the announcement they had intended to make next week to beat the YES campaign to the headlines and destroy its impact.

"So, you spied on them? Hacked them?" said Caroline, surprised.

"Everyone's doing it now Caroline - don't be naive." said Rupert, preening himself.

"But Creative Juices, we handle the YES campaign. You've shafted them!" said Caroline, flabbergasted.

"They shafted me. They underpaid me for years, that pompous arse Rogers never gave me the time of day and used my expertise to win accounts and make a fortune. Call it revenge if you like. I didn't go looking for it, Techfix approached me." replied Rupert, oblivious to what was going to happen next and virtually drowning in a sea of self-obsession.

"Well I don't see it like that, Rupert. I see it as it actually is. That you've broken the law, spied, trodden on someone who invested in you and let down all your friends and colleagues at the agency." Caroline was angry and outraged. Her suppressed anti-Rupert feelings rose up and demanded action from her sense of morality and pride. Morality and pride activated vocal chords and leg muscles and Caroline got up swiftly, looked at Rupert and said

"I'm off. For good. I ain't living with a spy and a traitor." She ran to the bedroom to pack. He didn't try to stop her. His ego-trip was too far gone for that. He needed to be with someone who worshipped his abilities, not criticised them. He remained at the table, sipping his drink. She re-appeared ten minutes later looking flustered and angry, lugging a suitcase and two bags. She was hurriedly making for the door, her desired speed slowed by the weight and awkwardness of her luggage.

"Want a hand?" said Rupert sarcastically.

"Not fucking likely!" she spat back. He had never heard her swear before.

***

Jackman called Peter.

"I suppose you've heard from Gethin? How the fuck this happened is beyond me. But I don't believe it was a coincidence."

Peter started to reply but Jackman, clearly irritated and in a hurry, cut him off.

"I have more news for you Peter. The decision has been taken that the referendum on Wales becoming an EU member state will be a digital one - so, conducted online." Peter hadn't needed the clarification that digital meant online but Jackman, a civil servant, always communicated with clarity to avoid misunderstandings which might implicate him in the future.

After the call Peter and Dougal spoke for twenty minutes on the phone, their second conversation that morning about recently acquired news.

"I hope this news is better than what you told me earlier." said Dougal grumpily, referring to the Jingo Lipstein announcement which was tearing through the media like a sprinter on steroids.

Peter told Dougal about the digital referendum adding for his own perverse enjoyment the clarification that this meant 'online'.

"Oh well that's great. So, we are locked into a digital contest without our key digital expert and knowing that the YES campaign has serious cyber-security breach! Whoever is bugging the YES campaign - or indeed us - and I'm looking into that - could have the skills to tamper with an online election!" Dougal neatly summarised the situation.

"True." said Peter. "But we have no choice. Welsh Government need to be seen to be independent. They would have no interest in the fact that there's been some foul play between the campaigns. And we have no proof that someone who may simply be a low-end hacker could intend to infiltrate or corrupt a democratic election. It's like suggesting that a shoplifter could commit a murder the next day."

He may have been right, but things still didn't look good.

Chapter 15: Pinot Grigio

"I know you think it's Evan, Peter, but I don't know what you want me to say, or do. There is no proof." said Justine, who sympathised with Peter but felt agitated that he expected her to do something about it.

"Can't you call him?" asked Peter in a slightly desperate tone.

"Oh what, really? He'll love that! I dump him, he still fancies me then I call him up out of the blue, he hopes it's because I want him back and instead, I'm accusing him of a major crime?"

Peter muttered, digesting defeat.

"Sorry, Pete, I'm swamped with work. I didn't mean to snap." said Justine. The lockdown had caused a big surge in divorces. Couples who were used to having space to lead their own separate lives were now being thrown together in lockdown.

"I could do with a break for five minutes." said Justine walking over to Peter and hugging him. They had slept together last night. Happy that things were maybe getting back on track, Justine didn't want to feel she was giving Peter the cold shoulder this morning.

"Let's have a coffee." said Peter, talking to the top of Justine's head which was buried in his shoulder, mid-hug. They disengaged and walked to the kitchen.

"So, everyone's going stir crazy and getting divorced then?" said Peter carefully, aware that they had come close to being a divorce statistic a short time ago.

"Pretty much." answered Justine, opening a packet of home-made biscuits they had bought from a food festival before lockdown. As if to take her mind off divorces she looked at the packet.

"Home-made." she mused.

"How can they be home-made?" asked Peter. "If

they were home-made, you'd have made them at home. What's the name of the manufacturer?" Justine swivelled the cylinder around looking scouring for the details.

"Here it is. Latham & Dicks Foods, Coventry. You're right - it doesn't sound very homemade. Oh yes and here's disclaimer! 'Latham's Home-Mades - so fresh you'll think they were made next door.'

"What the hell does that mean?" said Peter "Next door? Well, next door to us is an empty house!" shouted Peter. Then, in another surreal moment, the likes of which currently formed the leitmotif of their relationship, Justine replied

"Yes, but Joe and Angela live the other side, they're nice. I can imagine she'd make lovely biscuits." Peter rolled his eyes. He loved this about Justine. She could switch from being hyper-intelligent to a little naive in a matter of seconds.

"Well, that may well be the case, but Angela didn't make the biscuits, a factory in Coventry did. And some ad agency spun a yarn to make them sound nicer than they are. What are they like, by the way?" asked Peter. Justine bit off a piece and started chewing, looking skyward as if she now had all the time in the world, was no longer a busy lawyer and was now a recently-qualified food taster.

"Bit soft. Maybe a bit stale." she said.

"Well bugger me, it must have been that long journey from Angela's kitchen, next door!" exclaimed Peter, with a little sarcasm.

They stayed put for another ten minutes, occasionally glancing at their watches, mindful of schedules but enjoying each other's company. Justine told Peter about the lockdown divorce surge, explaining the trends that seemed to be emerging. New couples, who were lucky enough to be already living together, rarely figured in the calls to divorce solicitors. Presumably they were happy shagging and drinking, on furlough from work and being paid for doing fuck all. No, the trouble area was for those who had been through that phase, started arguing then had kids, hoping that the kids would solve things and give them more in common. It worked for a while, but then one day they woke up and the kids had left and gone to uni. The couple were then forced back to where they had been twenty years ago, with nothing much in common apart from a modicum of physical attraction, mutual bills and household chores. So, these couples carved out partly separate lives - coming together in the middle of a Venn diagram for key events, like dinner or even sex. Then the sex fizzled, TV dinners replaced sociable meals and happy-coupledom became just a charade that they played-out whenever anyone came around. Of course, no-one could come around now - what with lockdown. And the separate lives that had been lovingly cooked up - a recipe of hobbies, affairs and friends - were getting as stale as a Latham's biscuit. These couples quickly came to the conclusion that their relationships only worked if they didn't have to see much of each other and remained in their bit of the Venn diagram for as long as possible. Affairs didn't really work over Zoom, neither did badminton or golf. So, they either put up with it and fell into a hopeless, loveless lockdown routine, or they called time on the relationship and called in the official receivers: The divorce lawyers.

"It makes me think and hope we had a lucky escape." ventured Peter. Before Justine could answer Peter's mobile called. He glanced down at it.

"I'd better take it." he said.

"Caroline? Yes, I am fine thank you, Caroline. And you? How are you getting on? Is it harder working remotely in the creative world?" asked Peter, surprised to have a call from the quiet girl in the studio with the new jacket and haircut.

Justine looked at Peter as his expression changed to one of concern. She could only hear his voice.

"Well how do you know?" Then a pause (whole) Caroline spoke.

"What's the name of the company?" asked Peter. Caroline spoke again this time for much longer, clearly answering more than his question. The phone call ended with Peter's assurance of her anonymity and his gratitude.

"Well?" asked Justine, who seemed to have forgotten all about her waiting world-be divorcees.

"It seems you were right." said Peter, clearly very

surprised.

"It appears that a small company that one of our ex-employees joined, is responsible for the hack. Apparently, he was an integral part of it, though the boastful little fucker would probably say that anyway." snarled Peter, remembering his dislike of Rupert.

"So, not Evan Tomkin?" Justine asked cocking her head sideways, as if to make a point.

"It would appear not." replied Peter flatly.

The news had cast a new atmosphere over morning coffee and both Peter and Justine took this change of vibe as a cue to get back to work. Peter wondered why Caroline had called him instead of Dougal. But then any director would do, he supposed. Back in the kitchen he picked up his mobile to relay the news to Dougal. Then he had a thought and put it down. It was better to spend a few minutes thinking about the news so he was prepared with advice, rather than relay the basic information. In his haste, his logical mind had slipped out of gear, but now it was back. He googled the name of the company Rupert was working for - TechFix 49. Companies House listed it as being formed six years ago. It was a small company, so much of the financial information was not available. Peter wasn't used to investigating companies and began to wonder exactly what he was looking for. Then he spotted an option that read 'People'. He clicked it and it led him to a page where the officials of the company were listed - directors and company secretary. To his shock, both names read the same: Evan Tomkin.

Peter sat back in the uncomfortable kitchen chair which was no replacement for its swivelling leather office cousin. So, Rupert had left to work for Tomkin - an alleged ex-hacker - whose company had hacked the YES campaign's server. Surely, though, it would raise alarms bells with at least one staff member that the company was carrying out illegal activities?

***

A day later Peter was relaying the information to a Police Officer, with Dougal also on the phone call. The Police Officer was sympathetic but pointed out that the evidence was flimsy. Whistle-blowing by an angry ex-partner was often done out of spite and frequently lacked truth. OK, she could make a statement and yes they would investigate, but hackers were clever and covered their trails and potentially all that would happen would be that Caroline would leave people wondering whether she had blown the whistle on Rupert purely out of spite.

The Officer went on to question a motive and how - as Peter had wondered - apparently bonafide employees would have knowingly entered into an illegal act. Dougal explained that Tomkin - who owned the company - was a member of the NO campaign and that Creative Juices were handling the promotional campaign for the YES campaign. For good measure he added that Tomkin was 'a known hacker'. The Officer questioned the validity of this claim and Dougal admitted that it was rumour. The Officer conceded that, overall, there were a number of factors - many subjective - that supported Peter and Dougal's allegation against Tomkin. The Cyber Crimes division of the regional police force would look into the matter, the Officer said, leaving no impression that they actually would. He would interview the YES campaign HQ next - he said - and sounded as if he wanted to finish his sentence with 'and if all they've got is a bunch of circumstantial evidence too, then we ain't wasting time on it'.

Another day passed. Peter watched Justine disappear into the office with her morning coffee, his mind momentarily distracted from work by the wiggle of her bottom in the cotton dressing gown she wore. His mobile rang and his morning glory vanished in a cloud of work-related smoke. It was the police. It was someone different this time, with a more authoritative tone. A Detective Inspector, it turned out. It also turned out that he was a close friend of Gethin Jones-Evans, chairman of the YES campaign. The matter was now in his hands and under investigation. He explained that the matter was potentially more serious than had originally been thought, though Peter and Dougal were to treat this information in the strictest confidence, whilst the situation was being looked into further. Dougal pressed as to why the seriousness level had been escalated, avoiding the temptation to suggest that it was because of Gethin's intervention. The reply came that there may be a connection with other cybercrimes, though it was too early to say. Both Peter and Dougal suspected that they were not being told the full truth.

A week passed and they heard nothing. A phone call to Gethin seemed the quickest way to an update.

"I spoke with Neil - the DI - this morning actually, Dougal. It seems that there is evidence, but much of it is circumstantial. They have interviewed Tomkin and some staff members and they all deny any involvement. They say that the company has begun to specialise in cybersecurity, and sometimes they are required to attempts hacks to test the security of a system. Your designer girl - who blew the whistle on her ex - well, that's good, but it's her word against his. We've interviewed him and he's denying it ever happened. So, it looks as if we don't have enough to go on yet. Which is worrying. So, I have instructed our tech people to beef up our defences, be very vigilant and I think we will just have to do our best." he said in a pragmatic tone.

"So, we just carry on?" asked Dougal, incensed that Tomkin and even worse, Rupert were - he perceived - getting away with it.

"I suggest we throw ourselves into preparing for the online election rather than wasting further energy on this." said Jones-Evans flatly, effectively closing the subject.

**

David was working at home. Alicia, on the other hand had been furloughed - effectively meaning that she had been sent home as her place of work was closed. No-one, it seemed, would want office stationery and photocopiers when there were no offices open. Alicia had argued that it could in fact be a big opportunity to service the new 'working from home' market, but her wise words had fallen on the foolish ears of her manager. So, she was housebound and getting a full wage, thanks to a government grant and a top up from her employer.

Every day, she worked through a list of chores from the regular to the real bottom-of-the-listers, like painting skirting boards in the bedroom. She and David met for lunch and did their permitted once a day outdoor exercise after work, usually in the form of a walk, or sometimes a bike ride.

First on the list of jobs today was watering the plants. She tried to keep David away from this task as he and the plants didn't really get along. There were several problems. Firstly, David didn't know which plants were real and which ones were artificial. She had tried telling him and even suggested a map with a key. You know, the ones in blue are plastic and the green ones are real - but he wouldn't have it. Then there was David's attitude to the plants. It mirrored his attitude to relationships, Alicia thought. A good patch with lots of regular attention, but short-lived and then a drifting into negligence. Then when negligence prompted a reaction - an argument or a dying plant - David would be surprised and over-lavish attention on either Alicia or the plant. In Alicia's case it was all too much and in the plants' case, well, they usually died from overwatering. David had jokingly pointed out that at least it wasn't the other way around. So, the plants became Alicia's domain.

David knew he would have very little work to do after a few weeks. Juice TV was grinding to a halt as taking camera out on location, or indeed anywhere, wasn't possible because of the Coronavirus rules. So, he dropped a gear and made the work he did have last a little longer. Being at home had advantages and disadvantages, he found. On the upside, there was no commute to and from work, his time was his own and as there was more of it. He got to do other things as well, like play the guitar - something he had neglected since Juice TV. On the flip-side, he'd had an overdose of Alicia - and too much of anything, no matter how bad or good - isn't really good for you, he consoled himself. A call from Dougal made him wish he hadn't taken his foot off the accelerator finishing his other projects. He needed to produce three new videos for the YES campaign in the run up to the election, which was now three weeks away. So, one video for every week, building the argument for Wales joining the EU and reaching a crescendo of enthusiasm and logic just before digital polling day.

Digital polling day was actually digital polling two days and part of the message was to help people understand how to vote not just what to vote. They required a unique code which would have been sent to them at the address at which they were registered to vote. The voting period had been extended to two days in case of overload and a potential system crash. Longer had been discussed, but voting has to be a snapshot of opinion and so limiting time was critical in case of events occurring that would bias the vote in another direction, during polling. This could be geo-political event, a terrorist attack - anything significant, especially if it were linked to the policies of one of the parties. Of course, any of these could easily happen within a day of polling but it was all about limiting risk. David had much of the footage to make the ads and where he needed more - for screenshots and general people scenes - he bought library clips.

The YES campaign didn't like the ads at first, claiming that they wasted too much time telling people how to vote not what to vote. So, in conjunction with Tim Hughes, the copywriter, Juice-TV went back with a mini-campaign that almost lampooned their feedback:

At Last, Something to Get Excited About: You know when to vote. **YES!** [x] You know how to vote. **YES!** [x] You know what to vote. **YES!** [x] *Vote YES - for a richer Wales*

The YES campaign liked it, though some had quibbled about the three YESs- arguing that it could be mistaken for an orgasm, particularly because of the suggestive headline. Juice-TV had come back with the answer that that was just another bonus and that being memorable was a key part of all advertising. YES collectively shrugged and accepted the point but expressed concern about the connection with Coronavirus because the headline about getting excited eluded to lockdown boredom which could be perceived as using the COVID-19 situation to their advantage, they argued. Juice-TV simply replied that time was now of the essence and the video just needed to be made. The YES campaign reluctantly agreed to the ad.

David told the story to Alicia one evening over dinner who simply said "Well I don't shout yes, yes, yes - and I don't think a lot of women do." David butted in without thinking about it.

"Well, some do." Alicia took this a criticism of her orgasming abilities and an argument ensued. She questioned how many women David had slept with in order to come to his conclusion and make it statistically robust. Alicia seemed eventually satisfied with David's answer of a) Whimpering is as good as shouting b) Two.

The YES campaign was live on social media within a day and receiving good engagement. The NO campaign was playing the Coronavirus card arguing that collective UK efforts were better and this applied to all external threats, like terrorism, or disease for example. Their ads were not as snappy as the YES campaign, but they struck a chord with COVID-stricken Wales. The deeper narrative from YES was that COVID-19 was going to wreck the economy and being part of the EU would make Wales far more resilient and able to recover quickly.

Once that narrative was played out on social

media the options polls tipped in favour of YES. The public were oscillating between health of the nation and wealth of the nation as primary drivers, but as the death toll began to fall eyes were turning to the future and the state of the economy. So, YES found themselves circumstantially better off. The Chancellor had issued a huge range of financial support for the struggling British public during COVID-19. Joe Average didn't care where it came from as long as he got it. He rarely thought about the economic future until the media began to explain to him that generations of people may end up paying for the financial consequences of the virus. What the YES campaign cleverly did was to play on this fear of troubled times ahead and suggest that being in the EU would make it much easier. Grants, subsidies and other handouts were talked about during TV interviews, but just referred to as 'economic support' in the advertising messages.

It was the perfect storm. The public wanted to be told that the economy in Wales was going to be OK - whether it was true or not. Then the YES campaign was given an unexpected boost. It was bittersweet, though, as it turned out to be somewhat embarrassing. The edgy, suggestive ad, known as the YES, YES, YES campaign was hi-jacked on social media and went viral.

Someone had taken the graphic of the ad into Adobe Photoshop and integrated into it a beautiful, bikini-donning 30-year old woman. Then, bizarrely, the popular anti-racist movement jumped in, objecting to the fact that the girl in the ad was white! To counter the problem, they produced a new ad, with a black woman replacing the white one. Their audience went wild for it and that ad went viral as well.

Mostly men interacted with the ad - that was clear. Creative Juices willed someone to create a version for women with a man in, but it wasn't happening. They couldn't suggest it to the YES campaign who were affecting a reaction of disdain, only to cover their delight that the suggestive campaign was a roaring success. So Creative Juices simply produced the version of the ad with an attractive, muscly, 30-year old man in it and launched it into the ether anonymously, adding the suggestion that 'Surely, girls just wanna have fun too?'. The popularity of the ad eclipsed the previous two versions as females sought to out-do their male counterparts. After many weeks of house arrest and pent-up aggression, Welsh males and females could finally play out their squabbles on a national digital platform. But it didn't end there. The ad began to circulate to the former UK and overseas, where it was adapted to other causes and

countries, powered by the internet and popular culture. Back in Wales though, the opinion
polls showed the YES campaign as clear win-
ners, with over seventy percent of the vote. It
would take a major error or a PR disaster now to
stop them from winning the referendum. Even
though the ad campaign had now grown its own
legs and in some cases morphed from clever to
lewd, with erections replacing elections and all
sorts of other connotations, all the publicity
was good publicity as far as the ratings for the
YES campaign were concerned. They were still
distancing themselves from it shrugging it off as
'modern times, digital light-heartedness and our
over-zealous ad agency'.

In the run-up to the referendum, both sides
fought hard to get their messages across. They
were lucky - more people were consuming
media than ever before, struggling to fill furlough time and receptive to fiction, fact, opinion, sensation - anything that transported them
out of house-arrest for a few moments. YES had
stolen the show with the YES YES YES campaign
- there was no doubt. Two days before the vote,
the polls still gave them a sixty percent share of
the vote - down from a few weeks ago when the
campaign was launched - but still very strong.
It seemed that YES was almost certain to win,
apart from the fact that, as a journalist pointed

out 'there are no certainties in politics. The adage 'A day is a long time in politics' predictably featured in a number of commentaries just before the voting period - as it was called.

Voting opened at midnight on Monday and closed at midnight on Wednesday. Government information campaigns urged people to keep trying if they weren't successful in voting first time around due to sheer volume of traffic to the website. Cleverly, the BBC staged an online debate between the two sides at ten thirty on the Sunday night. The debate and the wash-up discussion came to a close at midnight, just in time for voting to begin. The stakes were high, even with a solid lead in the polls for YES. Many people weren't working in the morning, no-one worried about staying up too late and pretty much everybody saw it as a viable form of entertainment. Such was the enthusiasm for it that online referendum parties were arranged as people wanted friends and family around them to watch the big show. Rather than watch it on a traditional TV, the participant party-goers had it streamed by the host and everyone shared the screen, commenting in the text box. Drinks were in order for these parties too and the more outrageous the better, social media had suggested. The Welsh nation needed some entertainment and even though the referendum was a matter of huge importance, sadly for the public, it may as well have been 'Britain's Got Talent'. The government quickly realised that the potential drain on bandwidth caused by these planned 'Drink and Decide' parties could impede the capacity of the network for would-be voters, all tried to vote at midnight. Happily though, they needn't have worried. The array of tiny thumbnails on screen across the country were happy to carry on the party and watch footage of 'The Year So Far' - a hastily edited programme put out at the request of the government to try to stagger the voting surge. Not all the drinks were outrageous. Most people couldn't be bothered, but there were still a few hundred images circulating on social media with the hashtag #drinkanddecide and an image with a bucket sized cocktail with a whole pineapple in it, or a fish-tank labelled 'Pinot Grigio' strapped to someone's back.

Rupert was beginning to regret leaving Creative Juices. The sweet feeling of revenge had passed quickly only to be replaced by a lingering bitterness over his split with Caroline. He missed the varied personalities in the agency - the creatives, the 'suits', the video-guys, the directors - everyone was different but it was like one big family. In TechFix, there were fewer people and apart from Gina, an Italian temp, everyone was a developer - and a little bit geeky. Rupert - geeky by most people's standards, seemed as flamboyantly outgoing as Freddie Mercury next to them. Working from home now didn't make it any easier as he hadn't had chance to really bond with any of his fellow colleagues.

Privacy and secrecy were the watchwords. The euphemism that Evan Tomkin used for them was 'discretion'. The veiled threat was that if you did suspect that there was anything untoward and suggest it in any way, you would very quickly lose your job. Tomkin likened it to the work of staff at GCHQ, in Cheltenham, who listened in to conversations across the world, in the name of national security. Employees there couldn't question the reason behind the need to 'spy' on certain channels and it was the same for TechFix people. They were told that TechFix had been hired to "penetration test" - to hack into or disrupt certain organisations with their permission, to test their security., Tomkin made it clear to his team that in order to maintain absolute anonymity and security, total discretion was still needed even though permission had been granted by these organisations.

The penetration testing work was never to be discussed outside the building. If anyone had a problem with that then they could quit and leave their generous salary behind. The developers were without exception, bright people, many of who suspected what was going on. Some of the original batch had left, pocketing the money and saying nothing. Those who remained observed a code of silence and an affected doubt that they were really breaking the law.

Tomkin occasionally worried that one of his former employees would turn into a whistleblower. There were only four of them. So, he periodically offered them highly paid non-sensitive PHP coding projects, on a freelance basis. TechFix was to all intents and purposes a general technology company, with a specialism in cyber-security, but as the security part grew the other work had often been left to the bottom of the pile as the small team were over-stretched, spying on or hacking people. Freelancing it out was a neat way of getting the work done whilst keeping potentially dangerous employees from talking. Tomkin was effectively a quiet, dangerous mega-geek. Harbouring the early-life challenges of an introverted personality, he had endured a difficult adolescence during which he was seemingly unattractive to women and was scorned by his male peers for his obsession with computers. Now he was the one with power.

Rupert was getting paid a lot of money over the election period. He was one of only two working on the project. It was bigger than anything he had ever worked on before. His common sense told him that what he was doing was illegal but his orders stated that it was part of a cyber-security procedure. Impulsively, he texted Caroline. No reply. The text had been a middle of the road one.

'Hi - how ru x?'.

Having waited five minutes for a follow up and not received one, he decided that he needed to say more. Not given to apologies, the best he could muster was

'I think maybe I did the wrong thing moving jobs. I am missing CJ inc. you.'

No answer. Rupert was determined by nature so he wasn't going to give up that easily. What could he share with Caroline that would make her speak to him or even forgive him? He picked up his mobile again 'I think I may be out of my depth and I'm not sure what I am doing is legal.' It worked. Caroline quickly came back with 'Why?' - nothing else. Rupert consoled himself that at least he had prompted some sort of reaction, but the conversation ended shortly afterwards when Rupert failed to give a reason.

The referendum result shocked everyone. A landslide win for the NO campaign hadn't been predicted by anyone. They had scooped eighty percent of the vote. It was almost farcical. The polls suggested a clear majority for the YES campaign and out of the blue a ridiculously improbable turnaround seemed to have happened. The YES campaign swiftly demanded a recount. The media speculated about election fraud. The NO campaign claimed victory. The whole thing was a shambles. Unless a reason for the mess came to light what would happen next was anyone's guess. A recount was being hailed as yet another opportunity for election fraud and some were calling into question the legitimacy of an online election. Wales was hanging by a constitutional thread.

Caroline couldn't believe that she was the one person who could unlock the problem. Shy, but principled Caroline. Surely this kind of burden wasn't meant for her? If she did make what she knew public, Rupert would certainly be in a lot of trouble. But her principles and what Rupert had done won out. She argued to herself that if she didn't act, she would forever have it on her conscience. Rupert wasn't the ring leader here. He was an employee and with a good lawyer that surely would get him off the hook? Truthfully, she missed him too, though she didn't like to admit it.

Chapter 16: Lettuce

After what he had been through in the last few weeks, the guilt of what he was doing, the loneliness of isolation at home and the regret of losing Caroline, Rupert had mellowed and begun to look at the future. Previously he had only thought of himself, tomorrow, himself, technology, himself, gaming, himself and more recently, Caroline. In the long period of reflection and loneliness he had created a life plan, a product of self-realisation and the unburdening of an emotional self that had been deliberately hidden for years as mechanism of self-defence. The destination of the roadmap or life-plan surprised him. Goals he had never aspired to were there with unwavering solidity: A proper relationship, a home, a future and a shared life, a family.

Caroline had unwittingly given Rupert a way to realise his dreams during their exchange of texts and subsequent phone call. It was a perfect storm, in terms of timing. His pent-up frustration, his longing for her, his guilt, his creeping self-doubt all came calling. And she had the key. But her conditions were prohibitive. Rupert was to confess to the police immediately. If he agreed, she would collect a statement from him and deliver it to the police station. For Rupert, it was bitter-sweet. His head told him to refuse. Would she turn him in if he did? And then what would become of him? If he accepted, he stood to get her back and build a life with her. But that might be after a long court case and a criminal conviction, which could include prison. He agonised over the pros and cons, but deep down he knew he had no choice.

Rupert's statement was complete. It had been written in thin green marker pen on two sides of A4 paper. Electronic communications would most certainly have been monitored, so every precaution had to be taken. Sending the statement would have serious consequences for Rupert. Not sending it would have serious consequences for the country. He had written the statement two days ago and decided to do nothing with it. But Caroline had changed his mind. What she had said during the phone call after their text exchange remained emblazoned on his mind.

Caroline shivered at the prospect of what she was about to do. Oddly, she was worried more about the consequences of breaking the social distancing, travel and contact rules than what might happen to Rupert, when he confessed to the hacking of a major referendum.

Social distancing was still mandatory, but she had been in close contact with Rupert until recently and the police station would probably have barriers in place. Even so, she was nervous as she headed off to Rupert's to collect the statement. What would happen if she were stopped by the police? Non-essential travel was banned under the lockdown rules. But surely the police were the very people she needed to see? It would sound ridiculous, though. She imagined what she would have to say to the police if they stopped her en-route to Rupert's.

"I am travelling to meet an ex-boyfriend who may become a future boyfriend who is also a penetration tester. Before you laugh, Mr Policeman, penetration testing is not what you may think. He has hacked the referendum to make the NO campaign win and keep Wales out of Europe. I am collecting a letter from him which I will deliver to the police station and effectively turn him in."

Caroline's head was rushing with disbelief, excitement and fear. Her hands were shaking as she drove to Rupert's. She collected the letter from him at the door and declined the invitation to go in. He handed her the unsealed envelope which she took with a hand that was donning a plastic glove. She hadn't looked at him directly until that point, she was too confused, upset and afraid. She took a deep breath.

"Thank you, Rupert. You have done the right thing. Now there is hope." And in a second, she was gone, leaving Rupert to ponder her esoteric reference to hope. Was it hope for them as a couple? Or for leniency by the authorities? Or for Wales? Or for democracy as a whole? Was she that clever that she had managed to sum up all those things in just one phrase? Or was he just damn good at interpreting words? His arrogance was still there, he realised.

She rushed to the car, clambered in and slammed the door shut, finally releasing her grip on the envelope that the stiff wind had tried to prise from her grip. Her over-active mind imagined Evan Tomkin hacking into some fictional weather computer and turning up the wind to rip the statement from her hands. She needed to regain control. To calm herself, before opening the envelope, she started the car, turned on the heater and the radio and sat back in the car seat, fumbling down the side with one hand to twist the wheel to recline the seat a little. She waited a few moments then reached inside the envelope and withdrew the sheet of paper, surprised initially by the green writing.

The handwritten statement read:

To whom it may concern

I have unwittingly become involved in a cyber-crime, which I profusely regret. Now that I am aware of the full extent of what has been happening, I am compelled to communicate the truth to you as well as confess my own involvement - albeit unknowingly. I wish to name the culpable person. I do this with difficulty, as that person is my employer, a Mr. Evan Tomkin of TechFix 49 Ltd.

Under Mr Tomkin's instructions we monitored the electronic communication and activity of the YES campaign - for the Wales independence referendum and also for EU membership.. I would like to point out that as a cyber security firm, employees were routinely told that the accounts that they were working on were with the full knowledge of the organisation in question. Our industry calls this process 'penetra-

tion testing', we refer to it as P.T. We were under the impression that this was a P.T. exercise only. My suspicions were raised as it was carried out in real time (even though we were told the server in question was only a back-up one) and we were asked to sign an extra, more detailed NDA as part of the assignment.

As part of the PT exercise, we gained access to the electoral server, discovered significant breaches and, albeit with some degree of skill, we were able to change the numbers involved. To be clear, we were able to alter the election results, and we did. The alteration was instructed to be enough for the NO campaign to win by a small margin, but for reasons that we are not entirely sure of, the margin was significantly larger than we anticipated. This may be down to human error, a bug in the system, algorithmic idiosyncrasies - at this point I do not know.

Detail aside, we altered the election result in favour of a win by the NO campaign. I understand that this is a criminal offence and I can only plead ignorance in my defence. I hope that the law will look favourably on me because of this communication which seeks to right wrongs and bring the guilty to justice. I offer every co-operation and include my contact de-

tails below. Please do not contact by email as this may be being monitored.

Yours,

Rupert Swann

Caroline slid the paper back into the envelope, straightened her seat and started the ignition. She fumbled in the glove box to check there were face-masks, gloves and hand sanitiser ready for when she arrived at the police station.

The car clock turned 3pm and the on the hour news started. The news items were dominated by the fiasco of the referendum, the decline in the economy and Coronavirus updates. The Welsh Government had issued a statement to say that they would be discussing the outcome of the referendum and making (another) statement next Tuesday. The carefully-worded initial statement acknowledged that democracy must be upheld, recognised that the outcome of a ballot gave the winner a legitimate democratic mandate to proceed as per their pledge or manifesto but added that these were 'uncharted waters'. It went on to say that the size of the margin of the NO vote compared to the pre-election polls had called into question the validity of the vote. Whilst the matter was being looked into in terms of technology, counting, people and processes, political life would continue as normal.

There were speculations about an independent enquiry. There was talk of digital elections no longer being credible and of the referendum having to wait until such time as a physical vote could be held. Behind the scenes at Welsh Government and both the YES and NO campaigns, lawyers and politicians worked at full throttle to pin down a constitutionally-robust argument that would uphold whichever side of the argument they were on. The Welsh Government at this point primarily wished to avoid further embarrassment and restore the status quo. The NO campaign argued the democratic right to their win. The YES campaign - well, that was trickier. Their argument was more subjective, based on the surprising margin and swing that had no political precedent in the UK. They suggested foul play, but diplomatically inferred that this may have been by a third party rather than the NO campaign themselves. But what political group or country could benefit from trying to rig a Welsh Referendum on membership of the EU? Was Russia involved? China? It just didn't make sense to people.

Only a small number of the NO campaign were involved with the appointment of TechFix 49. Alan Haines was the architect of the idea. He would have happily kept it to himself but the large spend needed to be authorised, so a handful of others technically knew about it. A few eyebrows had been raised over the expenditure on 'social media monitoring, assessment of YES campaign's digital and technical capability and ongoing observations about wider technological implications on the referendum'. That was how the initial quote had read.

Creative Juices were stuck in the middle. The YES campaign had instructed them that, on legal advice, all communications were to be approved by them before going out. The lawyers were getting twitchy about every press release and even every social media post. It was imperative that YES did not directly accuse NO of tampering with the election.

A day passed. Peter and Justine were heading for their usual appointment with the one o'clock news. Peter was making the salad at quarter to one and Justine was trying to extricate herself from phone calls and emails so she could join him. As if to pip the one o'clock news to the post, a newsflash popped up on Peter's mobile screen. His hands were full with a knife and a lettuce respectively, so he leaned over to see what the audible alert had in store for him. Craning his neck so he could see the screen without his hands leaving the safety of the chopping board he glimpsed the headline: Four arrested on Welsh Election Fraud Charges.

"Justine!" he yelled. "I think you need to see this. Minutes later they were watching it play out on the one o'clock news.

Haines - arrested. Rupert - arrested. Rupert's colleague, Den Marcum - arrested. Tomkin - arrested. The arrests had happened early that morning and all had been taken into custody on suspicion of election fraud. Suddenly Peter thought about Paula. What must it be like (to) for her to see her ex-husband arrested and reported on national TV? Was she OK? He wanted to call her, but he knew that door needed to stay closed.

Reporters from everywhere were all over it within hours. Phones rang. Questions flew. Everyone wanted to know the stories behind the faces of those charged. Welsh Government issued another statement saying that the statement that they had been intending to make on Monday was now going to be deferred for a further 48 hours, following the arrest of four people who were being questioned over election fraud.

Media that had been swamped with Coronavirus suddenly had a new topic to talk about. In the days that followed, no news came from official sources. There was an investigation, but no-one knew the details. Journalists filled the dead air and empty pages with interviews of anyone who had ever met any of the men and with their interpretations of the truth. Sketchy pen-portraits of Haines, Swann, Marcum and Tomkin began to jigsaw together. Social media dubbed the group 'Fraud Four'. The nation was glued to all media, eagerly digesting any new information - whether true or not.

Peter looked at his watch. 10.30am. Time for a break from work. But before he could get up and head for the fridge in search of some milk for a coffee, his portable electronic town crier stopped him with yet another newsflash. Newsflashes had been so common in the past week or so that Peter looked wearily at the device, as if to ask what the fuck it wanted now. He reluctantly picked up to read the headline. As he did, his expression changed from one of indifference to one of bewilderment. He called Justine - then he heard her on the phone. He re-read the news headline and checked it was correct online as the story broke across the world. Justine appeared.

"Peter - I was on the phone to a client!" she hissed, reproachfully. Then she looked at him and knew straight away that something was wrong.

"Peter? What's happened?" He still looked bewildered and struggled to find the words to sum up what had apparently happened.

"Someone has leaked information about how Coronavirus started. It happened accidentally - so it says. A lab - a commercial laboratory - was carrying out testing of a low-scale virus for use in possible biological terrorism, or war – we don't know which. Things obviously got out of control..." said Peter, scanning the next few lines, immune to their content after the impact of the initial news.

"Is it China?" asked Justine, still in lawyer-mode, firing questions. The news hadn't really sunk in yet.

"Not sure, but... " replied Peter, reading from his screen.

"But Wuhan? We know it started in Wuhan? In China?" snapped Justine

"Yes, China." Said Peter, his brain clicking back into gear as he skim-read the rest of the news, which was only appearing in brief, as it was still breaking.

"Outsourcing!" he exclaimed. "An organisation – we don't know which one... it could have been a country, or a group – it says - outsourced the testing and production of this virus for biological warfare or terrorism to a commercial lab in China. Not to the Institute there, but to a private business. And there is more..." Peter paused, scanning the screen.

"We have always said that everything gets outsourced and made in China and India. But I never imagined this." said Justine, waiting for Peter to relay more information.

"The whistle-blower says that a vaccine already

exists. Already exists!" Peter paused, shocked. "He - or she - alleges that it is being used successfully by the Chinese, though they are still claiming it is in "advanced testing stage". Their intention is to release it to the world as soon as testing is complete. All Chinese manufacturing facilities have been gearing up for mass production." Peter looked up at Justine, watching her eyebrows shoot high above her pretty green eyes in surprise. He continued:

"Ominously, further information is to follow." said Peter.

"Why? What does this whistle-blower want? Money? Bitcoin?" Justine asked.

"Nothing. His printed letter, which was delivered to the World Health Organisation by a hired third-party, simply said that his motives were entirely altruistic and for the benefit of humankind." said Peter.

"So, the Chinese will make millions by selling the vaccine? And what was the motive behind informing the World Health Organisation?" Justine said, her mind back in lawyer-mode.

"Maybe he's Wikileaks guy – those guys feel the public have a right to know things." said Peter, glancing up at the muted TV and suddenly looking puzzled as he read the rolling carousel of headlines. He appeared shocked again. Turning to Justine, his voice faltered and switched between emotions of disbelief, surprise, scepticism and optimism as he spoke.

"The Chinese government has intervened and announced that it is their intention, should the vaccine pass final testing, to produce and distribute the vaccine at minimal cost to the rest of the world, as a gesture of goodwill and harmony."

"Where does that leave us?" Peter mused rhetorically, staring at the TV. Then unexpectedly, Justine was holding his hand and pulling him towards her.

"Together, Pete." Then there was a pause. "I love you." she said firmly, infused with optimism.

Justine was fed up of being rational and sceptical and just wanted to hang onto the hope that she could close the door on the past year or so. She was back with Peter. A vaccine was on the horizon. Even though her lawyer-mind was looking for backstories and motives, her emotions took over and she began to cry. She didn't know whether it was happiness, relief, or both.

***

Months passed. Optimism grew. Stock markets rallied. Investors celebrated. Wales re-ran the election traditionally. The YES campaign won. Creative Juices prospered. Dougal celebrated. Wales left the UK. Wales joined the EU. The EU celebrated. Tomkin was tried and convicted and sentenced to prison. His accomplices, including Rupert, got off with suspended sentences. Paula moved to Bristol. Caroline and Rupert got back together. David and Alicia were married in a small church in West Wales. Morris carried on eating pistachio nuts.

And Peter and Justine lived happily together in Cardiff Bay, a stone's throw from Pizza Express.

THE END

Printed in Great Britain
by Amazon